AVERY

BILLIONAIRE BAD BOYS & BLUE COLLAR MEN
BOOK ONE

EVIE RILEY

Avery

Billionaire Bad Boys & Blue Collar Men Book 1

Copyright © 2025 Evie Riley

ISBNs: 978-1-77357-766-1, 978-1-77357-767-8

Published by Naughty Nights Press LLC

Cover Art By CDG Cover Designs

CHAPTER 1

CUTTING the ignition as soon as I threw my car into park, I let my head fall back to hit the head-rest behind me and closed my eyes.

There was a soft ticking sound as my car's engine settled. The silence filling the cab and causing my ears to ring wasn't the most unpleasant thing after being crammed inside of a car for hours on end and traveling to get all the way out here.

No, it was the fact that now that I was finally *here* and back in Ellington Heights, I actually had to deal with what I'd been putting off for the past four months—with no choice but to face it head on. I'd run out of time to stave off the inevitable and now I was going to be paying the consequences for it.

See, the thing about death was that it wasn't always about the grief and the coming to terms with that person no longer being involved in your life that was the shitty part. There were things outside of that emotional process that were just as big, if not more, of a pain in the ass than the actual burying of your relative and wishing them well in the afterlife.

Namely in the form of their estate.

My father was a complicated man and had lived the kind of life that most people tended to envy from the outside. The kind of life that would be slapped on the cover of magazines with salacious headlines and that had reporters lined up outside the gates to our family's mansion come sunrise.

He'd never let any kids, a wife, a well paying corporate job, or whatever responsibilities that went with any of those titles, stop him from living however he wanted to.

Mainly at the detriment to everyone around him.

Growing up, my relationship with him had been, to put it nicely, quite strained. Living in his shadow my whole life and then watching him completely destroy everything I'd ever known after the death of my mother, had erased any goodwill I had for the man, which carried over well after I became a legal adult.

So, on the day of his passing, when I'd received a phone call from his lawyer to talk me into coming back to Ellington Heights in order to work through settling his estate, I was met with a sort of crossroads.

Pushing it off had gotten me nowhere to delay the inevitable truth that I knew would be waiting for me once I finally made the drive back to my place of birth. His entire life was mess after mess and even in death, none of that was escapable.

The only difference now was that *I* had to deal with it.

Opening my eyes again, I stared through the windshield at the mansion that I grew up in and was forced out of the day I turned seventeen.

Fond memories were seldom things to be found within those walls. And while the staff that had been left behind to take care of me after my father had decided that jet-setting around the globe was a far more lucrative use of his time than continuing to raise his only heir by himself, had been good to me, their care levels were directly associated with their paychecks.

As I'd gotten older, I'd blamed them less and less for it. Their responsibility in keeping me alive and fairly functional was all that any of them had been signing up for upon walking through those large double doors. Any more than that was simply a waste of their time.

They had their own families to worry about, after all.

Sighing to myself, I slipped two fingers under the car door handle and popped it open. The hot afternoon breeze hit me instantly, soaking me in the high humidity that I'd long since forgotten about upon leaving this god-forsaken town.

My dress shoes crunched against the graveled drive leading up to the marbled steps. The familiar arched doors greeted me with their iron filigree accents curling around the glass panels.

At one time, I used to think that they were beautiful—a symbol of my mother's delicate touch that guests would see first thing upon entering our home.

Now, all I felt was deep dread.

The doors parted easily when I pushed at them, a small chime coming from deeper inside the foyer was all that awaited me. Soon, the telltale footsteps of someone rushing to the door, their shoes clapping loudly against the tile, beckoned me into shutting the door behind me and turning to face the hall leading down to the kitchen.

Our family's live-in chef stopped short the second she spotted me. She had a dirty dishtowel thrown over her shoulder, her black apron handprinted with flour and other powdered ingredients. Her wiry gray hair was thrown up in a messy style on the top of her head, pieces of it falling down the back of her neck.

"Well, I'll be..." she muttered. "As he lives and breathes."

I held back another sign in favor of plastered a smile on my face. "Good afternoon, Hazel. It's been a while."

She was in motion before I could even blink, ripping off the towel from her shoulder and curling it up a few times between her hands before snapping at me with it. It caught me right in the thigh, the pain biting my skin even through the fabric of my slacks.

"Ow!" I howled.

She snapped it at me again and caught me right above the previous spot, just as she would any other unruly child she came across. "Don't you 'it's been a while' to me, young man! You come waltzing in here like it's any other normal Tuesday night dinner. Ha!"

"Okay! All right!" I threw my hands up in surrender.

"You never call, you never write!" she kept going on. Her disappointed scowl was the stuff of nightmares—mine, to be exact. Even after I was accepted into college, I still woke up sweating some nights, remembering those long days spent at the dinner table while she lectured me about my homework.

"I've been busy!" I said, though even to my own ears, it sounded like a lame excuse. Mostly because it was one.

I'd stayed away from this place for many

reasons, only having been dragged back on the rare occasion where I'd felt the need to try and reconnect with my past and soon finding out that the old me, and my past along with it, had died the night my father had put me on a plane to Switzerland.

A lot could be said for being sent away under the guise of your only surviving parent giving you a 'better education' far, far away from the place you grew up in and the only home you ever knew. All the while having to find out through various online media that that same parent that had promised sending you away was for your own good was then found entangled in various affairs all around the world.

But I digress.

Hazel threw her arms up in the air out of exasperation. "For ten years, Avery?"

All right, it couldn't have been *that* long since I'd last visited. Right?

Recalling the last decade was fuzzy, but not for the fact that I had a shit memory. I'd tried hard not to think back on what I'd been forced to leave behind, rewriting those deep wounds with something that was far less easier to digest.

Such as forgetting any of it ever happened.

"Sorry," was all I could manage to come up with.

She sighed at me, shaking her head before pulling me into a tight hug. "I missed you, you know. Not that you care."

I clapped my hand against her back a few times. "I do care."

"Don't make me whap you for lying to me."

I winced.

When she pulled away again, she had a smile cracking through that tough scowl. "Are you here to stay?"

I wasn't really sure how to answer that. While in the long run, I'd eventually need to go back to my life in the city, for now, I had enough time to stay and sort through the mess left behind by my father.

Dedicating most of the last eight years to being a workaholic and getting to the top echelon had earned me some perks with my associates—namely in the form of taking an extended leave for the foreseeable future.

Though it could also be wagered that perhaps that wasn't exactly a *perk* so much as getting to do whatever I wanted by being in the top one-percent of the economy's income earners.

"I am for a while. Until I sort through the estate and whatnot," I said.

She nodded slowly. "You're staying here?"

I wasn't planning on it. "Ah..."

She nodded again. "Good. I'll have Janey make up a bed for you."

I slowly shut my mouth. There was no use in arguing with a woman like Hazel. Especially, when she had her mind set to something. Even as a grown adult, I felt reverted back to my teenage self, treated as if I were her own unruly child in need of discipline.

In a way, back then I'd needed someone like her around. With my mother buried in the ground and my father off doing whatever it was that had occupied his time after she'd passed, Hazel had been one of the few to step up and expect better of me

She was determined to not let me fall into the 'rich brat' mindset and forced me to challenge myself in ways that no one else around me really expected me to.

Now that I was home again, I found myself

really missing this kind of structure—as sad as that was coming from a thirty-something adult.

"Thank you, Hazel."

She waved her hand at me, her expression softening. "Oh, stop. You go grab your bags and bring them inside. Ivan will bring them up to your room. I expect a full report of what you've been up to when you come back inside. Come find me in the kitchen."

"Yes, ma'am," I murmured.

Satisfied, she spun around on her heel and toddled back down the hallway.

Blowing out a breath, I made my way back outside to where I'd parked my car, fishing the keys out of my pocket to pop the trunk open. Upon rounding the passenger side to grab my smaller bag, my phone began to go off in my pocket.

I dug it out as my father's lawyer's number flashed across the screen.

Great. What now?

I punched the green button, sucking in a breath. "This is Avery," I said, once it was put up to my ear.

"Mr. McAllister," Ted Evans greeted. "How was your drive up from the city?"

"Long." Grabbing my bag, I looped the strap over my shoulder and hip checked the door closed. "Just got in. But I assume you're not calling just to check in on my travels."

He chuckled. "Straight to the point as always, I see. I wanted to run something by you. Going through your dad's paperwork, I noticed that there was something else that I'd missed when we were going over the estate. It seems he also has an off-property garage that has a few classic cars stored in it."

That had me blinking in surprise.

Classic cars?

Since when was my father ever into anything old?

That man was notorious for being a habitual upgrader, especially with his women.

What use would a couple of classic cars have in his possession when he was barely ever in the country as it was?

"How many?" I asked.

There was some rustling of paperwork before he said, "Looks like four."

Four more problems to deal with.

"Where is the garage? I assume that it's gated and I'll need a passcode to get into it."

"Yes. I can send all of that information over to you. I also have a set of keys here to open the garage but the facility also has a spare set that they'll let you borrow. I called already to let them know about the situation. You just need to show them your ID."

Checking the time on my Rolex, I noted there was still a little bit of time in the day that I could run over there and see what exactly I was going to be forced to deal with. The only problem now was that I had no fucking clue about classic cars outside of my slight knowledge from when I was a teenager.

My heart squeezed at the memory, driving me to push it back into its box in the back of my mind and lock the damn padlock before I was forced to unpack that shit that had been long since buried.

Clearing my throat, I said, "You have any recommendations for places around here that can assess cars like that?"

The sound of his fingers moving across his keyboard filled the speaker. "There is a repair shop that's known for working on classics. It's called *Carmichael's Body Shop*. I'll send you the info."

"Thanks. I'll head over there now and talk to them."

Pulling the phone away from my ear, I ran a hand across my face, massaging my thumb and pointer against my eyes.

Classic cars...

What the fuck?

As if my life could get any less ironic.

CHAPTER 2

BRANDON

"ALL RIGHT, Mr. Nelson. That'll be $86.50. You want to pay cash or card?"

The old man in front of me grumbled something under his breath that sounded a lot like *"this is fuckin' highway robbery"* before throwing a few bills and a handful of change onto the counter.

I forced a smile on my face and slid the money across the counter, the register chiming with a pleasant sound as I opened it up to deposit the cash inside. The funny thing was that out of anyone in the surrounding area, I was the cheapest.

The receipt was quickly snatched off of the counter the moment I slid it across to him. "Have a good day, Mr. Nelson. The keys are in the ignition."

He grumbled at me again before turning and walking out of my shop, slamming the door behind him.

Sighing, I sagged against the counter where I let my forehead rest against the cool surface. Honestly, if I wasn't in this business to keep people from going bankrupt while trying to take care of their old beaters, I really would've contemplated selling out a long time ago.

All right, maybe that was a little dramatic.

I did actually enjoy the work I put into running this place, along with my customers who came and went along with their car needs. While Ellington Heights boasted plenty of the overly wealthy, Edgewood was a blue-collar working class population with not much money to squeeze out of the already relatively dry pockets.

Even if I wanted to stoop down to scum lord territory and start charging for my services like my competitors, there would be no point to. Not that I would in the first place, but dealing with people like Roger Nelson had me fantasizing quite heavily these days.

I supposed it was part burnout from work and part wondering if there was more to life than living in the back of my shop's garage for twelve hours a day. Most people my age were out starting families and getting married while I was too stubborn to waste my nights down at the local bars trying to look for anything that wasn't a casual one-night stand.

Instead, I buried myself in work like any normal habitual singleton and kept myself preoccupied in between periods of seemingly unending loneliness.

These days, I was finding myself more and more restless for reasons unknown. Though, I had a feeling that my sister's constant badgering also wasn't helping.

Back behind the door leading down to my office, the desk phone rang.

"Speak of the devil," I muttered to myself.

Pushing off from the counter, I headed toward the back of the shop. With my lobby empty and no cars up on the risers to work on, there wasn't really any excuse to avoid my sister's lunchtime phone call like I'd been doing for the past few days.

I loved her but damn was she a pain in the ass sometimes.

Settling down into my swivel chair, I lifted the phone off of the receiver. "Carmichael's Body Shop."

She snickered. "Why do you sound like that every time you answer the phone?"

Frowning, I said, "Like what?"

"Like you're trying to act all tough."

I rolled my eyes. Leave it to my sister to have an insult geared up the second I picked up the damn phone. "It was nice talking to you, Lila. Have a nice afternoon."

"No, wait! Don't hang up!"

Smirking to myself, I said, "What's that now?"

"Ugh, you're such a brat."

"Takes one to know one."

"Real mature, Brandon."

See, the thing about getting a sister later in life was that we never got to experience the sibling rivalry thing back when we were kids, on account that we didn't even know each other. After my mom married my step dad, and along with him came a bratty teenaged girl and her three older siblings that were two years younger than me, I'd been met with the realization that getting picked on wasn't nearly as bad when I had someone to dish it back to.

"So, what's up?"

She huffed at me. "Did you get a chance to look at those dating profiles I sent your way?"

Holding back a groan was a Herculean effort.

While I appreciated my sister accepting me for who I was without question—to the point where she was constantly asking me about who I was seeing—since getting engaged, she'd begun to go into overdrive worrying about my plus one. Going so far as to have a *matchmaker* create profiles for me to look at of all of the guys within a fifty-mile radius that had dating potential.

Never in my life had I ever thought I'd have someone trying so damn hard to set me up with someone because they were terrified I was going to die alone.

"No, I've been kind of busy."

Lila groaned. "Brandon, come on. I think this batch is really good! There's some definite cuties in there."

My nose wrinkled involuntarily. "I hate the way you just said that."

"My matchmaker tried giving you both options this time around. Since she wasn't really sure what your *preferences* were, and frankly, neither was I, so she got you cute guys and super manly—"

Oookay.

Time for this god forsaken conversation to end.

"Bye, Lila."

"Hey, wait!"

Thankfully, the alarm at the front of my store chimed, signaling a new customer. "Gotta go!"

Setting the phone back down onto its cradle, I leaned forward to rest my head in my hands. As if my love life couldn't get any sadder, my poor sister was taking it upon herself to try and set me up herself. She had no faith in me to find someone to bring to her wedding and had resorted to *paying* to find me a date.

Although, I couldn't exactly blame her. We were both late bloomers when it came to our love lives—mine for completely different circumstances than her just being picky as hell. She'd eventually found a really nice guy that treated her well and wasn't about shoving her into the housewife box the second he put a ring on her finger.

Lila was a career driven person through and through, much like I was. We both found solace in what we did for a living, and changing lives, even on a micro scale, was fulfilling. Though, now that we were both in our thirties, it was getting harder to watch everyone else around me move on with their lives while I was still stuck.

I loved my career, don't get me wrong. But sharing my life with someone else was also a need that had gone unfulfilled for a long, long time.

That last person that I'd ever wanted—or rather, *envisioned*—a future with had left Ellington Heights and never looked back.

I'd love to say that my teenage heartbreak had been left in the dust but even now, a damn decade and a half later, it still ate me up sometimes when I was lying awake in bed staring at the water stain on my ceiling.

By now, the world had since moved on and it was my turn to do the same. Even if that meant complying with a damn *matchmaker*.

Sighing, I lifted myself up from my chair and headed out to the front of the shop.

There was a man standing in the waiting area with his back turned toward the counter, his arms crossed over his chest while he stared out the dingy window that I'd yet to get a rag and a Windex to since spring hit.

He wore an expensive looking suit that hugged his body perfectly in that old money kind of way. His dark blond hair was just long enough to touch the top of his collar, thick and silky looking, even in the natural light spilling in from the window in front of him.

"Can I help you?" I asked, leaning against the counter.

He wasn't the kind of guy who usually frequented my shop. Any of the city-slickers who blew through here were more prone to sticking to the chain shops a town over from this one, finding their ritzy reputation worth more of taking a risk than one like mine that barely had any kind of online presence outside of a Google overview.

When he turned away from the window to look over his shoulder at me, his eyes widened.

He was handsome—an angular jaw that was dusted with stubble, blue eyes that I could spot even from here, and full lips that curled back as his mouth opened.

"Brandon?"

My brow rose. "That would be me." Usually people weren't too inclined to use my first name, seeing as how it was my last that was stitched onto the patch on the front of my uniform. "Can I help you?"

He let out a soft laugh, shaking his head. "Wow. I wasn't expecting to see you here."

Weirdly enough, this man looked familiar. The problem was that I couldn't quite place my finger as to why.

"Well, considering I own this shop, I would hope that people would be expecting to see me here."

His mouth opened again and then closed, his eyes softening. "You did it."

Did what?

"Shit," he muttered, rubbing a hand over his face. "Sorry. I don't know why—*Avery.* McAllister."

Av—? I shot back from the counter.

Holy shit.

There was no way.

My eyes pinballed over him again, taking him in once more. He looked so different, but not in a bad way. He was grown up, more mature, since that last time I'd seen him back when we were teenagers. He looked like a *man* now. Gone was the scraggly seventeen year old that was permanently impressed into my mind and with it replaced him with *this* version.

"Oh," was all I could manage to say.

Avery's face pinched slightly as he dropped his hand. "Sorry, that must be really weird. I hope I'm not interrupting your day. You probably don't even remember—"

"I remember you." The words came tumbling out of my mouth before I could stop them.

Fuck, *how could I forget?* This man had been my best friend for nearly a decade. He was the first person I came out to when we were fifteen and the first guy I'd ever had a crush on long before I even knew I was gay.

How the hell *could* I forget Avery McAllister?

He looked relieved at my words. "You do? Good, good... it's been a while."

All I could do was nod at that, my words failing me.

Avery being back in town was nothing that I

could've ever predicted. When he left for boarding school at seventeen, we'd kept in contact through letters for a while but that had soon dried up once we'd both graduated school respectively.

I always wondered what happened to him, figuring that he'd made a life for himself out in Europe and never thought once about coming back, even though I'd lie awake every night until I got accepted into trade school, wishing that he'd magically show up at my door.

Back then, I'd had a lot of wishful thinking surrounding my former best friend.

The pressure of being a growing teenager, soon-to-be young adult, while having a father like Avery's wasn't without its struggles. I'd seen the news articles, the flamboyant magazine spreads and gossip columns with their salacious headlines, detailing a billionaire's fall from grace slowly over the years.

It was such a spectacular spectacle to witness from the sidelines that I could never imagine actually living like Avery was forced to.

That was why I'd never grown angry for the decisions he'd ultimately made in staying away.

Who could really blame him, after all?

"Are you... in town for long?" I asked.

His shoulders deflated slowly. "I'm honestly not sure. I don't know if you heard about my father passing away, but I'm here to settle his estate."

"I did. I'm sorry to hear about that. How are you holding up?"

Avery shrugged. "Fine."

Not that his answer was at all surprising. Even back then, Avery was never a fan of his father. "That's good to hear. He leave you a lot to deal with?"

He rolled his eyes. "Yeah. Actually, that's why I swung by. His lawyer mentioned that you may know some things about classic cars. Which, now that I know it's you, I would say I'm in expert hands."

I couldn't help but smile a little bit at that.

It was a well known dream of mine back in the day that I'd wanted to buy and fix up old classic cars, turning them from rust buckets back to their former glory. Right before Avery had left for boarding school, I was in the process of saving up enough money to buy one from a junkyard two towns over.

Two months after Avery was gone, I bit the

bullet and bought it. Worked on it for an entire year restoring it and fucking loved the entire process. It sold a year after that to an older gentleman who still, to this day, would send me pictures of him taking it down to Florida for the colder months.

"Didn't know your dad was into classics," I said. "What are they?"

"No idea. I haven't gone over to look at them yet. They're being stored at an off-property garage."

Looking over at the clock on the wall, I noted I still had about two hours of the shop being open. With no outstanding appointments for the day, I could essentially pack up and leave with him to go check out what exactly his dad had stored... but something was telling me to pump the brakes, to take a step back and *breathe* before I got involved.

I wanted to. Damned if I wasn't ready to leap over this fucking desk and grab Avery by the hand and march out that damn door. But getting too deep into anything with this man was a bad idea. Especially since he seemed like sticking around wasn't exactly in his future plan.

Why do that to myself?

Judging by the way he looked, he clearly had a life he was going to eventually want to get back to.

"Unfortunately, I won't be able to tell you anything without at least looking at a picture," I said.

"Why don't I shoot you some?" He pulled out his phone. "You can give me a rough estimation."

I hesitated before I asked, even though I already knew the answer, "For what?"

"Obviously to sell." He laughed.

Right.

Obviously.

Clearly Avery was looking forward to getting back to his life from before his father's passing. Ridding himself of everything that could possibly tie him back to Ellington Heights was the plan, not heading down to *Sack's Bar* to grab a beer and catch up like old times.

This man may have shared a life with me once long ago, but he was a stranger now. One that I had absolutely no idea about.

"You can send them to my email." Frankly, not giving out my phone number was more for my sake than his. Having the ability to text him whenever was setting myself up for failure.

"Oh." He looked surprised, though he recovered quickly. "Yeah, of course. Just type it in here and I'll send them your way."

When he slid the phone over to me, a contact entry for me was already pulled up. Right below my name was my old landline that had been out of use for well over a decade. I hesitated upon seeing it, my fingers twitching over the phone's screen.

Why keep that?

What was the point?

Nostalgia?

Rationalizing any of this was stupid. Yet I knew for a fact that the second my head hit the pillow and sleep refused to claim me tonight, this goddamn contact was going to haunt me.

My fingers felt clunky as I typed in the shop's email. After a few long seconds, I finally returned the phone to him. "Take as many pictures as you can. I'll let you know what I think and then we can go from there. If they're in good shape, I do have a few buyers that I know who are always looking to add to their collections."

Avery smiled. "Of course. Thanks again, Brandon. It was really good seeing you."

Yeah, I wished I could say the same.

Thankfully, another customer parking in front of my shop and coming in through the front door saved me for the second time today. As the door alarm chimed, Avery backed away from the counter; his promise to contact me was soon lost in the complaints of my new customer filling the small space.

I watched him through the window as he climbed into his sports car—an Audi series, of course—and pulled away from my shop, disappearing into the slow moving traffic.

Avery McAllister being back in town was an omen I'd never been expecting. Spelling the downfall of my entire life if I wasn't careful enough.

CHAPTER 3

AVERY

SNAPPING the last photo to attach to the long-running email I had pulled up on my phone, I felt a sense of peace wash over me.

For the first time since starting this entire process of disentangling my father's laundry list of fuck-up's, running into Brandon Anders—now Carmichael—was by far the best accident I never thought would happen.

We'd grown up together in this town, spending practically all of our waking moments together and being so ingrained with each other's lives that it was impossible to tell where he began and I ended.

There had been plenty of times that people had accused us of being together that we'd laughed off, even after he'd come out to me. I never cared. None of that ever changed what we had between us—a rock solid friendship that was unshakable until I was forced away and slowly cut off from everything that I knew.

For some reason, it never occurred to me that he may still be in Edgewood. Having left the area myself, I figured he'd do the same.

He'd looked good—still had those soft features that used to get him into trouble while we were in high school with the guys that were too chicken shit to admit that they thought he was pretty.

Seeing him all grown up was a shock, but a good one.

Sending off the email, I slipped my phone back into my pocket and pulled the garage shut. The keys the facility allowed me to borrow were hanging off of my finger by the key ring, both of them clinking together while I walked back to my own car and climbed in.

The off-property garage was about fifteen

minutes away from the McAllister residence, located in a highly secure facility with guards that were monitoring the property 24/7. Getting up here and showing all of my credentials had soon granted me access to my father's rented space, allowing me to see just what had been collecting dust for the past few months since his death.

According to the property manager, the last time my father visited the garage was several years ago, leading me to believe that after the purchase of these cars, he'd set the rent on auto pay and promptly forgot about them.

While I wasn't that savvy on classics, they seemed to be in relatively good condition. So whatever buyers Brandon had in his books would soon be getting a call once I'd gotten the all clear to sell them.

I was excited for what he had to say, mainly because I was eager to talk to him again. His wariness back at the shop wasn't lost on me at all, however I was ready to chalk that up to the odd situation that brought us together in the first place.

Showing up at his work so out of the blue like that was no doubt jarring, especially when there had never been any type of correspondence after we'd lost touch. He didn't seem freaked out, which was a positive.

It spelled good things for our future.

Pulling around to the admin office at the front of the facility, I dropped off the spare keys and then headed out. There was a good possibility that I'd be back sometime soon. Pictures could only do a car so much justice and with how Brandon used to be when it came to working on things, he was a hands-on sort of guy.

I was excited for him to come with me, if only for an afternoon. I was dying to catch up with him, to know what exactly was going on in his life over the past decade and a half.

As soon as I pulled out onto the main drag running through town, my car's alert system chimed with an incoming call with my ex-wife Carrie's name attached to it.

Tapping on the phone icon on my steering wheel, I said, "Hey you."

She laughed. "Hey there, stranger. How was your trip?"

"Fine. Long. The air up here feels like I'm breathing in a straight tank full of pure oxygen."

"I bet that's doing wonders for your brain power."

"I'll be crunching stock numbers in my sleep."

She laughed again. "Glad to hear it. You doing okay, though? I bet it's weird being back there."

It was. More than I thought it would be.

Carrie knew much about my gripes when it came to my father. Our relationship was always volatile, but she got to witness front and center how toxic we could be with each other. The day we'd gotten married, my father had decided that bringing his flavor of the week as his plus one would hardly be noticed.

If we were any family other than the McAllisters, I might have been willing to let it go for once.

However, we were never so lucky.

Reporters had shown up in droves for the chance at a glimpse of our wedding. Two powerful conglomerate families coming together in a formal union like ours was the kind of news that happened very seldom. Something that my father very much knew when pulling the stunt that he had.

Our fight had been horrible, resulting in my

father, along with his date, being banned from the property.

That was the first time I'd cried in front of Carrie during our entire two and a half year relationship. My disappointment in my only living parent not attending my wedding through actions of his own doing had been the tipping block to send me right over the damn edge.

Still to this day, I had no idea why she ever went through with marrying me. Maybe she felt sorry for me—recognizing the lonely child that still lived inside of my man-sized frame. Or maybe it was a classic case of obligation, the pressure of which had been placed upon her shoulders by her own family.

Either way, I'd always be forever grateful for her sticking by my side through some incredibly tough times. Even if it did eventually end in us divorcing.

"I'm all right," I finally said. "I certainly won't complain when everything is said and done."

"Yeah, I hear you. When you do come back, we'll get together so you can tell me all about it over lunch. Eva misses you."

Instantly, I felt myself softening. "You get her in with that early development school yet?"

"We're still on the waiting list. Ryan said that if by next week we don't hear anything, he's totally flashing my family name at them."

Both of us laughed together.

Coming from a wealthy family myself, I tended to try and not wave my status around to get whatever I wanted. Not for any particular reason outside of the dying need to want some kind of normalcy that aligned with the rest of the world.

I was no stranger to my own privilege. Having grown up with a silver spoon in my mouth and living among the working class of Ellington Heights had shown me that much at a young age. *Brandon* had shown me that quite clearly.

However, I would be lying if I said that sometimes being the son of a billionaire didn't come with quite the expansive list of temptations.

And Carrie was no different.

"We do what we can for our kids," I said.

She let out an exhausted sounding sigh. "Too

true. You okay if I call you after Eva goes down for bed?"

"Yeah, of course." The offer to read her daughter a bedtime story was on the tip of my tongue, quickly squashed once I remembered the conversation I had with Carrie a few weeks ago about our boundaries.

"Great! I'll call you then," she said and then ended the call.

My fingers drummed along the steering wheel while I edged my car through a four-way stop.

I hated feeling shut out of Carrie's life.

Her fiancé, while not at all on our level in terms of family wealth, treated her well. After our divorce, Carrie had—much like me—stayed out of the dating pool for quite some time, only ever branching out when her friends had decided to set her up on a blind date with her now fiancé.

He was a nice guy. Wasn't all that interested in her family, outside of getting to know them like any normal boyfriend would while dating. Seemed to genuinely care for my ex the way she'd always needed to be. And didn't seem to mind that she and I were still good friends.

In my book, that was enough for me to approve of him.

After the birth of her daughter, though, things seemed to change. It was gradual at first. Subtle comments here and there. A guiding arm away from me whenever I got too close to the baby, or he felt like I was becoming too involved with helping Carrie navigate early motherhood while he was working overtime.

Carrie had done so much for me over the years in terms of helping me navigate my world out from under my father's thumb. Repaying her in kind by stepping in where her fiancé lacked was second nature and never needed to be asked of me, despite Ryan's growing attempts to keep me away.

I bonded with Eva. Became like a pseudo uncle to her. She was such a wonderful little girl that I couldn't help but feel that paternal love toward her.

And then it all came crashing down.

No longer was Ryan so casual in his attitude toward me. He'd grown overprotective of both Carrie and their daughter seemingly overnight. It was devastating to receive that phone call from

Carrie expressing that Ryan wasn't comfortable having me around anymore, especially in Eva's life, and that I needed to take a step back from their family altogether.

I'd been crushed.

My pseudo family ripped away from me in the blink of an eye.

Before that, I never thought about wanting a family. Once it was gone, I'd mourned the losses like they were dead.

I supposed in a way, that's kind of how it was. I wasn't allowed to go back to those times, no matter how much I missed them. I had to come to terms with my new reality, just like when I'd been forced to leave Brandon and my life in Ellington Heights behind.

There was a part of me that had hope Ryan would eventually come around. Then again, in his shoes, perhaps I would be feeling the same way. My fiancé's ex constantly popping in and out of the picture certainly could lead to some unresolved issues no matter how amicable Carrie and I were.

Stopping at the town's main intersection, I pulled out my phone to send Carrie a quick text to tell her that it turned out, I was going to be busy tonight, only to be distracted by the email notification on my top bar.

Pulling it down, I saw Brandon's name listed.

Immediately, I tapped on the notification.

'Hey, Avery. Thanks for the photos. From them, it seems like the cars are in great shape, so you should have no problem selling them. However, I wouldn't be able to give you any kind of estimate on what they're worth unless I actually look under the hood. Where is this garage located? Is it local? I'm going to have to meet you so that I can get a better look. Let me know what your schedule is looking like for this week so we can figure something out. Best, Brandon Carmichael.'

My heart leapt in my chest.

I'd missed him so goddamn much.

Even the stilted professional language he was using was charming.

Behind me, a car leaned on their horn, causing me to jolt up and realize that the line for the light was already gone. Tossing my phone into the passenger seat, I stomped on my gas and continued through the light.

Once I was home, I'd email Brandon back and set up a time to meet him.

I'd only be in Ellington Heights for a little

while, but in the meantime, I'd soak up as much time with him as I could before I'd be forced to say goodbye once again.

CHAPTER 4

Brandon

"You buckled in?" Avery asked the second I was finally situated in the passenger seat.

"Yeah, all good."

"Excellent." The tendons in his hand moved as he flexed it over the gearshift, putting the Audi into reverse, and backed out of the shop's parking lot.

"Nice car you got." The remark was off-handed, meant for a throwaway kind of line that most people used when trying to fill up the awkward space. In this case, though, I absolutely meant it.

"Thanks. Bought it at the beginning of this year. Cash, no interest. Got a good deal."

Jesus... Imagine having a cool 100k lying around that could be spent frivolously on a sports car.

He had one of the newest models that were suped-up with the long paneled touch screen spanning from the driver's to the passenger's side, displaying all sorts of modules that were tempting me to reach over and fiddle with.

The interior was black leather with a sharp orange trim that looked sleek despite it being a little more unconventional in terms of style. The engine rumbled pleasantly, leading me to believe that, taken down a long stretch of highway, this thing could do numbers on the speedometer.

He drove stick while we moved through traffic, handling the gears expertly in a casual sort of way that kind of got me a little horny.

Okay, maybe a *lot* horny.

The thing about Avery was that he made most things look effortless. His ability to command anything that he could get his hands on—this car, an entire goddamn room full of people, whatever it was—went unmatched.

That trait of his was one I'd always admired.

With years between us and our lives being completely foreign to each other, I was glad that this fact had somehow remained true.

"How was your first night back in Ellington Heights?" I asked.

"All right. Felt weird being back in that house."

I imagined so.

Regardless of Avery's tumultuous relationship with his father, being away from a place you'd once spent every single day living in, had to have felt strange. I'd lived in this town for my entire life and I still found myself having déjà vu moments from time to time since moving all the way across town.

"Was the staff happy to see you?" I asked, forcing my eyes away from the hand gripping his gearshift.

"I think so. It's hard to tell since everyone's still shocked over my father's death. I don't think any of them really thought he'd keel over in the way that he did. A man like that you'd expect to live till he's eighty.'

"That's true." I paused, then asked, "Did you? Ever expect him to..."

Avery was quiet for a moment, his eyes

fixated out the windshield to the intersection's light up ahead.

Perhaps that was the wrong question to be bringing up so soon into us talking again. I'd been reeling since he'd come into my shop, nonstop thinking of all the things I'd wanted to say and ask him that it'd driven me nuts.

My curiosities weren't exactly an excuse to be asking him such personal questions anyway. No matter how close we once were. Death and grief were tricky things, as were coming to terms with the process of living through them.

How could I, someone who had no contact with him until two days ago, be expecting him to answer?

Before I could apologize, Avery spoke.

"Yes and no. He certainly wasn't going to live *that* long but I was also surprised he passed before he turned sixty-five. For some reason, I feel like he was still pretty young. Or maybe I'm just getting old." He let out a soft chuckle, shifting again to accelerate as the light turned green.

The sound had my stomach knotting. Fuck, maybe it was a bad idea to let him drive me over to the place. Being enclosed in a space like this wasn't exactly giving me much room to put distance between us.

It's funny how feelings never truly go away, no matter how much time has passed. A teenage crush carrying well into adulthood was pretty sad, if not downright strange. No wonder my sister was determined to hook me up with someone. She probably saw right through my pathetic 'I'm okay being single' act.

Avery pulled us up to a facility that had a gate and an attendant waiting for us. After passing over our credentials—mine in the form of my shop ID—we were let through without any issue and soon driving up to a garage toward the back of the property.

The units were built on either side of the main road, carved out in sections with smaller drives running down them for access. Avery's was one of the last garages on the property, a large four-door that was painted a soft yellow cream to match the surrounding ones.

Getting out of the car was more a relief for my pounding heart than anything else. I sucked in a deep lungful of air, trying to get myself under control before I made more of a fool out of my own pride.

Avery's door slammed shut behind him. He then fished a pair of keys out of his pants pocket as he strode over to the left garage door.

Unlike the day he'd come into my shop, he was wearing a more casual outfit though still looked quite expensive. His slacks were looser fitting and were cuffed at the bottom, the color of which matched with his black knit top that was fitted to his chest perfectly under a bomber jacket that he left unzipped.

He looked *damn* good which was unfortunate news for my poor libido.

The garage's door screeched horribly when he lifted it, causing us both to wince.

"You'd think a place like this would have automatic doors," he drawled.

"I imagine it's in case of a power outage. People can still access their things no matter what, like in the event of a hurricane or something."

Avery snorted. "That may be true. Not sure why someone would need four classic cars during inclement weather."

Coming up behind him, I peeked around his shoulder to see the first car. A low whistle spilled out of me.

A 1957 Chevy Bel Air in turquoise. The ultimate classic. The classic of *all* classics.

"Mind if I..." I nodded to it.

He stepped back from the doorway. "Please. Go ahead."

Shooting him a brief smile, I stepped up onto the small lip leading into the garage and moved around the space. The car's paint job was in good condition, as were the tires—black with that infamous white trim around the hubcap. Peering inside of the window, the interior was much the same in terms of condition while nothing out of the ordinary jumped out at me.

"Was your dad planning on driving these cars around? Is that why he bought them?" I asked.

"I'm not sure. The guy down at the gates was surprised when I showed up the other day to take pictures. Said no one's been up here for years."

That was odd.

To have something this beautiful just sitting here rotting away was a damn shame. There were way too many people in this world that would kill for a car like this and actually take good care of it.

Rich people always had it way too easy.

Leaning back from the window, I came

around to the front of the car and felt around near the grill. The latch for the hood was just under the lip of the grill, making it easy to pop and get the thing open.

Avery came over quickly to hold the hood up, which almost had me leaping out of my damn skin, while I grabbed the stick and slotted it into place.

"Thanks," I said, letting it go.

"Yeah, no problem." His gaze darted around the engine. "So, what's it look like?"

Leaning over the lip of the car, I tugged out my flashlight to shine it over a few spots, testing things along the way. The oil was definitely in need of a change, as were some of the old fluids still sitting in their pipes. The engine block looked fairly new, as well as the battery, although that was most likely dead considering how long Avery had said this car was sitting here for.

Kneeling, I ducked under the car to take a look at the undercarriage, seeing no crazy rust spots or missing catalytic converters that had been recently sawed off.

"This one looks pretty good," I said, standing again. "Want to show me the others?"

He nodded.

Going next door to the other three garages, he pulled them open for me, revealing a 1966 Chevy Chevelle, a 1932 Ford Coupe and another Chevy Bel Air but in black.

"For someone who wasn't at all interested in driving these around to show off, he sure had some taste," I mumbled.

"If he had one thing going for him, it was the right to brag about something." Avery's eyes crinkled slightly.

Too true.

That man was a damn shark when it came to showcasing his wealth.

But I supposed, coming from a billionaire family kind of ended up rotting your brain one way or another.

Pulling up the hood of the Chevelle, I noticed immediately that this one was definitely not as well preserved as the Bel Air. Poking at a few spots, it was clear that not only would a lot of the smaller pieces need to be replaced such as the timing belt. But the engine wasn't looking too good either.

And that was simply a guesstimation based solely without starting up the actual car to see it in action.

"Uh oh. That face isn't very promising."

My body stiffened when Avery came up from behind me and leaned over the side of the car, our shoulders briefly brushing together. He was warm, even hidden under his jacket. A shiver rolled up my spine, causing me to clench my teeth tightly together.

"I can't really give a good opinion unless I bring it in for a full work up."

"You didn't say that about the other one. Which leads me to believe you've got some kind of idea."

I did. But not one that was solid yet.

Anytime a customer came into my shop with some kind of problem, I had at least two running theories. Rarely was I ever wrong on either prediction as most problems skewed one way or the other.

However, a situation like this one was a bit out of the norm. I wasn't in my shop, putting a customer's vehicle up on the stilts and hooking it up to my code reader to see what the hell was going on.

Instead, I was in a garage with nothing but my flashlight to help me.

What I *really* should've done was bring my

entire tool belt. *That* would've been the smart mechanic-thing to do. But no, I'd been immediately distracted the moment Avery had arrived at my shop looking good as hell while my coworkers all shot me knowing looks as we both headed out the front door.

"What I'm predicting is probably going to be expensive. Like I said, I can't say for sure but this one is in rough shape just by looking under the hood. You'd have to get it towed to wherever you're planning on taking it, which is going to be more money. Labor will probably cost a lot, too. This is all to say that you may want to cut your losses and sell as-is and let some hobbyist take on the costs."

When I turned to look at Avery, I found him staring at me with a strange expression. He didn't move for what felt like an entire minute of heavy silence. As he finally did so, it was to tilt his head to the side.

"Are you... not interested?" he asked.

"Interested in what?"

"Fixing the car, Brandon."

My stomach tightened as my name rolled off his tongue. "That's not what I said."

A small smile crossed over his lips. "Oh. I see. You're telling me you're expensive."

"No, I—"

Where the hell did he get *that* from?

He cut me off. "It's fine. I don't mind paying."

Now it was my turn to stare.

Sure, Avery was well off but was sinking close to what the car was probably worth even... well, worth it?

Not many people who didn't have a passion in car restoration would agree. There were plenty of things that could go wrong during the process, leading to more headaches and cash being burned.

"I don't think you're understanding me," I said.

He laughed. "I'm understanding you perfectly fine, Brandon. I can afford it, trust me. The only hold up would be if you're willing to work on it for me. If not, then yes, I'll probably just end up selling it as-is like you suggested."

"What? Why would I be the only one you'd be willing to have work on it?"

He shrugged. "I trust you. And I trust that you won't needlessly fuck up because you are looking for a bigger paycheck. Like I said, I can afford whatever you want to charge me. But I *hate* people wasting my time."

Well, I guess I couldn't fault him for that.

I had no idea what Avery did for a living now, but given his expensive looking suit, expensive car, and overall bland attitude when it came to money, led me to believe he was somewhere in the financial world.

Probably running it, no doubt.

Still, wasn't it kind of sudden to be asking me to help him with this project? After all, we barely knew each other any more. How was he to know I wasn't some kind of grifter now?

"You're awfully confident in my skills," I mumbled.

He leaned closer to me, barely a hair's breadth between us as he said, "Why won't you let me trust you?"

My heart slammed in my chest.

Oh god.

Why the hell was this happening?

I was supposed to be over this two fucking decades ago. Hell, I was never supposed to fall for a straight man to begin with. And now here I was, doing the same goddamn thing all over again.

Was my heart content with never learning?

Or was I some kind of closet masochist?

"Uh..." I needed to get away from him. Put some distance between us before I did something monumentally stupid like asking him out on a fucking date. "It's not..."

"Not what?" He tilted his head, those stupid blue eyes of his that always reminded me of sapphires, staring back at me patiently.

"I have a job. To do." Even to my own ears, my words were stilted. "At the shop."

"Do you run it by yourself?"

My head shook mechanically.

"Okay, how about this. I fund whatever your shop's paycheck would be for the next however long it'll take you to look at all of these cars, restore them, and then fix them up for me to sell. How's that sound?"

My jaw dropped to the ground. "My *entire* shop... Avery, you're fucking kidding me. I'm not letting you do that."

He frowned. "Why not?"

"You—I." What the *fuck*. "I have customers."

"Okay?"

Oh my fucking god. This man.

This stupid fucking rich billionaire brat.

Of course that would be his response.

'Who cares, Brandon. Just send them somewhere else! I'll pay you to shut down your whole shop.' is exactly what he would say to me if I let him.

Which wasn't going to happen. I wasn't going to let *this* happen. Paying for my fucking shop to close down so I can fix his goddamn cars... who does that?

"Avery," I gritted through my teeth.

He sighed. "How many people are working for you?"

"Four."

"Okay, so have one run the shop with your regular customers and the other three can help you. Or... two. I don't know. Do you get a lot of business? Edgewood isn't *that* populated."

Using my fingers to massage my aching eyeballs, I let out a long sigh.

I hated that he was tempting me with this. The whole point in agreeing to come out here and assess the cars was to get him a quote, maybe throw in some advice, get him in touch with some of my past clients and then send him off on his merry way.

There was no room in that equation for him to be weaseling his way into my life any more than he'd been doing already.

But *damn*, being able to work exclusively on these cars without having to worry about a paycheck, or my employees staying afloat, would be an absolute dream. Honestly, that *was* my dream before reality gave me a long hard slap across the face once bills began to accumulate.

You couldn't run a successful business on classics alone—there just wasn't that big of a market to keep up with the cost of materials for restorations, and maintaining an overhead in the process.

This situation was different, though. Avery was filthy fucking rich and was offering the opportunity of a lifetime. I'd be a damn fool not to take it.

At the same time, I was afraid to.

Not that he would ever be that kind of person to hold money over someone's head but the possibility that by the end of all of this, he came out unsatisfied would weigh on me more than I cared to admit. I didn't want that kind of guilt eating away at me. Not with him involved.

I had enough of that living through my twenties.

"Brandon." Avery reached across the space between us to grab my arm. "Why don't you think about it?"

Just as I was about to tell him I couldn't, his phone went off.

He sighed. "Give me a second."

I tracked him with my gaze as he walked away, pulling his phone out of his pocket to answer it.

I couldn't do this. Work for Avery, technically, while living the dream I always wanted to. It would be stupid to put my business on hold, even if the bills would still be getting paid.

I'd be a damn fool to accept.

Right?

CHAPTER 5

Avery

WALKING TO MY CAR, I tucked the thought of Brandon's hesitation toward my offer away in the back of my mind.

It wasn't really any of my business that, instead of jumping at the opportunity to work on a known passion of his while not having to worry about the cost of a paycheck, he was digging his heels into the proverbial dirt for whatever reason

Even if it severely bothered me.

Him having a life in Edgewood, far removed from the one we shared together in Ellington

Heights, was understandable. As was him wanting to run his business without someone like me coming in and bulldozing everything to shit. He clearly had a system going and disrupting the flow of that wasn't exactly winning me any favors.

Why doesn't he want to spend time with me?

That traitorous thought.

It plagued my fucking mind uselessly.

My phone buzzed in my pocket, distracting me from my thoughts. I dug it out and punched the green icon with my finger.

"This is Avery," I said into the phone.

"Mr. McAllister, it's Ted Evans."

"Hey, I was just about to send you an email. I've got someone looking at those cars."

"Ah," he cleared his throat. "Well, that's good. I take it you've got an expert with you, then?"

My brows knitted together.

What was with the weird tone?

And asking me an obvious question like that?

Sure, Ted was typically one for small talk but not in the way that it made him almost seem like he was trying his best to avoid bringing something to my attention.

Alarm bells went off in my head immediately.

"What's going on?" I asked.

He chuckled. "Astute, as always."

Turning to glance over my shoulder, I spotted Brandon poking around the third car, his flashlight moving along the trim of it while he squatted toward the rear on the passenger side. Watching him work up close like that had been both nostalgic and a little eye opening.

He'd always had an eye for the smaller details —taking in the bigger picture and then breaking it down into smaller, more digestible pieces. I'd adopted and used that technique countless times in my professional life. But nothing would compare to the master of it.

"There's been some... news," Ted finally said.

"About?" I needed this man to spit out what he was clearly stalling on telling me. Either way, whatever information was going to come next was going to upset me. How much was the real question.

Ted calling out of the blue without so much as my follow up email regarding anything about my father's estate was troublesome, to put it lightly.

He sighed. "I just got off the phone with *Alexander Steele's* law office. It seems one of their clients has just filed to contest your father's will."

"*What?*" I snapped. "Who?"

Were they out of their fucking mind?

I was my father's sole heir. Unless he had a bastard child without me ever finding out about it, his entire estate was owed to me. Not to mention *I'd* been the one that had to deal with all of his bullshit for the past thirty-plus years.

No one else would ever get to claim that 'privilege'.

"Her name is Ana Liapovich," he said. "She's a Russian model that claims she and your father were married when he passed and is now seeking to claim some of the estate as a surviving spouse."

My mouth dropped open, rage pouring through me.

Of fucking course.

Why had I never expected this?

People coming out of the woodwork the second my father's passing was made public news in order to try and get some kind of claim to whatever it was that they thought was owed to them was absolutely ridiculous.

None of them—his inner circle, women he'd dated, people he'd promised fortunes to—were entitled to jack shit. No one but me and the staff back at our family home.

"The only woman that man was ever married to was my mother," I said.

"She claims she has proof of their relationship. If she's able to produce a valid marriage license, then she might have a case."

My jaw ached from how hard I was clenching it. "And how much do you believe this woman?"

"I can't say for sure but the way her lawyer spoke, it seemed quite legitimate."

Jesus fuck...

Digging both of my fingers into my eye sockets, I let out a long sigh.

Leave it to my father, that even in death, he would complicate my life more than he already had so far. Of course, his reputation for being a notorious playboy wasn't something that ever went unnoticed. Not to the public and certainly not to me.

He wasn't one to take his 'retirement' years and spend them alone, sitting in a mansion behind the tall gates of our family mansion while drinking himself into an early grave.

Though at the same time, he'd also never had any interest in sticking around for long in the lives of whomever he was dating. Even the woman he'd brought to my wedding had been dumped within the month and soon, he was spotted with someone else—an Ibizin princess, if I recalled correctly.

So who was to say that any of what Ted was telling me could be proven?

The issue was this: if this Ana Liapovich *was* able to produce a legal document or marriage license that stated she was now my father's widow, I'd be forced to negotiate with her.

The money wasn't the issue—lord fucking knew I had enough of it already. It was the principle of the matter that someone coming in and staking their claim over a piece of my family's legacy without actually having to bear the burden of its weight for as long as I had was downright infuriating.

Who the fuck did this Ana Liapovich think she was?

"Listen," Ted cleared his throat. "I'll keep you

updated. I don't expect to hear from them for a few days. Once the documents are sent over to me, I'll run through them and then we can go from there. I only wanted to call you to give you a head's up in case this woman tries to show up at your doorstep."

I dragged my hand over my face. "Thanks for the warning."

"Of course, Mr. McAllister. Send me the details of those car estimates, too, and I'll have them put together with the rest of the files."

I let my hand drop from my face, my eyes instantly locking on to the back of Brandon's body again. He was bent over the hood of the third car, waist deep in checking something out on the side of the engine with his flashlight and some other smaller tool that I couldn't exactly make out was what from here.

However, that's not what my eyes were focused on. It was the fact that his ass was perked up in the air, the round shape of it pronounced with the way the fabric of his pants were pulling tightly over it.

Flustered, I turned away. "Uh, can you actu-ally hold off on that? The guy I'm working with says they might need a lot of work. I don't want to go throwing in estimates if this woman does turn out to be legit."

"Oh. Yes, that's true. I'll keep the information off the books for now."

"Thanks."

"Of course. I'll call you again with any updates."

Shaking my head, I pocketed my phone and scrubbed my hands over my face a few times. All of this mess with my father was making me fucking delirious.

Since when was I into checking out any man's ass, let alone my former childhood best friend's?

I needed to get laid.

That was the real issue. I had too much tension built up in me from work and then coming down here to deal with this mess. The last time I'd had anyone warming my bed was... well, a while ago. *Too* long, apparently.

When Brandon leaned back from the car again, I found myself heading back over. "How's it looking?"

He glanced over his shoulder at me and then clicked his light off. "Well, it's not horrible. These were certainly kept in good condition when they were first bought. The problem is that since your dad never came up here or had anyone doing regular maintenance on them, the sitting wear and tear is what's going to need repairing. The problem with older cars is that they need a lot of daily TLC to keep running. Modern cars aren't as touchy."

Nodding along to his words, I slid both my hands into my pockets. "You think about my offer?"

He let out a soft snort. "In the time it took you to take your phone call?"

I winced.

All right, maybe that was a little too soon for me to be asking. But sue me, I was eager to have Brandon back in my life, if only in a short-term capacity. I missed this, the energy between us. It felt both like coming home and breathing in a fresh lungful of air after having been kept stagnant for so long.

How he was able to do that to me—to make me feel like this—I'll probably never know. Dissecting it to death like the rest of the relationships in my life felt taboo, like I would be somehow breaking a magical illusion that I wasn't quite ready to peek behind the curtains and figure out just yet.

"Sounded serious," he said, nodding to me. "Your phone call."

"It was."

He eyed me carefully but didn't press me further for details. I appreciated that about him. He was clearly curious about the situation but wasn't so crude that he'd go out of his way to dig the information out of me.

I hated when people did that.

Seemed Brandon hadn't forgotten that.

"My lawyer, or my father's I guess, just called. Told me that apparently there is some woman claiming to be his widow. She's contesting the will."

His eyes widened. "Do you know her?"

"No. She's some Russian model. Honestly, as much as I don't want it to be true, it doesn't surprise me. You know how he was after my mother died."

Brandon nodded slowly, his gaze drifting back toward the car in front of us. "What are you going to do? You think it's legit?"

"Possibly. And I'm not sure. The information has to be verified first to start any kind of legal battle."

"So... you're going to fight her, then? If it is true."

Normally, if any other person were to phrase it that way, I would've taken it as an attack. A *'so you're actually going to deny that poor woman her right to the estate? What an asshole'* type comment that would've no doubt set me right off.

For him, that's not quite the way it was meant and I knew that. This was more so Brandon's way of subtly fishing for answers, wanting to get into my head and figure out what my course of action was. He'd done it countless times when we were kids, reframing my thinking in a way that was more constructive and less emotional—as I tended to get when things were overwhelming me.

Back then, I'd hated it. I'd hated how he'd full-stop me from lashing out and raining my fury down on everything that was in the way on my war path like I'd wanted, like my instincts were screaming at me to.

That was how my father had been, and

learning by osmosis, I'd become quite the little tyrant myself. Until I met Brandon.

His approach to life wasn't soft, it was firm. There was no hand-holding or *there theres* that would eventually end up coddling whoever it was he was trying to work with. For me, he'd kept me from turning into a person that I would one day hate looking into the mirror and facing.

He'd changed me and molded me into someone who was forced to step out of my anger and look at the bigger picture. Even when I vehemently refused to at first.

Brandon would never know how much him doing that impacted me—changed me for the better. And in turn, I'd never be able to thank him enough for it.

"I want to see what she's asking for," I finally said. "If it's money, whatever. She can have it. But if it's anything more than that, then I'm going to fight her. Her being entitled to anything regarding my family's legacy is off the table."

He nodded slowly. "Makes sense."

The bitter *'she hasn't earned it'* burned on my tongue.

No amount of me trying to explain those

feelings would make sense. Even to someone like Brandon, who probably knew far better than anyone what my childhood had been like.

He lifted his hand to check the watch strapped to his wrist, frowning at it. "I need to get back to the shop. If you can have these towed, that would be great."

My eyes widened. "So, you're taking the job."

He froze, only for a moment, before quickly shoving his flashlight and the other small tool back into his uniform pockets. "Yeah. We'll discuss terms later once you've gotten the cars to the shop."

Oh man.

This was going to be perfect.

"Excellent. I'll get them towed immediately. Let me drive you back to the shop."

He seemed hesitant again, but then nodded once. "Sure, thanks."

Fishing my keys out of my pocket, I helped Brandon yank the garage doors down and locked them behind us. Excitement bubbled up in my chest. Despite Ted's shitty news, my feelings for Brandon's acceptance of the project were quickly trumping that.

However long it took for him to work on them—I didn't care. I'd fund the next five years if I had to.

As long as I got to have him back in my life, no matter how temporary, I'd do anything.

CHAPTER 6

AVERY

THE NEXT MORNING, I found myself up bright and early with my coffee in hand and a list of towing companies pulled up on my laptop.

After the first two of them had declined service with some bullshit excuse about not having enough trucks available, *Pete's Towing* came through as my Hail Mary. They only took two hours to get enough trucks in the area with towing capacity, and with called-in permission from me to the guard down at the garage site, my father's cars would be showing up at Brandon's shop come noon.

Since dropping him off yesterday, I couldn't get the zinging thrill of excitement out of my veins.

I wasn't going to be around much for when Brandon would be working on the cars, however, it gave me plenty of excuses to drop by and spend time with him while under the guise of checking in on the progress.

I tried not to think negatively over his hesitance, chalking his reaction up to being the jitters of rekindling a long lost friendship. After all, it wasn't like Brandon was known to be the type of person to jump headfirst into things.

He was cautious by nature, even while wearing his heart on his sleeve at times.

That was what was always so charming about him and what drew people in wherever he went. I doubted that personality trait had been wiped from him, despite the years passing by.

But that was something I could work with —having to earn back our friendship. Being forced to leave abruptly and then us losing contact that same year had more than likely soured him toward me in an understandable way.

Blowing back into town and into his life so

suddenly probably wasn't doing me many favors, either.

In the grand scheme of things, what I hoped for was another chance at this friendship. To show Brandon that us being apart had hurt me just as much as it had him. I'd had to fill the void left in my heart with too many things to count at this point, all of which paled in comparison.

We could never go back to the way things were—us as innocent kids trying to navigate this big scary world with nothing but each other to rely on—but I could damn well try and get us back to somewhere close.

Next to my arm, my phone went off. I lifted it from its spot on the arm of the couch, expecting the towing company's number to flash across the screen.

Instead, it was someone else entirely—their contact ID being the last one I ever expected to see come scrolling across my phone's screen.

Well, well. Look who it is...

"Long time no talk," I said after clicking the round green button.

The man on the other end of the line chuckled. "Oh, come on. Give me a break. I've been busy."

Funny he could say that while in the past, my same excuses would get me a disappointed sigh and a guilt trip that would end in me paying for an entire bar tab after a night out.

I could already feel the damn hangover settling at the base of my skull just thinking back to those times. Didn't miss them one bit—the hangover or the ridiculous partying I'd inevitably been dragged into. Though, I suppose that's what I got for befriending two fucking extroverts who took joy in seeing me suffer.

"Too busy to call me back, I see," I quipped. "Don't tell me you've got another houseman distracting you from picking up the phone every once in a while."

"Funny. And I like to call them wait staff, you privileged ass."

Smirking, I said. "Spoken like true new money, Knight."

"Oh, fuck off, McAllister. You seem to have gotten that silver spoon stuck too far up your ass."

That had me barking out a laugh.

He could be so damn dramatic.

Sliding the laptop off of me and settling it

down onto the couch, I stretched my legs out in front of me before rolling onto my feet. Teasing Marlow Knight mercilessly was one of my favorite pastimes. Especially, when it came to us battling it out about which side of the tracks we both grew up on.

Coming from the same small suburb of Ellington Heights, but having met officially in boarding school halfway around the world, was the wildest thing I'd ever experienced in my short seventeen years.

The old adage that Hazel was always fond of quoting to me as a kid, how small this world truly was, never quite hit until the day I'd gotten my room assignment and walked in to my new roommate sitting on his bed and discovering it to be Marlow.

He'd filled the void Brandon had left behind quite seamlessly. Helping to ease the pain of losing someone so important and leaving behind the only life I ever knew.

Coming from new money, unlike my family, was an added bonus. While Marlow wasn't able to relate to my struggles growing up as a trust fund baby, he certainly knew how difficult life could be while navigating relationships where money was a deciding factor on whether people wanted to stick around or not. Which unfortunately, had been a startling realization the moment both of us had stepped out into the real adult world.

I stood at the window facing out to the back of the mansion's property, overlooking the crystal clear, Olympic-sized swimming pool. "So, what brings you to calling me so early in the goddamn morning?"

"I knew you'd be awake," was his simple reply. "I heard you came blowing back into town and didn't bother telling anyone. Let alone your *friends*."

That had me sighing at my reflection in the window.

Despite his rather cavalier tone, this was Marlow's way of scolding me just like he'd done many times before. There wasn't exactly a question as to *how* he knew about me coming back to my—or rather, *our*—hometown, since it was pretty obvious that he'd heard about it through the grapevine consisting of our staff.

But rather, it was all a matter of principle.

He wasn't a relatively patient person, a flaw in most financial analysts these days, and even giving me two and a half days to settle in was generous of him. So, calling like this was more of a formality.

The next time, I'd most likely find him showing up to bang on my damn gate.

"Is this you telling me you miss me?" I teased.

"You're full of yourself. Silas was the one who missed you."

That had me rolling my eyes. "Don't hide behind him."

"Never could. He's too short. And he'd rather throw me to the sharks."

"Funny coming from you when I can see clear over both of your heads."

He scoffed at me. "Are you coming out tonight with us or what?"

I loved ragging on him. As the one only three inches taller than my companions, it always gave me a sense of satisfaction to knock both of them down a few pegs on something as simple as height when they were getting a bit too rowdy for their own good.

With all three of us typically having our heads shoved too far up our asses at times due to our insane wealth, a little heckling now and again kept us all humble enough to not be completely insufferable to be around.

I checked the time on my watch, noting I still had time to run over to Brandon's shop and catch up with him about the cars before I'd unavoidably get roped into whatever Marlow clearly had planned for tonight. And as much as my instincts to hunker down and avoid everything at all costs until the situation with Ana Liapovich got settled, it was only going to make my restlessness worse.

What better distraction than to head out to whatever bar I was going to be dragged to and finding myself a woman or two to blow off some steam with?

"Text me where we're going and I'll meet you and Silas there tonight," I said.

"Great." The grin was obvious in his voice. "Hope you've got the day off tomorrow."

How ominous.

"We'll see."

"Famous last words," Marlow said, right before ending the call.

I shook my head, letting out a chuckle, and pocketed my phone.

Hopefully, Marlow's warpath would lead me to getting laid tonight.

Fuck knew, I needed it.

CHAPTER 7

I HEADED down to Brandon's shop a little after noon. There were no signs of the tow trucks I'd called in to bring my father's cars down. However, upon peeking in through the back of the garage after I parked my car on the side of the building, I spotted all four of the vehicles inside of the shop with two of them already up on risers.

Three guys were working around them all, their motions in tandem with each other as they chatted over the radio blaring a classic rock song that sounded vaguely familiar. A good sign so far.

With Brandon not among them, I made my way back around to the front of the shop. The door was already propped open by a small brick, letting the fresh air in from outside, and allowing me to sneak in without ringing the alarm bell above it.

Brandon was behind the counter as I'd expected, leaning with his hip propped against the side of it and his arms crossed loosely over his chest. There was another man standing with him, his back facing toward me as he leaned forward on both of his hands, getting very close to Brandon.

There was something in the way the man was speaking, a hushed tone that was hard to hear over the remnants of the music from the back of the shop slowly seeping into the main lobby. While not as noisy up here as it was back there, it was still enough to notice.

The scene playing out in front of me made me stop short. I watched as Brandon's smile, the one that I hadn't seen in literally *decades,* cracked through his usual somber expression that I'd gotten used to seeing over the past few days.

A buzzing filled my head at the sound of his

laugh, prompted by whatever the man standing in front of him had said.

His happiness shouldn't be coming as this much of a shock to me. I'd seen him delighted plenty of times in my life, even if it was eons ago. However, this situation, for some reason, caused my hands to fist at my sides.

"Are you sure I can't take you with me tonight?" the man was saying.

Brandon shook his head again, a bemused expression replacing his wide smile. "I've got a lot of stuff to do tonight. But I'll definitely take a rain check."

"Fair enough." The man leaned back away from the counter and out of Brandon's personal space. "I look forward to it."

My heart slammed hard in my chest when they both turned toward me, the man looking neutral while Brandon's expression twisted into something that looked both shocked and bewildered at seeing me standing here in his shop.

Almost as if I was some kind of ghost haunting him.

Was that how he saw me?

An unwelcome pest?

I tried to not let that expression on his face

bother me. I knew I failed to do so the second the other man turned around with a promised, "I'll see you soon," before he turned and strolled out the open front door.

The silence that followed was fucking deafening.

Who the hell was that guy?

It wasn't my business. Not yet, at least. We were still on rocky terms, and even if we weren't, I'd been so far removed from Brandon's life that I didn't exactly have any legs to stand on in demanding he let me into his personal life.

For all I knew, he had a fucking long-term boyfriend or whatever occupying his time and bed.

I hated that it bothered me.

What business did I have intruding in on Brandon's life like that anyway?

"Friend?" I asked, stupidly.

I was praying that he'd tell me yes, just a friend and nothing more. That the man who'd drawn a laugh and a smile out of him was someone he knew in passing and not the person that had replaced me after I'd left.

The thought of sharing that space was like a knife to the heart.

"Uh, kind of," he said, glancing away from me.

"What does 'kind of' entail?" I tried to make my tone casual—despite my clearly raging jealousy over the possibility of having been replaced.

"My sister is trying to get me to take a plus one to her wedding. That was one of the guys her... *friend* is trying to set me up with."

I blinked. "Sister?"

Since when—

"Ah..." Brandon dropped his arms to his sides, letting out a half-chuckle. "Yeah, my mom got remarried. Her husband came with a few more kids."

When?

The question rattled inside of my brain, so loud that it had me holding back a wince.

So damn much had changed in the time that we'd stopped communicating. Both of our lives had forked into two separate directions, and now that we were back in the same town again, I was trying my damnedest to force our paths to cross once more.

Frustrating didn't even begin to cover it.

A sister.

A new father.

What the hell else did I miss?

"Congratulations to your mom," I said, flashing him a fake smile.

"Yeah, it's been interesting. We went from our family of five boys to being one of nine kids. All four new ones are female, too. Let's just say there's never a dull moment, especially since they all still live close by."

"That does sound like quite a big change." As an only child myself, I couldn't imagine my father bringing home a new wife and a gaggle of kids. That was the stuff of my nightmares growing. "All younger than you?"

He shook his head. "Older. Me and my sister, the youngest of their bunch, are the only ones close in age."

Why set him up was the real question. Brandon was a good looking guy, more so than most guys I knew. Imagining that he had any kind of trouble pulling interest from others seemed rather impossible. Unless it was the location being the main issue.

Ellington Heights was certainly much bigger in terms of population than most of the surrounding ones were, but it was still considered a small suburb by far compared to the city a few hours away. Which made for few opportunities for someone who was gay, I'd imagine.

There were plenty of fish in the sea when it came to my sexuality. Though perhaps Brandon couldn't say the same. Maybe that's why his sister was sending him romantic prospects like a damn singing gram.

"Well, I hope it works out between you two." I flash another fake smile his way, hoping I pulled it off despite the coiled tightness in my belly. I wasn't even sure what bothered me about it all, but something niggled at the back of my mind either way.

Brandon threw me a weird look, once that had my stomach churning over. "Thanks..."

Desperately wanting to change the subject to something way more neutral, I said, "So, I see the cars arrived."

"Yeah, just a bit ago. They're in good hands with my guys."

I had no doubt about that. Or with him handling everything personally, either. Brandon would never let something like this screw up on his end. Whether I was looking to make an absurd amount of money off of these vehicles or not, they were still my property—which is exactly why Brandon would treat them with care.

"Keep me updated on what's going on with them. You're free to do what you need to in terms of getting them back into working condition."

Hell, if they all turned out needing to be junked and stripped of their parts, that was fine with me, too. It wasn't like I was banking on the possibility of selling these things off at a high ticket. My bank account would, as sad as it was, hardly see a dip in funds whether the situation went good or poorly.

He nodded. "Of course. I'll call before we do anything to them."

The tempting offer to tell him to not bother with calling me and to stop by my place instead was right on the tip of my tongue. We weren't there yet, clearly, but that didn't stop my heart from wishing it so.

Now that I knew he was in the market for dating, his time was even more precious to covet.

"I'll let you get back to it." Pulling away from the counter was hard, as was forcing the words out of my mouth.

If I had it my way, I'd hang around the shop

and soak up as much of his time as I could. Damned be the consequences on either of our sides. Pathetic, of course, no matter how you dressed it up. But that's how I'd always been. Desperate to keep him focused on me and no one else.

No wonder we were always accused as teenagers of being an item.

What kind of person does that to their best friend?

Monopolizing their time like he owed me something?

He never dated in high school, probably because of me and my ridiculously overpossessive tendencies.

Jesus, how the fuck wasn't he resentful of me?

Was he?

Secretly?

He flashed me a quick smile. "Sure. I'll see you around, Avery."

The expression on his face calmed my inner turmoil somewhat, keeping it down to a dull roar inside of my head. "I'll be around. Whatever you need."

I backed out of the shop, putting some

distance between us before I did something stupid like ask him to come with me later tonight to my hangout with Silas and Marlow. The last thing he probably wanted was to see me outside of our usual haunts.

Not to mention my friends interrogating him about our past. Silas especially. The man would never pass up an opportunity to learn any and all embarrassing stories about me that he could get his hands on.

Subjecting Brandon to that would be cruel and unusual.

Getting back to my car, I pulled out my phone again and quickly texted Marlow.

Me: Meet me downtown. We're starting tonight early.

CHAPTER 8

WIPING the grease from my hands on the rag I usually had thrown over my shoulder, I took a step out from under the Chevelle's undercarriage and stared up at the main body of the car. With it being on the risers like this, one could hardly tell the work that was going to need to be put into this in order to get it road ready.

I'd had my fair share of rust buckets through the shop since opening, and this wasn't close to any of the worst ones I'd seen. However, from a financial standpoint, it was going to need a pretty penny invested into it to get it back to its former glory.

With Avery telling me, or rather reassuring me, I guess, that money wasn't an issue, I had the freedom to do what needed to be done in order to get all four of these cars back on the road. While it was certainly a dream of mine to do so, I still couldn't help that nagging guilty feeling of somehow taking advantage of him.

Sure, he'd asked *me* to complete the job but half of me was betting on the fact that his ignorance when it came to cars like this was eventually going to end in him taking quite a loss no matter how much he preached that he didn't care.

Maybe that's the working class in me.

Caring about things like bills and finances were quite laughable in the eyes of someone like Avery McAllister. I doubted he'd ever struggled a day in his life to pay a bill, let alone blow enough money to send most people in Edgewood into a heart attack.

Was that catty of me to think, or simply the truth?

Avery had never been one to flaunt his wealth, unlike his dad, which is what made him different among all of the rich upper class that came from Ellington Heights.

He was down to earth, knew that hard work was far more valuable than an easy paycheck, and appreciated the time and care that went into a job like mine.

Unlike most of the people that were within his stratosphere.

I stretched my arms over my head, my joints popping back into place with a few audible cracks. Spending all day bent over these cars, while satisfying in figuring out what the hell was wrong with them, left me sore.

Like most blue collar workers, mechanics had a tough time keeping their bodies from breaking down from the years of manual labor that had us bending and contorting ourselves into weird positions that would eventually end up retiring us quite early into the game.

Being young, I tried to keep myself as mobile as possible, not wanting to end up like the man I'd bought this shop from whose crippled back had me wincing every time we met up to discuss lease terms.

Craning my neck back to look at the time on

the large clock hanging at the back of the shop, I sighed.

It was well past dinnertime, which left me fending for myself in terms of takeout. I had a habit of doing this, staying way later than my entire shop and finding out the hard way that every business around me had long since closed up by the time I'd decided to put the socket wrench down and take a break.

The rest of this work could certainly wait until tomorrow. Fuck knew, I had plenty of time to work on it.

I wasn't sure how serious Avery was about the whole, paying for my shop while we fixed up his cars thing outside of him giving me his word. I wanted to believe him, trusted that he wouldn't screw me over due to his sincerity.

How long the offer would last was up to him, though. At a moment's notice, he could decide that the cost was outweighing the benefits by a good margin, forcing my team into getting back onto our daily grind.

None of that would be a bad thing—just throw a proverbial wrench into my plans.

Relying on anyone like that, even my former

best friend, as a business owner would be stupid anyway. No matter our history.

Noises from the front lobby had me whipping around.

Charlie had been the last one out of here, closing up the shop behind him while leaving me tucked safely inside. Or at least, that's what I thought he'd done.

So, unless he or the other two were back for some reason, I had an entirely different issue on my hands.

I grabbed one of the heavier tools off of my bench, carefully creeping my way to the front of the shop. Down the hall that led into the main lobby, I could hear shuffling and someone cursing under their breath, both of which had my heart racing.

If it were any of my guys, they would've at least announced themselves and come straight back to greet me. Whoever this was had either stumbled into the wrong place or was looking for trouble.

I tightened my grip around the metal handle as I made my way down the hallway. There were no lights on in the front of the store and only the soft glow of the shop from behind me illuminated my way. As I came up behind the front counter, I saw a figure moving in the darkness, their body swaying slightly.

Drunk?

My gaze darted over to the front door, partially open.

Right as I reached to flick on the lights, I said, "You've got five seconds to leave or I'm calling the cops."

"Arg...!" A pair of arms came up to curl around the man's head as he winced.

I stared at him for a long moment, recognizing both the voice and the clothes. "Avery?"

"Bright..." he mumbled.

What the hell?

Setting my tool down onto the counter, I came around the side of it and grabbed his arm, gently lowering him into one of the waiting room chairs. He swayed in his spot, practically doubling over the second his ass hit the cushion and causing me to have to grab him by the front of his shirt to sit him up right.

His eyes were bleary as he blinked at me a few times. "S'you..."

"Jesus, how much did you drink? Tell me you didn't drive over here, Avery."

Without waiting for his answer, I gazed out the front windows to try and spot the familiar Audi.

"No... no... s'at the bar..."

Glancing back at him, I asked. "Your car?"

He nodded.

Sighing, I let go of him. "Why are you here? And how the hell did you get in?"

"The door." The answer was followed by a confused look.

I rolled my eyes.

Drunk people were so annoying to deal with sometimes.

Leaving him to sway on his chair, I headed over to the front door and yanked it shut, pulling at the latch until it locked again and trapped us both inside. Nothing *seemed* broken... so either Charlie was an idiot and forgot to latch the lock all the way or Avery was somehow clever enough to pick the lock while drunk and let himself in.

Why the hell was he here again?

"You didn't answer my question," I said, turning back to him. "Why are you here?"

He smiled. "Came t' see you."

I hated the way my heart stuttered at that. "How come? Worried about your cars?"

"Nah."

He leaned back until his head was resting against the window behind him, both of his eyes fluttering shut. I had half a mind to yell at him for trying to fall asleep in my lobby at ten o'clock at night and scaring me half to death by breaking and entering.

But as he hummed a soft song to himself, I found my own heart melting just a little bit. Avery was always too charming for his own good.

"You're not going to answer me, are you?" Walking over to him, I stopped in front of his chair and reached out to put my hand over the top of his head. His hair was just as silky feeling as it looked, tempting me to run my hand through it.

His eyes fluttered open again. "I did."

Wanting to come see me... for what, though?

To hang out?

I found that hard to believe. Especially with him coming here after clearly visiting a bar.

"Did you go out with someone tonight?" I asked.

He nodded. "Friends. From Ellington... They asked 'bout you...'

"Me? Why?"

He grinned. "'Cause I told 'em 'bout you."

My face flushed.

It was all innocent. It had to be. He'd obviously told them that I was working on his cars and nothing more. Probably bragging that he got an entire shop dedicating the next few weeks exclusively in getting the cars back on the road so that he could sell them.

I hated the way my mind was filling in the blanks with more romantic intentions, trying to read between the lines to decipher if he was bragging about me in a friendship sense or something more. I doubted it was either of those things and more likely my first theory.

So then why the fuck was my heart so hell bent on pretending it was something more?

That was the problem with having crushes on straight men. They weren't ever going to reciprocate any feelings, let alone read into situations that could be misinterpreted as romantic. I doubted any of his buddies were hassling him for reconnecting with his childhood best friend and asking him what was going on between us.

Unlike my dumb ass.

"Aw, what's the face for...?" Avery reached out and pinched my cheek. "I don't like it."

"What face?"

"Y' look sad, Bran. Stop it."

Ugh, leave it to drunk Avery to see right through me.

"Maybe I'm annoyed that you showed up at my workplace wasted."

He barked out a laugh. "Nah. You missed me."

I did. Desperately.

I missed the dumbass shenanigans we used to get into when we were stupid teenagers. Sneaking off to parties and then ditching them once we found the stash of alcohol and pilfered a bottle so we could go hang out in the woods and drink by ourselves. We always had way more fun with just the two of us than being surrounded by a bunch of people we grew up with.

Back then, I'd deluded myself into believing that I could get Avery to fall in love with me. That by being his best friend was somehow a cheat code into turning him gay or getting him to question his sexuality long enough to realize I was perfect for him.

Clearly, that had worked out real well for me.

"Come on..." I stepped back to offer my hand. "Let's get you home."

He slapped it away from him. "Can't send me away. Came all the way here... to hang."

"It's ten at night, Avery. You should be in bed."

"Not old."

I huffed out a laugh. "That's not what I meant. You don't relax in bed before you go to sleep?"

He pinned me with a weird look. "No."

Of course not. He was always too restless for that sort of thing. "Let me bring you home."

"No."

"You can't stay here. I'm leaving for the night."

Avery's face pinched together in a painfully sorrowful look. "Oh..."

Even without him meaning to, he guilted me into wanting to take care of him.

What did it say about me and that deeply unfilled void that craved being needed?

Outside of anyone else, I would've called it a day and told them to get out or else they'd find my wrench being thrown at them.

But not with Avery.

Never with Avery.

He was always a damn exception.

"Kind of sounds like you're avoiding going home," I said.

He nodded quickly.

Bingo.

Not a surprise, either. Being surrounded by the memories of your past and the things that could no longer be were probably both haunting and disconcerting. Even with as great of a relationship that I'd had with my mother, I couldn't wait to leave the nest.

Avery had no such luxury. He'd been forced to go back to that house and be confronted by everything he left behind.

I wondered how much of it changed?

Stayed the same?

How much did he recognize that brought those same agonizing memories back, and how much was new and startling to come to realize that life moves on with or without you?

As sad as it was to leave my mother's home, I at least would never feel suffocated there.

"You can sober up at my place, how's that sound?" Offering him another hand that was quickly taken, I heaved him up out of his chair and steadied him while he swayed into me.

He was quite a bit taller than me which was

much more obvious being this up close to him. He smelled nice, outside of the soft fragrance of alcohol coloring his breath.

Before I could move away from him, his arms wrapped around my waist, pulling me into his chest. He tightened his hold on me, not letting me escape or wiggle free as he lowered his face and buried it against my hair.

Oh. My. God.

My entire body was on fire.

It's just a hug. Relax. He's drunk. He won't even remember this in the morning.

But I would.

This was going to be imprinted into my damn DNA as soon as he pulled away from me. We'd never had a touchy-feely kind of relationship outside of the subtle brushes of our hands when passing things back and forth, or Avery's shoulder resting against mine as we sat on the bus together heading off on a field trip.

I'd soaked all of those moments up, knowing that what little crumbs I'd been fed would have to last me until the next time Avery's guard was down and he let me in again.

God he smelled good.

"Bran..." he mumbled. "You like your boyfriend?"

Boyfriend?

"I don't have one."

"That guy... earlier. Was makin' goo-goo eyes at you."

He readjusted his hold on me, tucking me flush against his body so that I felt every inch of him. My nose was nuzzled up against his shoulder, taking in that intoxicating scent of his in waves that were starting to make me dizzy. One of his hands came up to rest against the back of my head, cradling me gently.

My tongue was too tied to respond, my brain too fuzzy to even try to form words at what he was saying.

"I don' like 'im..." he mumbled into my hair again. "That guy."

"Why?" was all I could manage to say.

"You were mine first."

I slammed my eyes shut.

The *'he's drunk'* mantra was only taking me down so far from this absolute high I was getting. Hearing him say things like this, the words that I'd fucking fantasized about for longer than I ever cared to admit to anyone, let alone myself, felt like a fever dream.

What the fuck was I supposed to say to that?

How could I?

Swallowing with my dry throat, I said, "You don't mean that."

"Do too," he argued.

"You're drunk, Avery."

"So?" The annoyance in his tone was obvious.

I moved my hand around him to find the center of his back, where I then patted him a few times. "Okay."

Maybe complying would get him to let go of me and give me some room to breathe. I was already getting hard against his leg, my cock painfully crushed between him and the other side of my jeans.

If he didn't feel any of that, it would be a damn miracle.

The urge to rut against his leg, grab him by the back of the neck and haul him into a sloppy kiss, was overwhelming. To the point where I was actually considering it like a fucking lunatic.

See, this was the problem with being so close

to Avery like this. He allowed me to throw all reason out the window and act impulsive.

How the hell I managed to never do anything stupid when we were kids and ruin our entire friendship was a goddamn miracle.

"Ugh," he muttered. "You always do that."

"Sorry." Even though I had no idea what I was apologizing for.

"Take me home."

A shiver rolled down my spine. "Gotta let go of me first."

He grunted again but finally, slowly, let up on his hold over me.

I wiggled free, taking several steps back while quickly turning away from him on the off-chance that the tent at the front of my pants was fucking obvious, even to a drunk man.

I brought my hands up to scrub at my face, carding my fingers through my hair as I let out a long, slow breath. "Let me grab my keys and we can go."

Not waiting for him to answer me, I quickly scooted around the counter to the back of the shop to flip all the lights off and grab my stuff from the office. Avery was waiting patiently by the door, his gaze glued to me the second I came down the hallway.

He swayed slightly but wasn't in danger of falling over from the looks of it. Leading him out by his arm, I gripped tightly around his biceps. I locked up behind us and carefully ushered him over to my truck.

"You able to make it up there?" My question for more of a half joke, half concern.

To my surprise, Avery was nimble enough to throw himself onto the bench on the passenger's side and haul himself up. The sight had me shaking my head and shutting the door behind him.

This was going to be a long ass ride home.

CHAPTER 9

B RANDON

R OUSING A VERY AWAKE — WHO ' D fallen
asleep on my shoulder the minute I'd gotten the
truck out of park and pulled onto the main road
—I killed the ignition and slipped my seatbelt off
of me.

He slowly blinked his eyes open, was
mechanical in the way he sat himself up and
shook his head a few times to wake up. I had half
a mind to reach out and rub his shoulder out of
comfort, already feeling sympathetic to the hangover he was bound to wake up with tomorrow
morning.

Although it wasn't really *my* problem per say, I still found myself concerned for him.

"Come on, let's get you to bed." Pushing open my side of the truck, I climbed out and let the door slam behind me.

Avery didn't move inside of the cab and merely squinted at me through the windshield. Him being so drunk had me wondering what exactly had tipped him over the edge like this. Usually, he wasn't one to get more than tipsy, let alone being so far gone that he could barely recognize where he was.

Or rather... that's how he *used* to be. I supposed I really had no clue if he was some kind of alcoholic or heavier partier nowadays. I could only speculate about it based on what he used to be like a long time ago.

People were prone to change, after all, and continually trying to fit him into a box he'd clearly outgrown wasn't fair on my part.

At the same time, though, this also seemed like some kind of cry for help. Perhaps his father's death was finally hitting him. Or maybe he was coming to terms with no longer having that man looming over his shoulder and was finally feeling free enough to go a little crazy.

A combination of both?

Who knew.

I wretched open Avery's side, beckoning him over to me. "Come on, let's go."

He frowned. "You're mad..."

"What? No, I just don't want you throwing up in my truck."

"You don't like me..."

I sighed. "Avery. Get out of my damn truck."

He slowly scooted over, swinging his legs around, and then heaved himself off of the seat. My eyes widened as I reached out to catch him, only just barely steadying us both before we careened down onto the driveway and ended up in a heap.

Avery's arms came around me again, tugging me closer until I was pressed up against him once more. His face was buried in the crook of my neck, his warm breath ghosting over my skin and sending a shiver rolling up my spine hard enough to make my entire body twitch.

"Don't hate me."

Not being able to help myself, I ran my fingers through the ends of his hair. "I don't. Whatever gave you that impression?"

"S'cause you don't want to be around me."

"To be fair, we don't really know each other anymore."

"Hate that," he mumbled.

I couldn't help but smile a little. "Is this you trying to tell me you want to be best friends again?"

He nodded.

Truth be told, I wasn't sure I could handle that.

The more likely scenario was that now more than ever, I was going to make my feelings obvious enough for him to pick up on, no matter how hard I tried to suppress them from not only him, but from myself as well.

It wasn't fair of me to put that kind of pressure on him in any sense, but especially with him still dealing with his father's estate and the mess that came with it.

What sense would throwing my own drama into the mix make?

None whatsoever.

Able to wiggle out of his hold this time, I grabbed him by the arm and led him up the front steps to my house. It was a small thing, no wider than a trailer, but was something that I proudly called home. The outside's curb appeal could certainly use a little work, but who the hell had time for that anyway.

Unlocking my front door, I ushered Avery inside and flicked on the hallway lights. I pointed to where the shoe mat was, taking off my own and then waiting for him to do the same before I tugged him down the hallway.

"You can take my bed," I said, pushing the door open to my room once we reached it.

Like the rest of my house, the master bedroom was pretty small, but with it only being me here, I never found the need to complain about it.

Why have more room that would just remain empty?

Avery's gaze was curiously darting around the space, taking everything in all in once as I turned the fan and light on. Once I let go of him, he wandered over to my dresser, picking up some of the small photo frames I had sitting there to inspect them.

Pictures with my mom and brothers from childhood, a few of me and my sister, and the rest of our siblings, along with one of Avery and me —all of them were neatly set side-by-side in a uniform row that looked quite out of place in my undecorated room.

When he picked up the one of us—a fishing trip we'd taken one year where both of us caught the smallest bass you could ever imagine—he traced his finger over the glass in a languid motion. Like he was trying to memorize it.

I watched him quietly, keeping my distance over by the door.

He set the frame down carefully, stepping back while looking over his shoulder at me. His eyes were half-lidded and slow blinking, the kind of expression that most people would think was Avery trying to make eyes at them.

I knew better, though. Knew to not give into whatever pathetic excuse my mind was trying to come up with in order to cross the distance and pull him into a kiss.

"Bed?" he said, finally turning back to it.

"Yeah." My voice was hoarse.

He settled down onto the edge of the mattress, putting both of his hands on his thighs while spreading his legs wide. He eyed me expectantly, a strange expression coming over him.

"You want a change of clothes? I think I've got some oversized stuff."

When he didn't answer me, I took that as a sign to grab him a pair anyway. The worst thing he'd do was not wear it.

Pulling a pair of wide legged pants and a t-shirt from my dresser drawer, I crossed the room to hand them to him. "All right, well, I'll grab you some water and then leave you alone."

Avery's brows pulled together. "Alone?"

"Yeah, I'm going to take the couch."

He let out an annoyed sound, snatching the clothes from my hand. "No."

"No what?"

He tossed the clothes onto the bed, both of his hands suddenly grabbing me and yanking me clear off my feet. I stumbled and slammed into his chest, both of us tumbling backward. Avery was flat against the mattress and I was laid out on top of him.

My face burned at the position, and even more so when I felt myself growing hard again.

For fuck's sake.

"Couch." He huffed. "What the fuck."

"What's wrong with me taking the couch?" I tried to sit up, failed immediately when his arms tightened around my waist.

"Stupid," was all he said before rolling us over, pinning me under him.

"*Avery*," I spat out—but even to my own ears, I was barely sounding just above desperate.

He settled against me, resting his entire body on mine like an oversized weighted blanket. One of his legs was hooked under mine, causing our hips to practically be pressed flush against each other. His one arm was curled around my body, his shoulder acting as my chin rest while I fumbled to wiggle out from under him.

"Don't you dare fall asleep like this," I said. "I'll fucking kill you."

He only laughed, burying his face in my neck. "S'kay."

No, it fucking isn't!

My cock was begging for me to reach down and unbutton my pants and fist my hand around it. Blueballs were nothing compared to whatever torture *this* was.

Humping his leg like a fucking horny dog was exactly what my brain was screaming at me to do. Just to get an ounce of relief. As long as I could breathe in his scent, I could get off just like this.

How fucked up was that?

I groaned.

"Shhhh," he said. "Sleep."

"Easy for you to say," I mumbled.

God, what would Avery even do if he found out how much he turned me on?

Freak out, probably.

Run for the hills?

More than likely.

Then again, what other chance would I ever get to be this close to him again?

Even without the grossly sexual tension that was clearly one-sided on my end, Avery wasn't one for physical affection at all, no matter the circumstances.

Was it wrong of me to take advantage of this?

To convince him to spend as much time like this with me as possible?

Before he sobered up and realized that keeping people at arm's length was better than ever letting anyone in.

Maybe this would have to be enough for me. Simply holding him as he slept while I listened to the sounds of his soft breathing in my ear.

Reaching up from behind, I tangled my fingers in his hair and gently stroked through the long lengths.

"Go to sleep, Avery."

But I didn't need to tell him that at all, because soon, his labored breathing tapered off into steady even breaths and his body relaxed against mine while he fell asleep.

This would have to be enough for me, no matter how much it was going to hurt me come morning when he inevitably pushed me away with some lame excuse and tried to play all of this off as some drunken stupor.

At least I'd remember it. At least I could hold this moment in my heart for the rest of my days and look at it fondly despite the heartache attached to it.

I loved this man more than he'd ever know.

And sometimes, that needed to be enough.

No matter what.

CHAPTER 10

Avery

THERE WAS a stark difference between going out for a few drinks with a couple of friends and catching up while we eyed the bar for singles and getting shit-faced drunk while being reminded of the fact that I was painfully striking out at every turn.

While I'd never had any difficulty in pulling interest from women at bars, *nothing* had been striking me no matter how much Silas and Marlow were egging me on in an effort to also get me laid.

The sad thing was that apparently my pent

up frustrations were obvious to pretty much everyone around me, including them, which had me wondering if Brandon had also picked up on it somehow.

Having that question teased in the back of my mind the entire night was the final nail in the coffin of me ending up stumbling out of the bar earlier than expected while both of my friends were finding themselves entertained with a couple of guys they'd been invited to play pool with.

I hadn't had the heart to try and worm my way between any of that—not wanting to bring down the vibes with my obviously overly intoxicated behavior that was getting eyebrow raises from both Silas and Marlow on multiple occasions.

And once I'd seen an out, I'd gone for it.

That's how I'd somehow found myself wandering the streets of Edgewood until the doors to Brandon's shop were staring me right in the face. To be fair, I'd only planned on trying to the handle on the off chance that it'd be unlocked, which to my surprise it *was*. And then I'd only planned on stepping inside to use his phone to call a rideshare.

But that wasn't exactly an easy task to accomplish with how fried I was.

Brandon *actually* still being there so late at night was a small miracle. One that I felt that whatever God was actually out there had somehow blessed me with. His mussed up hair and the single grease stain that was smeared across his cheek had made me melt, causing me to foolishly beg him to take me home like some stray cat hoping that their new human companion would spare them an empty box to sleep in for the night.

Never did I expect to find myself in bed the next morning with our limbs tangled together and my face buried in his neck while I breathed in his slightly salty and musky scent. Or the fact that my morning wood would be pinched between our bodies, throbbing with the need for any type of friction to relieve the pressure that was building in my balls.

Brandon's soft and labored breath was the only thing that soothed me and my raging hard on. His chest rising and falling against my mine, his breathing that fell in time with me, and the small ticks in his limbs that coincided with whatever he was currently dreaming about.

Being pressed up against him like this—like we were a couple of fucking ferrets tangled into a mess of a pile together—it felt good. Warm and welcoming. Coming home after a long day out in the cold and finding solace by the fireplace.

I *could* chalk all of this up to my hangover and my inability to invite any of the women who approached me last night back home with me so that I could finally find some fucking relief. There were too many excuses in my head the entire night, none of them mattering now that I was trying not to grind my hard on into my former best friend's thigh and get myself off.

What would even happen if I tried that, anyway?

Sometimes, I really envied Silas and Marlow. Out and proud of themselves as gay men who took no shame in finding what they wanted and taking it home with them. While I wasn't gay myself, I always found that quality in them was something that I lacked. I'd been so stuck in my ways for so long that at this point in my life, I wasn't sure *what* I wanted.

Carrie had been my ticket to figuring it all out. Marrying her had made sense for both my career and my family's legacy. When it all came crumbling down, I'd felt lost for so long that work had seemed like the next best thing to bury myself in.

And now it was almost three years later and I still didn't know what I fucking wanted.

Nothing made sense.

Nothing but *Brandon* made sense.

What did that mean?

What was so special about the friendship that we had together that made it so hard to let it go?

Brandon shifted under me, letting out a long sigh while rolling his body into mine. The motion of it sent a zing of pleasure shooting straight to my boner, forcing a hiss out of me as I fought the urge to move with him.

Oh, fuck me...

I was too comfortable in an agonizing kind of way. Not to mention my hangover was making me a little dizzy. What I really needed to do was roll over and go to the bathroom so I could rub myself raw over the fucking toilet.

With my arm pinned under him, radio static shot through my limb the second I tried to move it out from under him. Flames licked at my skin from the blood finally returning to my poor arm, causing my shoulder to cramp up in the process.

I used my other arm to sit up slightly, and the loss of the weight on his chest had Brandon moving once more. His legs crushed my thigh between them, holding me in place. That's when I felt something else brush up against my hips. Hard and tenting the front of his pants.

He moaned softly in his sleep, the sound a wonderfully enticing thing that had my mouth dropping open to suck in a surprised gasp of air.

As I stared down at where we were entangled, my brain began to short circuit. The collective symphony in my horny brain egging me on and telling me that just a little bit more friction and I'd finally find what I'd been chasing after since last night.

I knew I was going to monumentally regret this.

I didn't care.

Lowering myself down on top of Brandon again and burying my face into the crook of his neck, I breathed in deeply. God, he smelled fucking good. I was tempted to open my mouth and lick at his skin, which I had a feeling would taste salty and slightly bitter from him working at the shop all day.

Under me, Brandon's hips clashed again with

my own, rolling in a slow motion that had me seeing stars.

"Fuck," I whispered against his neck.

I needed to come so fucking bad it was boarding on painful. Matching his rhythm, I ground myself against him until I could feel the hard line of him hidden under his jeans. That had me gasping in his ear, the unexpected shot of pleasure building at the base of my spine.

I'd never had any questions about my sexuality, never found my own gender appealing, let alone want to rub my dick against another one like this. It felt so good, to the point where I didn't even care that another man was currently getting me off.

"Ahh..." Brandon whimpered.

Hearing him like this, in an intimate way, was something that felt forbidden—wrong in a way. Like I was intruding on a private moment that I wasn't meant to share with him. We'd only been open to a point about our hookups in high school, and with not much experience under either of our belts, we'd had very little in the ways of bragging rights.

So what Brandon was like in this kind of setting was foreign to me. Yet it did nothing to deter my balls from squeezing out enough precum to wet the front of my slacks in an embarrassing way.

My hips snapped into his, pulling a moan from my own mouth.

Oh, fuck. I was going to come just like this. Humping my former best friend like a thirteen year old who just discovered the beauty of an overly squishy pillow and a cock slicked with half a bottle of lotion.

So close…

There was a gasp and then his hands were slamming into my chest, thrusting me back hard enough to send me sprawling off the bed. Nearly hitting my head on the way down, I snatched the side of the nightstand for purchase, only missing the corner of it from slicing my forehead open at the last second.

My shoulder hit the floor first, my legs still hanging up onto the bed as I tried to blink away the black spots forming in my eyes from my headache.

"Oh my god— *Fuck.*" Brandon's face appeared over the side of the bed. "Are you okay?"

I only groaned in response.

"Just, uh, stay right there," he said, scrambling off the other end of the bed.

His footsteps moved around his room and then disappeared down the hallway, leaving me to slowly peel myself up off the floor in a humiliating show of stupidity. Well, that was one way to kill a boner...

Mortified wasn't even going to cover what I felt at this moment.

What the hell was wrong with me?

Just as I slumped back onto the bed, I heard Brandon coming back down the hallway.

His eyes were downcast while he stretched his hand out to me, a glass held in one and a fist full of something in the other. When I opened my palm up toward him, he quickly slapped a few tablets of meds on it and then all but shoved the glass of water at me.

"For your hangover," he said, refusing to even glance in my direction.

Oh, I'd royally fucked up.

Popping the pills quickly and downing the entire glass all in one go, I carefully handed it back to him, saying, "Thank you."

"Yeah, no worries."

There was a heavy pause that fell over us,

enough to make my body want to twitch as the anxious feeling inside of my stomach was twisting it into knots tight enough to make me feel nauseous.

There was no doubt about it, he was definitely freaked out.

And why wouldn't he be?

It wasn't like it was an every day thing to wake up to your straight, former best friend humping you like a fucking dog in heat. No matter what delicious sounds were coming out of your mouth because of it.

Jesus fuck.

'Delicious'?

I needed my head checked.

Sighing, I said, "Brandon—"

"I should probably shower." His words instantly had my mouth snapping shut. "Got to work soon."

Swallowing the bitterness on my tongue, I forced myself to stand. "Yeah. Of course. I've got a rideshare coming already."

He only nodded and quickly stepped out of my way. When we finally made eye contact, his face flushed a dark rosy color and he turned away once more.

"Have a good morning," he mumbled.

The second I was out the door and had it firmly shut behind me, I fought the urge to look up at the sky and curse at it.

Fuck my life.

CHAPTER 11

BRANDON

THE PAPERWORK in front of me was a complete blur as I stared down at it. The words jumbled into an unreadable ménage of nonsense that made less sense the longer I looked at it.

I'd been at this for hours now, with the pen pressed to the same damn line that I'd re-read probably a hundred times. My mind was elsewhere. Far, far away from my shop where I was tucked inside of my tiny little office pretending like this morning never happened.

The memories were like a punch to the gut, leading me to drop my pen and slap my hands over my face in an effort to drown out the groan of despair that tumbled past my lips.

Fuck.

Fuck, fuck, *fuck*.

How the hell was I stupid enough to have a goddamn *wet dream* about the man that I'd inexplicably let into my bed?

To the point where I'd been humping the shit out of him in real life and had almost come right before I'd managed to wake myself up out of it.

Avery had trusted me to take care of him after I'd taken him home—not expected me to come onto him while he'd sought comfort from me after what had been a very troubled few weeks for him.

The poor man was looking for a friend in his time of need, and what did I do to repay him?

Practically cream my own fucking jeans while I dreamed of him sucking me off and telling me that he'd been waiting do that since high school.

Slumping over my desk, I let my head smack down onto it, relishing the pain that followed. He was never going to talk to me again. There was no way we could come back from this.

What was I even supposed to say in defense of myself?

Sorry, Avery. I've been in love with you since we were fifteen, please forgive my horny brain in thinking that you were a part of my wet dream. Oh yeah, and I still have those about you, too.

Oh my god. I was lucky he didn't punch me the second I let him go. Hell, I was lucky he wasn't showing up to the shop right now with a towing company behind him ready to load up his dad's cars to be taken to another shop where he knew the owner wouldn't try and make the moves on him.

A hand clapped down on my shoulder, causing me to jump right out of my own skin.

"Jeez!" Charlie launched himself back from my chair, both of his hands held up in defense. "You didn't hear me callin' ya?"

"No." Slumping back in my chair, I said, "What's up?"

"That black Bel Air's got a rusted out exhaust system. I found the parts online but you gotta authorize it since it's comin' from a specialty dealer down in Michigan."

I held in another sigh. On top of that, I was also going to have to contact Avery about it, too.

Scrubbing a hand over my face, I asked, "You got a total already?"

Thankfully, Charlie pulled a folded up piece of paper out of the pocket of his uniform and handed it over to me. It was several sheets of printed out pictures of the parts that we'd need to order, along with totals scribbled in the margins of each one and a phone number for the shop located at the very top of the bunch.

"Thanks. I'll handle this while you get back to the other ones."

"Right on, boss."

Watching him slip out the door and down the hall, I spun back around to my desk and tossed the papers down over the payroll sheets. There was no way I was at all ready to face the music in calling Avery up and trying to talk shop while pretending that this morning was all a bad nightmare.

I had a slim chance of even getting him to answer my phone call in the first place, and if I did end up actually getting him on the other line, I was petrified to hear the disgust in his voice.

I knew controlling myself around him would be difficult; I just never took into account that my own body would betray me so heinously.

Sighing, I grabbed my phone off of the desk and flipped it over, noticing that I had a missed call from one of my brothers—Jonah. Curious, I tapped on his contact and let the dial tone pick up.

"Hey, he's alive!"

Unfortunately. "What's up?"

"Wanted to check in on you."

That was fishy. The only time anyone was ever worried about me was when I'd go AWOL for a little while in order to get my own mental health back in order before I accidentally made it everyone else's problem. But that hadn't happened in months.

"I'm fine," I said, slowly. "Something going on?"

"Lila called me."

I groaned. "No."

Jonah laughed. "Oh, come on. You didn't think she would blab to the whole family that she's been trying to set you up for weeks? You underestimate her ability to keep a secret."

No, what I really underestimated was how big of a deal she was going to make this whole me going stag to her wedding. Apparently, not taking her seriously the first time she'd threatened to get our whole family involved was my first mistake.

The second being calling my brother back without acknowledging his own ridiculous nature when it came to encouraging Lila's over the top behavior.

"Maybe I'm just not feeling it," I answered back, petulantly.

"You don't really mean that."

I didn't, but no one else had to know that. "Why is it that *I'm* the one getting singled out here? Both Marie and Reece are single right now. And I'm pretty sure Jace just broke up with his girlfriend."

"I'm pretty sure they just got back together," came Jonah's quick response.

That had me rolling my eyes. "Can you focus? Who cares about that. Don't you see the unfairness to this situation?"

Jonah sighed. "Bran, we're just worried about you. You've been perpetually single for your entire life. Lila wants you to find happiness."

"Through a *matchmaker*?"

"What?" He laughed. "Crazier things have happened. Look at Sara. She got married to Tom after knowing him for three weeks."

Okay, that was probably the worst example my brother could've ever given me. Not only was my half-sister a hapless romantic, but she was impulsive as hell.

Taking a trip up to the mountains after getting fired from her big-wig job in the city, she'd ended up getting herself snowed in in this little remote village out in the middle of nowhere for three entire weeks until the county next door to them had enough manpower to plow everyone out.

In that time, she'd ended up bunking with the manager of the motel she'd been staying at, getting a little more than just cozy by the fire-place with him. By the time she'd come back to Edgewood, she'd had a ring on her finger and a damn baby in her belly.

Five years later and those two were still crazy in love with another little one on the way.

"That's not the point." I forced the words out.

What I *really* wanted to say was that there *was* no point.

To any of this.

I wasn't going to magically get matched up with my soulmate and fall madly in love with him and run off into the sunset while we laughed and canoodled the entire way to our honeymoon destination.

My soulmate wasn't some man that sought the help of a matchmaker and had hope of one day finding their true match. Or even really believed in the power of love at all.

Honestly, my soulmate probably never existed in the first place. I'd been cursed to forever fatefully find myself obsessed with the one man I could never have. Therefore, denying me of a soulmate for being stupid enough to let myself fall into this trap in the first place.

It was my own dumbass fault for getting my emotions too entangled with Avery's at such a young age. Imprinting on him to the point that infatuation paled in comparison to the kind of obsession I felt for him.

By now, I was in too deep.

If after an entire decade of having not seeing each other had done nothing to dull these feelings, then nothing ever would.

Not some matchmaker setting me up with a handsome guy who was determined to sweep me off my feet. Not some man trying to talk me up at one of the bars downtown while hoping to convince me to come back to his place with him for a nightcap and a quick roll around in the sheets.

And certainly not some poor son of a bitch who had already buried his demons in the past and healed himself of the kind of future that eventually awaited me.

"Okay," Jonah's voice drawled. "Then what *is* the point?"

"Never mind. It's not important. Look, if Lila's actually that dead set on forcing me to go with this guy she picked out, then whatever. Fine, I'll do it."

"Don't sound so morbid. You're not walking the plank here."

That's exactly what it felt like, though. A proverbial gun being held to the back of my head while my sister chanted 'kiss him!' in the background.

Or worse: *fall in love.*

"Just... *try* it, Brandon. One date. That's all we're asking. Mom's also worried about you, you know."

Ugh, I hated this guilt trip. Mainly because it always worked. Jonah knew that. I knew that. This was the pain about having older brothers.

They knew how best to push your buttons and get you squirming enough to agree to whatever crazy plan they'd concocted. Which, in this case, was apparently to get me back into the dating world.

Or, I guess, into it in the first place?

My casual hookups weren't exactly counting as a defense for me at this point. If anything, they made my life seem that much sadder.

The only silver lining to any of this was that none of my brothers knew that Avery was back in town. That information was something I'd like to keep hidden for as long as possible. The second the rumors of that got to floating around my family, I was done for.

My brothers knew how devastated I was when he left and they'd waste no time hesitating in trying to force us back together again, especially under the excuse of *for old time's sake.*

No amount of protesting would change any of their minds, either, so there would be no point in fighting them on the matter, regardless of how awkward things were between Avery and me now. It wasn't like I could explain, *hey so I might've sort of accidentally came on to him and now I think he hates me* without there being a million questions followed right after.

With no way to defend myself, I was merely digging my own grave at that point.

Why hand any of them the shovel to then bury me?

"Brandon?"

Clearing my throat, I said, "Yeah. I'll give it a try."

"Atta boy. Tell me how it goes."

"You want a play-by-play in the group chat, or..."

"Ha, funny. But now that you're offering, yeah. I do. Everyone will be stoked to hear about your date."

I really needed to keep my mouth shut. "Fine."

"Good luck, little brother."

As soon as the other line disconnected, I tossed my phone down onto my desk.

Agreeing to a date wasn't *that* big of an issue, but leading him on was. Max was a nice guy and wasn't screaming any kind of red flags at me so far.

If anything, *I* was the red flag in this scenario.

He'd seemed eager to take me out. Something that I *should* find flattering. Yet all it did was make me want to dig my heels into the ground more so than usual. I hated that about myself—any man showing me an ounce of interest outside of just sex, was automatically dismissed and put in the 'do not trust' category with no hope of getting out, no matter how much they showered me in gifts and affection.

It was a tiring process that seemed never-ending in my mind, with few ways to stop it.

Eventually, I did want a family of my own. A big one like the one I'd grown up in. I'd never been shy about that fact to anyone, especially with my siblings, which was probably one of the many reasons I was being pushed to date in the first place.

They meant well. They always did.

I needed to trust the process.

What other hope did I have in trying to wring Avery out of my system?

Spending time with him wasn't helping and seemed to only make my obsession with him worse.

If there was a slim chance that I could poten-tially find a sliver of that same feeling with someone else, then I needed to take the plunge regardless of my own hang-ups about it.

Because, at this point, I had nothing left to lose.

Grabbing my phone again, I scrolled through my contacts until I found Lila's matchmaker and the number that she'd forwarded me into order to get in touch with Max.

Typing out a quick message to him, I hit send before I could think twice about it and then set my phone face down on my desk again. Within seconds, it buzzed, causing me to flip it over once more.

Max: Hey, Brandon! Yeah, I'd love to :) Are you free tomorrow night? Ellington Heights has that local band performing at the park. I think it's some kind of festival going on. There are supposed to be a bunch of food trucks and things to do while walking around. I'd love to take you, if you're up for it.

Actually, that sounded kind of fun.

Sending my response back to him, I folded myself back into my chair and let a long breath leave me.

Guess I had a date tomorrow.

Hopefully, I wouldn't fuck it up.

CHAPTER 12

AVERY

BRANDON'S EMAIL was the last notification I
expected to receive after taking an unnecessarily
long cold shower the second I got back home.

I'd planned on wiping the memories, along
with my shame, down the drain and punishing
myself in the process. An appropriate response to
my otherwise failed attempts at whatever the
fuck happened back at Brandon's house and the
inevitable fallout because of it.

Freezing myself to death was on the dramatic
side of things, more than I cared to admit, but it
had done the job in forcing everything but the

need to get warmer from my mind by the time I shut the water off and wrapped myself up in a towel.

I'd made the mistake of checking my phone once I'd stumbled back into my bedroom again, discovering an email waiting for me, and soon realizing how easy it was to unravel all of the hard work I'd done in locking up those goddamn memories and throwing the key away in the process.

Or so I thought.

Attached to the email were a couple of pictures, the message with it reading: "*The black Bel Air needs an entire new exhaust system. Here is the quote. Can order and have parts in by Monday.*"

And that was it.

Collapsing down onto my bed with only the towel to keep me from completely soaking my bedsheets, I stared up at the ceiling and wondered where the fuck I was supposed to go from here.

It shouldn't be that much of a shock that Brandon was still willing to work on these cars. His integrity to finishing up a project showed significantly in how he led all aspects of his life.

Half-assed was not in his forte, and neither was abandoning something halfway through after committing to it in the first place.

His message wasn't a good sign. The clipped tone and the professionalism that had none of the friendliness like the emails he'd sent me before this were telling. He was uncomfortable with me.

"*Fuck.*" Gritting the word through my clenched teeth, I fisted my hands into the wet lengths of my hair and tugged on them hard enough at the roots to hurt.

How could I come back from this?

Realistically, approaching him at his business would do fuck all in terms of soothing the tension between us. It wouldn't look like me coming to him as a friend, concerned about our relationship after a major fuck up on my part.

What it would come across looking like was me cornering him and pressuring him into forgiving me for my crude-ass behavior.

How the hell was I supposed to explain myself anyway?

Me, a straight man, humping my gay best friend like a fucking dog.

But oh god, the way he moaned. Those soft,

breathy sounds that whispered over my skin and tickled my shoulder while I had my face buried in his neck. I'd never felt another cock rubbing against mine in my entire life, but in that moment, it'd felt fucking fantastic.

The hard ridges of him lined up with my own, grinding together while each thrust of my hips into his brought on that building sensation at the base of my spine.

What would've happened if a different scenario went down?

If Brandon had woken up and instead of being freaked out and pushing me away, he'd been surprised but delighted to continue.

It isn't until I feel my balls squeeze that I realize I'd somehow snuck my hand under my towel and fisted my already hard cock. Squeezing around it, I shifted my hand up from the base, moving to circle around my leaking tip and back down to spread it along the length of me.

Imagining one of Brandon's calloused fingers coming up to grab at my hair and force me down into a kiss had me closing my eyes to picture it, my hand tightening. Our tangled tongues coming together to taste the inside of each other like we were memorizing the details.

I'd never thought about kissing Brandon before this. Hell, it'd never crossed my mind to get so close to him that our bodies brushed together, let alone grinding against him intentionally until we were both popping boners.

His hitched breath had done me in, gotten me curious into exploring an unknown territory that I'd otherwise left unclaimed until that very moment. Hell, I never thought that there was anything *to* explore.

I'd been as straight as the day was long for my entire life with nothing to tell me otherwise.

So what the fuck was changing?

Loneliness?

Nostalgia?

Whatever it was, it wasn't making the ache in my balls any less painful.

Rolling over onto my stomach, I kept an arm against the mattress for balance while propping my hips up from it. With my hand still fisted tightly around my cock, I reared back and then snapped forward, fucking myself into my hand and imagining a tight hole instead.

Getting past that first ring of muscles, I buried myself deep down inside, my eyes sliding shut while I recalled those breathy moans. He'd sound like that with his head pressed down into the mattress, my fingers tangled in his hair while I held him there and fucked him nice and raw.

His hole would take me greedily. He'd beg me to come inside him.

My back stiffened, that familiar tingling at the base of my spine coming on hard.

With a groan, I exploded in my hand. Cum spat out from my slit, coating my fingers and sheets in a complete mess that had me collapsing face first against my bed. I laid there for what felt like ages, until my spend began to dry and my breath was no longer coming in quick bursts.

I cracked my eyes open, and then reality slammed into me.

Peeling my hand off of my softening dick, I held it up while rolling to the side, surveying the absolute mess I left behind. I'd never come so much in my life.

Being turned on and ignoring it was one thing, but giving in and touching myself?

Fuck. I needed a damn shrink.

CLEANING up my bed while balling up and tossing my old sheets like a humiliated teenager down the laundry chute, I dreaded the sound of my phone going off by the time I stepped back into my room.

There was an innate possibility that, given the dread filling my stomach with unease while I retrieved my phone from where I'd tossed it after stripping my bed, the person on the other end of that line was about to deliver me with some horrible news.

Call it superstition or intuition, however it mattered. I never tended to question those things that had been gifted to me by my mother.

"This is Avery McAllister," I greeted, settling back down onto my bed.

"Avery, it's Ted Evans."

Jesus fuck.

Of all things.

"You hear back from that other law office?"

He sighed into the phone. "I did. Got the documents in my inbox this morning. They look legit. I'm getting them authenticated in the meantime, but I wanted to call you and let you know."

Pinching the bridge of my nose was only

doing so much for my oncoming headache. Despite Brandon's attempts at helping me circumvent a migraine, it seemed that my stress levels were determined to give me one anyway.

"What does she want?" I asked.

"A meeting."

"With me?"

"Yes. I imagine to discuss terms, but probably, more informally, to meet you."

That had to be some kind of shakedown tactic.

Why else would a random Russian model be interested in meeting her dead husband's adult child?

She'd had no interest before this, let alone enough to invite me into some kind of relationship with her before my father had passed.

While I wasn't sure on the exact timeline on when they'd gotten married before my father's passing, the fact that I'd never heard of her to begin with was telling.

Either he'd neglected to let me meet her for a specific reason, or she simply had expressed to him in wanting to keep distance between us. Fine by me, except now that this was a matter of my father's wealthy estate, suddenly the introductions were integral.

"And if I have no interest in that?" I asked.

"Unfortunately, I do need you down here during the discussion. Since she's contesting your father's will, I need all parties present."

I sighed. "When and where?"

"I'm setting up a meeting the day after tomorrow. If you can get down here early, we can go over what you're willing to bring to the table in terms of negotiating if it comes down to that. She may simply ask for money and be done with it. But until that happens, I want us both to be prepared for the worst."

A smart move, even if it was rather unfortunate timing.

Still, it would give me a much-needed distraction from the rest of the problems in my life.

"All right, I'll be there."

"Excellent," Ted said. "I'll see you then."

I tossed my phone away from me, and my world tilted backward until I was flat against the mattress.

I prayed that this woman was only after the money. That I could handle.

Anything else and I'd blow a gasket.

CHAPTER 13

BRANDON

QUIET NOSTALGIA WAS A PRETTY ironic name for the band currently playing on the gazebo stage at the center of the park. Ironic in the sense that the longer we wandered around the festival listening to their bluegrass music, the more I was falling into a weird funk that was killing the mood.

Coming over to this side of the lake wasn't something I did very often nowadays, as most everything I needed was within the small radius of Edgewood. Crossing the bridge to get to the ritzier side of our area felt both off and out of place now that I was no longer coming over here to hang out with my best friend on a regular basis.

And even then, I'd always felt *othered*.

Coming from a working class family and a single mom raising four kids all on her own, Ellington Heights had been less than kind to any of us. We'd gotten more noses turned up at us and biting remarks thrown our way that bordered on harassment, simply by existing within the same stratosphere as the rich and privileged and daring to think we were just as good as them.

It was a sad reality to be thrust into at a young age, but had toughened us up for what the real world would eventually have in store for us.

Meeting Avery had been my saving grace.

At least until I screwed it up by falling in love with him like an idiot.

"Brandon? You okay?"

The second a hand brushed against my arm, it sent me jumping in the opposite direction.

"Shit, sorry." Max held up his hands apologetically. "I didn't mean to startle you."

Slapping a hand to rest against my racing

heart, I let out a slow breath. "It's okay. I didn't mean to space out like that."

He shot me a sympathetic smile. "Not one for crowds?"

Well, that wasn't exactly it.

It wasn't like I was partial to anything.

The problem with being back in Ellington Heights after avoiding it like the plague since graduating high school, was that coming back here was slapping me in the face with the fact that this damn place held too many memories. Having been friends with someone like Avery whose restless spirit kept us from staying stagnant for too long, we'd explored this place from top to bottom and then all over again.

There was no stone left unturned, no back alley left unchecked.

We'd woven ourselves into these streets and left pieces behind when we both eventually moved on and never looked back.

Being brought back here on a date was fucking me up in a way I hadn't considered before agreeing to do this in the first place.

A complete oversight on my part.

Before this, I figured what was the harm in going to a local music festival that had a bunch of kids running around and stalls where you could get things like your face painted or henna.

Coming here was the perfect opportunity to get to know someone on a neutral playing field, and instead, I was too busy wasting my time reminiscing on days long since passed. To the complete detriment of getting to know someone outside of my small scope of regulars.

Was that at all fair to someone like Max who seemed like he was trying his damned best to keep up the conversation while I lagged behind pretending like I wasn't being absolutely haunted by every step we took?

Fuck me, honestly.

"The crowds are fine. It's been a while since I've been back here, is all," I said, trying to force myself back into the present.

Bypassing a small stand with lemonade and freshly popped kettle corn that smelled divine, I wished I was actually in the mood to be walking around getting to know Max while we played the twenty questions game like he'd suggested when we first got here.

He wasn't a bad looking guy and, so far, seemed to have a nice enough personality. If I wasn't so hung up on the past, I could see myself exploring something with him. Instead, I felt like we were killing time until he eventually got sick of trying to engage with me.

"Oh, that's right. Your sister mentioned to the matchmaker that you used to hang out with a friend over here." Max smiled.

Of course she did.

"Yeah, it wasn't as bad. The lifestyle over here isn't much different from what I grew up in. People are just more fast-paced and eager to make a lot of money, whereas Edgewood values quality over quantity. At least, in my opinion."

"True. Although, I'm native to East City." He let out a laugh. "So I can't exactly say I get the rivalry."

Rivalry was an odd choice of words to use, though I don't suppose he was exactly wrong in his observations. While *I* personally never saw it that way, I'd also been spoiled in terms of having someone from Ellington Heights as a close confidant for much of my pivotal years.

The same couldn't be said for others, such as my brothers, who had stuck together for the most part. Being the youngest, I'd had the unique pleasure of fending for myself.

As we passed by a small gathering of kids

dancing around in a circle, I turned to him. "Can I ask you something?"

He flashed me a warm, dimpled smile. "Anything."

"Why a matchmaker? You seem like you wouldn't have any trouble finding someone to date. You're friendly and outgoing. So, I'm curious why you decided to go that route."

To my surprise, Max suddenly turned bashful. "It's kind of hard with my job. I travel around the state a lot, so not much time to settle down and go out and meet people. I figured that doing the legwork was the hard part and if I could hire someone to do that for me, nailing the rest wouldn't be so bad. Thank you, by the way, for the compliment."

"How often do you travel for work?"

"Out of the year? I'm gone a collective of about four months. That's obviously not all in one go, but for a lot of people, the time away can be a lot."

Hm. Not the best kind of environment to be raising kids in.

Unless, of course, I also began to travel with him.

Giving up my shop was a difficult thing to think about.

I hardly knew this man, but if I continued to date him and did eventually develop feelings for him, how would any of that work?

Him traveling so often wasn't exactly the kind of untethered relationship I was looking for. But at the same time, was my refusal to see past my own shit forcing me to miss out on something that I may regret passing up in the future?

Something that could turn out to be a beautiful partnership if given the chance to explore?

I'd worked hard to get to where I was in life. Dreamed of teaching my kids the ins and outs of the car business while my spouse encouraged us along the way.

Yet, the way I was going about things, that dream of having a family was getting farther away from me the more years that went by. I figured by now, I'd at least be married, or at the *very* least, had someone in my life long term.

Neither of those were my reality at this point.

Was this a sign from the universe currently staring me right in the face and blatantly waving around a giant flag to get my attention and I was just too stupid to open my eyes and see it for what it was?

It was hard to tell from my limited perspective.

"Is that, uh... something that would be a turn off for you?" Max asked.

Shaking myself out of my thoughts, I gave him a small smile. "Not necessarily. You know I've got a business over in Edgewood, so I was just thinking about the logistics."

"Right, of course." He surprised me by grabbing my arm and ushering me to the side when a large group of teenagers barreled on by. But instead of letting me go once they were gone, he kept his grip on me. "Brandon, we don't have to jump into this right away. I don't mind testing the waters with you until you feel more comfortable."

I felt the urge to blow out an exasperated breath.

Why did I get the distinct feeling that my sister had not so subtly mentioned to the matchmaker that I was some kind of flight risk, easily spooked by commitment?

It wasn't true, obviously, as I'd wanted a marriage and kids since I could remember, but that wasn't going to stop my family from thinking the complete opposite when I'd hardly had any dating history under my belt to prove to them otherwise.

"I appreciate that."

Slowly, he let go of my arm. "My contract doesn't start for another month and a half. So, I'll be here until then."

I nodded, picking up the subtlety of his hint: spend the next month and a half together and see how it goes.

Maybe long distance after that wouldn't be a bad thing. Dipping my toes into the dating pool certainly made for a nerve-wracking experience and with him gone for a while after this month was up, it would give me time to reflect on if this was actually something that I truly wanted to give the old college try.

My sister's wedding wasn't for a while, anyway.

Pulling in a lungful of air, I nodded again. "Okay. That sounds good to me."

His eyes widened slightly. "Yeah? Really?"

"Unless you've got someone else lined up on your roster."

That drew a laugh out of him. "Not at all. Just you, I swear."

"Lucky me."

He brushed his fingers against my cheek, running up to where the shell of my ear was, and tucked some of the hair there behind it. I felt my face flush from the sudden intimate gesture and stayed still while his gaze traced my features.

I was no stranger to people finding me attractive, most of the time, though, it was a few beers deep and with some shitty old country song playing in the background of a crowded bar that always way overcharged on their drinks.

Being covered in grease and grime daily from work wasn't exactly the best mating call I could be putting out there, so this kind of attention was a little on the foreign side.

Aside from Avery, apparently.

Fuck, why was I always looping everything back to that man?

I hated it.

If I could bleach my brain and scrub it clean from all of the infected areas he'd burrowed down into, then I would do so in a damn heartbeat. Instead, I was stuck constantly being reminded of what I couldn't have, with no goddamn end in sight.

Max moved his fingers underneath my chin, curling them around to cup my jaw. "You want to get out of here?"

Actually, that wouldn't be a bad idea.

Sure, heading back to my place to get a little busy between the sheets was probably getting a little ahead of ourselves, but at the same time, if it meant being able to actually relieve the ache in my bones that had settled there after my morning with Avery, then I was all for it.

Right as I was nodding and opening my mouth to invite him back to my house, I heard someone from behind me say my name—the tone full of what I could only describe as disbelief and annoyance.

Pulling away from Max's hold on my face, I spun around on my heel, spotting Avery standing ten feet from me with his brows knitted together and a deep frown settled on his face.

CHAPTER 14

AVERY

PUSHING through a crowded festival in order to grab a basket full of food truck meals and find out where the hell the kettle corn stand was, absolutely qualified me for some kind of mental compensation.

As a peace offering to Hazel and the rest of my family's staff for my piss poor mood all day today, I'd offered my services in running down to the park and grabbing one of everything that I could get my hands on and bringing it back for them to eat once dinner service rolled around.

With my house staff already exhausted from their long day, I figured that the least I could do was go out and grab everything for them instead of telling them to suck it up and brave the crowds before heading home for the day. At least this way, I could also pay for everything while ensuring that they were well fed before leaving the property for the night.

Some of my staff lived year round on the grounds but the majority had families of their own to take care of.

After having hit the last food truck and then following the scent of the butter and sugar permeating throughout the park, I finally made my way toward a quieter section and wound up face-to-face with the last kind of situation I ever expected to stumble upon.

Tucked into the alcove of an alleyway was the same man I'd run into at Brandon's shop a few days prior who'd seemed all too interested in flirting with my former best friend, and said best friend standing way too close for anyone passing by to mistake it for anything platonic.

Seeing Brandon's face cradled in some guy's hold like that had my stomach turning.

Why the hell was this guy allowed to touch him so intimately when he hardly knew him?

"Brandon."

That had him breaking out of the guy's hold and turning to the sound of my voice. His eyes widened the second he spotted me, almost like he'd been caught doing something he shouldn't have been with the way he quickly glanced away and then back to me again.

"W-what are you doing here?"

Like that fucking mattered?

"Could ask you the same thing?"

Brandon's mouth opened slowly and then shut. His cheeks were slightly flushed in the fading sunlight that was casting an orange glow over all of us. The colors in the sky were reflecting in those deep colored eyes of his, mirroring back a refracted version that I could stare at all day.

I didn't want to read too much into what I'd stumbled upon. But the longer I stood here, the more I was realizing that Brandon was most likely on a date.

Fuck, why did that make me so fucking annoyed?

Oh, right. Because he was currently avoiding me, and or, ignoring me.

I'd sent two emails after the one he'd sent me. One asking for more information about the car's status and two, requesting either a phone call or for me to come in and look at it. None of which were meant to question Brandon's integrity or his shop in how they ran things or the way that they clearly knew much better than me on how to repair these cars.

But in actuality, it was simply an excuse to see him to try and smooth over what I was now calling *The Incident*.

An entire day and a half had passed since then with no response sent my way. Figuring he'd gotten busy, I'd let it go. Though, clearly, I'd been dead wrong about that.

"Do you... know this man?" the other guy asked, his gaze darting between both of us.

The question made my blood boil. "Yeah, we do."

Brandon ran a hand over his face. "Max, can you give us a minute?"

The other guy evidently wanted to argue with the way his mouth immediately shot open, but at the last second he thought better of it and slowly shut it again and cleared his throat. "Yeah, of course."

The second those words left the guy's mouth, Brandon stormed over to me and grabbed a hold of my arm, yanking me away from the alley. He dragged me through the crowd, the sound of the music blaring drowning out anything that he might be saying to me while guiding us to wherever the hell he was headed toward.

I didn't bother fighting. Didn't want to anyway.

My basket banged against my thigh as we dodged and weaved through the throngs of people, the top layer of food nearly rolling out when I was yanked off of the sidewalk and to a small patch of grass closer to the parking lot.

When he finally stopped, we were a few hundred feet from where I'd caught him canoodling with whatever-the-hell that guy was.

Friend?

Boyfriend?

Lover?

Each title made me more nauseous than the previous one.

"What are you doing?" Brandon demanded.

"Excuse me?"

"Don't, Avery. You know exactly what I'm talking about. What's with the attitude?"

Sucking my tongue back against my teeth, I contemplated being brutally honest. That guy wasn't shit and Brandon deserved better.

Did I have any proof to back any of my opinions up outside of my own mother-given intuition?

Absolutely not.

So I resorted to the next best thing. "You're avoiding me."

His eyes went wide. "No. I'm not."

"Yes, you are. Don't fucking lie to me, Brandon. You think it's cute that you ignored my emails and then I catch you out here with what's-his-face?"

"Max," he supplied.

"What*ever*." Between the both of us, we knew why Brandon was avoiding me. Why he'd ignored me when I'd requested to see him in person or even talk to him on the phone.

Why bring it up when I already knew the damn answer?

It was my fucking fault that we were in this mess of a situation anyway. Blaming him was ridiculous and we both knew it. None of that was stopping my stupid mouth from continuing to run—fueled by whatever emotion was currently auto-piloting my goddamn idiot brain.

"Stop it," I said, my tone firm.

"Stop what?" his voice croaked back.

My hand tightened around the basket. "You know what. Don't play dumb, you're smarter than that."

God, what was I fucking saying to him?

That wasn't fair. I needed to stop before I actually ruined what little threads left we still had connecting us together. This fragile and delicate state could only handle so much before there would be nothing that either of us could do to fix it.

He swallowed visibly. "I'm sorry. For..."

My heart pounded in my chest. "Don't be. I'm not."

His lips parted in shock.

The confession wasn't planned in the slightest. In fact, I had no idea I felt that way until this very moment when the words were suddenly tumbling out of my mouth. But now that they were out there, it was hard to regret them, as disgusting as it made me seem for coming onto him the way that I had.

Causing any kind of discomfort for Brandon was the last thing I ever wanted to do. Yet, at the same time, I couldn't get him or what happened before everything went to shit, out of my head. I'd never been turned on like that before, never felt that out of my mind with desire that I'd practically come in my own pants just by rubbing up against another body.

His intoxicating smell, his provocative moans, the way he'd unconsciously moved his body against mine.

Every waking second my thoughts were filled with those moments.

He lifted a slightly shaking hand to his hair and ran it through the lengths a few times. "You don't mean that."

"Yeah. I do."

He was staring at me with those same wide eyes that he'd given me when I'd caught him with his date. Slightly guilty and slightly mystified that I was even standing there in the first place. What I wouldn't give to know what the fuck was going on inside of his head right now, to get a small glimpse of the whirling thoughts cycling inside of that big brain.

"You... I don't think you..." His gaze darted away from mine, a slight flush coloring his cheeks again.

"Don't fill in the blanks. I said what I said." Whatever that meant. At this point, even *I* wasn't sure what I was talking about.

All I knew was that I didn't want Brandon to take what happened and hate me for it.

Brandon's chest was rising and falling quickly, like it was hard for him to catch his breath. He focused on my mouth for a long moment and then moved his gaze back up to make eye contact with me.

"Avery..."

Something deep and warm formed in my gut. I gave in to the urge and grabbed his arm, hauling him closer to me until we were nearly chest-to-chest. His small gasp shot right down to dick.

What the hell was happening to me?

I wanted to reach up and cup his face like that guy did. Replace his touch with my own so that Brandon remembered *me* instead. I supposed I'd always been a little possessive of my best friend, even back then, but it simply never seemed as prominent since we hardly hung out with anyone but each other.

There had been times when I'd had to chase people away from him, though. People who were much too interested in soaking up his valuable time that was meant for me only. I'd had a monopoly on it and intended to keep my position as lord over it, regardless of whoever else tried to come along and fight me for it.

They never lasted, though. Most people tended to give up too easily, even if it was something that they desperately wanted.

I doubted Brandon ever noticed any of that back then. He'd been way too busy with school, me, and his family to pay attention to anything outside of his bubble.

Which was fine with me.

Now that things were different and those same possessive feelings were cropping up, I had no way to relieve them other than to pray that I was enough to get Brandon to focus on me instead of everything else.

So far, I was striking out.

That didn't mean I was about to give up, though. I wasn't like the rest of them. I knew what was in front of me. I knew what having

Brandon in my life meant and what it felt like to lose him. I couldn't deal with that again.

I *wouldn't*.

"After your date, come to my place," I said, slowly letting go of his arm.

He let out a small, choked sound. "Avery."

"I'll be waiting."

CHAPTER 15

Brandon

Going over to Avery's house after my date would be a monumentally stupid idea.

Ditching my plans with Max *in order* to go over to Avery's would be even stupider. Especially, when Max had made it very clear that he was interested in coming back to my place to get to know me better on a more *physical* level.

We had a month and a half to figure things out. To see where all of this was going and to get to know each other enough to better judge if an eventual long distance relationship was worth the headache or not.

I'd agreed to try. I'd agreed to actually push myself out of my comfort zone to get out of my own way.

So then why the hell was I sitting outside of the McAllister gate with my window rolled down at the code box?

Because I'm a fucking idiot. That's why.

I knew the code. Had it memorized since the day I'd first been invited over to this ridiculously opulent mansion for a sleepover. I bet it hadn't changed since then—the date of his mother's birthday—and I would find that gate creaking open once I punched it in.

Practically every weekend, I'd take the bus across the bridge and walk the quarter mile it took to get here from the bus stop. Never once complaining whether it was rain or shine that greeted me as soon as I stepped down those steel stairs.

Not when after I'd finally made my way up to those front doors and found them already being pulled open by an overly eager Avery with that familiar smile on his face, beckoning me inside with the same kind of eagerness that brewed inside of my own chest.

Later on to discover that it was the heart-pounding beginning of a years long crush.

Leaning forward, I rested my forehead against the steering wheel.

"Fuck me," I mumbled.

I should've gone home after ditching the festival and grabbed myself a beer to help me wallow in my own shame.

The painful truth was that whatever happened back at the park with Avery had put me into a daze. The kind that had me going back to Max and telling him that I'd needed to get home because of a long work day in the morning. I barely cared about the sullen expression that had fallen over him, or the way he'd not-so-subtly glanced over my shoulder to where I'd disappeared with Avery minutes before.

If he could tell something happened, he'd been polite enough not to mention it. All he'd asked was that I called him in the morning to set up a time to see each other again.

Honestly, he was a fucking gentleman.

One that I'd refused to go home with because I was a goddamn masochist.

I'll be waiting.

My stomach tightened at the memory.

Why the fuck had he said it like that?

Why had he *looked at me* like that?

Like he was...

I stopped the thought, jammed on the brakes and derailed the entire train before it could even leave the station. Pushing any kind of narrative when it came to Avery would only lead me into reading between the lines on things that were otherwise perfectly able to be explained away.

He'd said it himself: he was annoyed that I'd avoided responding to him about the cars. That was the simple answer with no bullshit. There was nothing else to it. No matter how much I wanted there to be.

Avery was a simple heterosexual man with his mind only on getting his father's affairs in order. Trying to read between the lines about anything else was only me projecting my own shit onto him.

He wasn't jealous. He wasn't the type.

The mic connected to the code box crackled suddenly. "Brandon."

I just about jumped out of my skin. With wide eyes, my head whipped around to stare at the speaker connected to the box.

"Get up here," the voice demanded.

Ahead of me, the gate buzzed loudly and then began to swing inward, allowing entry without me even having to enter a code at all. Scrubbing my face, I turned back in my seat and shifted my truck into drive, ignoring the way my hands shook while I gripped the gearshift.

This was so fucking stupid.

I was so fucking stupid.

What was supposed to happen when I got up there?

Get on my knees and beg him to forgive me for the other morning?

Or worse, act like it never happened and never address the giant elephant in the room.

I wasn't even sure which option would suck more. Both of them sounded equally horrific in their own ways.

Reading Avery was difficult these days. He was a stranger, a man who was as foreign to me as Max, but with a ton more baggage that I felt personally responsible for on some level.

It wasn't fair to carry this deep-seated guilt when *Avery* was the one who left, who chose to cut off contact with me once he got comfortable in Switzerland. His promises had turned empty the moment he'd realized he was better off living his fancy, privileged life with no room for someone like me in it anymore.

I'd ultimately served my purpose. I'd given him what he needed while he was here. Him coming back and reconnecting was nothing more than utilizing his resources. After all, he was a businessman at heart.

What better way to get a job done than use an old contact?

One he trusted.

So, again.

Why was I here?

When I finally made it up the long drive and parked my truck out front of the walkway leading up to those familiar filigree doors, I left my keys in the ignition and just sat there. There was still time to turn around and leave, make up some half assed excuse as to why I couldn't come inside to talk.

Would he be mad?

Probably.

Did I care?

Unfortunately.

That was what happened when your traitorous heart refused to see the situation for what it was—a rehashing of things that were better left in the past.

Except that didn't stop me from slipping the keys out of the ignition and shoving my door open. Or listening to the sounds of my own two feet crunching through the graveled drive that led up to the main walkway.

Fuck me and my weaknesses.

If I were a stronger man, I would've stopped all of this to begin with. Refused him service the second he stepped into my mechanic shop and sent him elsewhere, ridding myself of the problem at the start.

Or better yet, gotten a hold over my own impulses, and called him a damn rideshare to come pick him up instead of taking him back to my place because I couldn't bear to part with him at the time. Not getting myself lulled into a false sense of security with him falling asleep on top of me and acting like some kind of fucked up version of a security blanket.

For far too much of my life, I'd relied on him to give me comfort. Even after he'd gone, his memories were the only thing that I'd held onto during my darkest times. When they'd begun to fade, I thought my feelings would soon follow but clearly that had been a pipedream in itself.

When my foot hit the first step, the doors to his family mansion parted and there he was, standing in between them waiting for me. The déjà vu hit like a freight train. Both timelines—then and now—collided together, creating a dizzying feel as I climbed up the steps one by one.

His expression was carefully blank, betraying nothing while he tracked me slowly. This all felt like a cat and mouse game, a push and pull that I didn't remember signing up for, let alone agreeing to.

And yet, I still climbed those fucking stairs until I was at eye level with him, a hair's breadth between us. Those remarkable crystal blue eyes of his bored into me, right down to my very soul. Reading me right down to my bones.

A shiver raced up my spine.

I loved the attention. Hated what it did to me.

He said nothing as he stepped back, waving an arm to let me through. The hesitation in my step was momentous, barely even noticeable, but still somehow had Avery's carefully guarded expression morphing into a frown.

This place was so familiar that it was painful. The same marbled floors that shone brilliantly under the warm light from the massive crystalline chandelier. The exceptionally tasteful decor that were the only remnants left of Avery's mother. Hazel, who was storming down the hallway leading from the kitchen galley, a towel thrown over her shoulder.

Oh fuck.

"Brandon Anders!" I winced at the stern tone. "Is that you? You better have a good excuse as to why it's been sixteen years since you've come around here!"

Before anything could be uttered, I was swept up into a tight hug that had me bending down in order to accommodate for Hazel's shorter frame. The life was practically squeezed out of me, sending a wheeze to be coughed up.

"First Avery," she was saying, "And now you. I can't believe this. Both of you all grown up and still no calls and no letters."

I had no idea what on Earth she was talking about. Though judging by the way Avery's face was slipping into an amused expression, he must've been given the same lecture recently, too.

Hazel was always like a pseudo-mother to

him, and me by extension. She treated Avery well growing up. Kept his head on straight and his ego in check—personally determined to not let him turn out anything like his father. Which she'd absolutely succeeded in doing.

She should be proud of the man she'd molded him into. I certainly was.

"Sorry," was all that came out of my mouth.

I wasn't going to bother with any half-assed or lame excuses. I didn't have any that would make sense, let alone grant me forgiveness in the eyes of Hazel for practically cutting off all contact the moment Avery stopped responding to my letters.

What would the point have been to keep torturing myself like that?

It was easier to sever the infected limb and hope that it'd heal on its own.

She merely huffed at me, shaking her head in the process. "You're both lucky I'm still very fond of you."

Wasn't that the truth.

We'd gotten away with a lot when we were kids for that very reason. Probably too much so, looking back.

Hazel slipped the towel off her shoulder,

waving it at the both of us while spinning on her heel. "Come back to the kitchen. You can catch me up on your life while I finish prepping for the week."

"Actually," Avery finally spoke. "We'll join you in a bit. I need to show Brandon something that I've been meaning to give to him."

My stomach churned.

I knew what that was code for: *we need to talk.*

It had to happen eventually, except now that the time was here, I was freezing up, my instincts telling me to turn around and rip open those doors and run back to my truck. It was the coward's way out, but at least it would save me from whatever rejection was waiting for me upstairs.

Avery's hand slipped around my arm, a gentle tug that began to nudge me in the direction of the grand staircase leading up to the second floor. Resisting him was futile, as was trying to make up some excuse to join Hazel in the kitchen instead.

Staving off the inevitable, no matter how painful and embarrassing this was going to be, would only make the fallout over this that much worse.

At least I could wallow on the couch with a cold beer once I was finally home.

With the sound of Hazel's heels clacking back down the hallway to the kitchen, I was pulled up the stairs and down the hall to Avery's room—the last door on the left. Upon stepping into the room, I was taken back through time.

Hardly anything had changed over the decades since the room's use. The bed set and curtains were still the same brocade fabric, dipped in a dark hue of blues and greens that complimented the rich color of the floor's carpet. The room's wallpaper still had that slight silky sheen to it that always felt smooth against my skin when I'd run my hands along the subtle pattern, barely noticeable until you were up close to it.

Across the way was Avery's old school desk, the surface cleared completely aside from a small stack of files that looked new in comparison to the school books that were usually sitting on top of it. The door to the suite's bathroom was open, the lights shut off, but I knew if I walked in there, that same brassy gold hardware would still shine under the amplified lights with not a single fingerprint to be seen pressed against their surfaces.

Avery let go of my arm to shut the door behind us, leaving my side in order to shrug off the quarter sleeve shirt he'd been wearing when we'd run into each other at the festival.

My eyes darted away quickly to purposefully avoid staring at the defined lines of muscle running along his back. Instead, I focused on the wall next to me as he headed for his walk-in closet.

There was a single photo frame still tacked onto the wall, a familiar one that I remember I used to spend so much time memorizing, waiting for Avery to step out of the shower or for him to come back up after being called away to answer for whatever ridiculous misdeed his father had made up that day.

Inside of it was a picture of a young Avery and his mother, Leanne, her arms circled tight around him while they both wore large grins on their faces while facing the camera. I loved picking out the pieces of her that reflected in Avery, the parts that were now the only living memory that she ever existed.

Back when she'd passed, Avery's father had all but wiped her from existence, leaving hardly anything behind aside from the surface-level traces that could've easily been passed off as the artful eye of an interior decorator.

The day after her funeral, family photos were taken down and shoved into some long forgotten box now left to rot somewhere down in the basement of this mansion, along with trinkets, clothing and anything else that could serve as a stark reminder of her. And just like that, it was like she'd never stepped foot inside of this house to begin with.

This was one of the only remaining things that were left.

I knew Avery missed her. We all did.

His father would've preferred if we all forgot about her. I don't think he ever accounted for how many people she'd impacted during her short thirty-two years on this Earth. And now he was lying cold in the ground, too, right alongside her.

When I finally turned away from the photo, I noticed Avery was already changed and sitting on his bed, watching me. His face was back to that neutral expression he'd worn when I'd first arrived, the only difference now was his fingers tightly gripping his pant leg.

I pulled in a slow breath. Might as well bite the bullet and get it over with. "We need to talk."

He merely nodded.

Silence fell over us.

Apparently, neither of us wanted to go first with popping the bubble that was the elephant in the room. This was the part I hated about being the more upfront one out of the two of us. I hated confrontation, but when it came to bringing up issues, I was usually the one that had to get the ball rolling.

"So—"

"Were you two out on a date?" he asked.

My brows knitted together. "At the festival?"

He nodded again. "You mentioned before your sister's friend set you two up. Was that your first date?"

"Uh..." Folding my arms around myself, I let my body weight shift to my right foot, planting it firmly against the carpet. "You could say that."

He went quiet for a moment, a small crease forming between his brows. "What does that mean? He harassing you for something else?"

"What? No. Nothing like that."

How did I even go about explaining this without sounding like a total failure in the dating world?

"We were... the friend of my sister's is actually a matchmaker. That's how Max and I got connected. My sister is determined to find me the 'perfect guy' to bring to her wedding."

"I see..."

My stomach churned again.

Why the hell was he so hard to read?

I used to be able to predict his every move—the very sentence that would next come barreling out of his mouth. This man in front of me was a book locked tightly with some kind of special key that I didn't even know the shape of, let alone where to find it.

It made for a confusing scenario, one where I was reading way too much into everything with no context clues to back anything up.

Avery rolled off of the bed and onto his feet. His strides were slow as he headed for me, a predatory sway to him.

I stayed rooted to my spot, too scared to move a single inch and break whatever tension was building between us.

"And is he?" he asked, his voice barely above a whisper.

My heart stuttered in my chest. "Is he what?"

Avery leaned close, his breath fanning across my face. "The perfect guy for you."

"I..."

How was I supposed to answer that?

I darted my tongue out to wet my bottom lip, a motion that Avery's gaze darted down to track before leveling with mine again. Something in his eyes shifted then, the uptick in his breathing catching me by surprise.

"I can't get it out of my head, Bran," he mumbled.

My throat felt parched. "Get what?"

"This." He grabbed at my hips, shoving me back against the wall to pin me there. A small gasp left me, my hands coming out to flatten against his chest.

What the hell was happening?

"I know you hated it." He was still mumbling, burying his face against my neck. "And I'm sorry. But I can't get it... *you,* out of my head."

A shiver raced up my spine. He ground his hips

against mine, the hard line of him digging right into my hip. I'd never been this close to him before—not like this. We'd hugged as boys, wrapped an arm around each other's necks as teenagers.

My teeth hurt from how hard I crushed them together, fighting the urge to draw him even closer so I could sink my teeth into his shoulder, leave a permanent mark there to prove to the both of us that this was real.

But it wasn't. It couldn't be.

"Fuck," he muttered into my neck.

CHAPTER 16

Avery

I was in trouble.

Pulling in a deep lungful of Brandon's intoxicating smell wasn't enough. I wanted to taste him, to drag my tongue up his neck and make my way to those pouty lips of his and see just how soft they were pinched between my teeth.

I couldn't stop the slow thrusts, letting my eyes fall closed with each press of my dick against his, hardening until it was almost painful. Some primitive part of my brain was overtaking the rational side of me, the one screamed to take a step back and let Brandon go.

His fingers were wrapped around the front of my shirt in a death-like grip, another delicious sounding gasp falling from his lips the moment I gave in and let my tongue swipe at the skin right below his ear.

Oh, fuck.

What would happen if I reached down between us and pulled both of our cocks out and began rubbing them together?

How many more sounds would come tumbling out of Brandon's mouth?

What other noises was he capable of making while being turned on?

Hands shoved at my chest hard enough to knock me back. I stumbled, just barely catching my own footing before I ended up ass-backward on the floor. Panting, I swallowed thickly while trying to blink the cloudiness out of my vision.

The tent in the front of my pants was obvious, there was no way to get around that. Even if I wanted to try and explain it away, what was no point. Not when I'd just been grinding up against Brandon like that.

Fuck, he was going to tell me to go to hell.

I'd be lucky if I didn't get a good fist to the

face before he ran out of here and never saw me again.

His eyes were pinballing between my own, searching for something that I wasn't too sure he'd end up finding no matter how hard he looked. There was no rational explanation to any of this—none that I could articulate, at least.

Whatever happened to my brain the morning after going out with Marlow and Silas had caused some fundamental change in me. One where getting turned on by my childhood best friend's soft moans and the smell of his sweat-soaked skin was completely normal.

The first step Brandon took toward me had some hesitation behind it. A tentativeness that wasn't lost on me, nor would be questioned. Clearly, we were walking on a thin tightrope here with neither of us knowing what the fuck we were doing. Where the fuck any of this was going.

He took another, and then another until he was close enough to me again to shove me backward. "On the bed."

My heart thumped in my chest.

Obediently, I stepped back until the back of my knees hit the side of my bed, tipping back until my ass was planted firmly on the edge of it. His hands clenched and unclenched into fists at his sides, an unsure expression passing over his face while he scoped down the length of me.

A part of me wanted to ask if he liked what he saw. The other didn't want to know. Rejection from him would sting like a bullet blasting through my body, mowing down everything in the path of its trajectory.

His clothes were slightly wrinkled from where I'd had a hold of him, the impression of my handprints just visible enough to me to stir up some weird psychologically possessive part of my brain that relished in the thought of marking him.

"Lie down." His voice was soft, barely above a whisper.

I scooted back onto the bed, doing as I was told, my arm coming up to prop my upper half up from the mattress to keep my eyes on him.

My cock throbbed painfully in my pants, begging for attention. Being this turned on was new to me. Hooking up with women was usually a one-and-done kind of situation. A get in and get out while making sure both parties got their rocks off by the end.

There was never any of this build up. The tight tug in my gut that only grew worse the longer I neglected touching myself or reaching out and grabbing at the person currently making it hard to breathe in here.

Was this just Brandon's doing?

Or something else entirely?

I'd never once questioned my sexuality in all of my years on this god-forsaken planet. Had never once felt the burning desire to pin him down and see how far both of us could take things until we called chicken and scrambled off each other.

So what the hell was any of this?

Some weird mistranslation in my brain that was converting my missing him into sexual need?

I held my breath when he climbed onto the bed, his hand resting against my chest and giving it a gentle push to make me collapse completely onto the mattress. My heart was beating so hard in my chest that it had to be audible.

Once he was settled next to me, Brandon moved his palm back down my chest to my abs, leaving a fiery line in its wake. Two fingers were then hooked under the band of my sweats, freezing there the moment my dick twitched under the fabric.

Fuck, this was actually torturing me.

Grabbing onto his wrist, I forced him to drag the band down past my hips, kicking myself up just enough to get it past the length of me and free my poor dick. It slapped against my belly, the head of it already oozing precum and wetting my t-shirt where it rested.

"Jesus," he huffed.

I had half a mind to be embarrassed. To apologize and tuck myself away and pretend none of this ever happened. But that naked hunger in his eyes stopped me from moving at all, keeping me still while he smoothed his hand down the length of me and then gripped me at my base.

He squeezed lightly, drawing another painful squeeze of my balls as more precum drooled from my slit.

A pitiful noise escaped me. I'd had plenty of blowjobs in my life. Some good, some bad. Some in between that bordered on indifference. All of them were a means to an end.

None of them had ever made me feel like this.

Brandon lowered his mouth until his lips

were hovering over the crown of my cock, his eyes darting up to meet mine briefly before he slipped it into his mouth. I nearly came then, the grandiose effort to keep myself from jacking my hips to drive myself deeper into his mouth was barely registering in my mind.

"*Fuck*." That hot, wet heat was going to kill me.

Obviously, Brandon would be good at this. He had the practice under his belt and however many notches that accompanied it. Anything involving a dick would be his area of expertise and I was the poor, unfortunate soul at his mercy.

He treated my cock like a precious thing, opening his mouth up just enough to curl his tongue around under the head and clean up the mess that had collected there. Tilting his head to the side, he dragged his lips down to where his hand was holding me up, leaving a wet trail behind that he used as a kind of lube while stroking me.

The friction from his hand, coupled with his mouth, was too much and not enough at the same time. I wanted more—didn't know if I could handle it, either.

Belatedly, I realized how hard I was gripping my sheets when my hands were starting to cramp up. But letting go meant that I'd be tangling my fingers into Brandon's hair and forcing that talented mouth back down onto my cock until my balls were shooting cum down his throat.

Fuck, that image in my mind was hot.

Why was it so hot?

He worked his way back up to the head, sealing his lips around it and then working me deeper into his mouth. He bobbed his head slowly, his cheeks a flushed red that matched the rosy color of his slightly swollen lips.

The second he snuck his other hand into my pants to cup my balls and roll them gently, I was done for. My hips jacked up, nearly choking him while I spilled into his mouth. My body strained from the effort, coming hard enough to have me gasping for air like I'd been held under water for ten minutes.

When it was finally over, I slumped back down onto the mattress.

"Holy shit..." was all I could think to say.

The last thing I heard while my eyes slid shut was Brandon's soft laughter.

CHAPTER 17

Brandon

My head was swimming.

The numbers on the timesheets in front of me were all but a blur despite my best efforts to focus on actually getting any of this paperwork done before close this afternoon. But no amount of putting my pen to paper was motivating me enough to work through the past month's worth of clock-ins.

All I could focus on was Avery.

He'd been too far gone in post-nut bliss to notice me quietly grabbing my things and leaving last night. I hadn't had the heart to stop by the kitchen to make up some excuse to Hazel for leaving so soon, nor did I bother emailing Avery when I finally got home.

Sticking around for whatever aftermath awaited me once he finally realized his former best friend sucked him off wasn't exactly the kind of conversation I'd been prepping myself to have when he'd invited me over.

In fact, that was the complete fucking opposite of what was supposed to happen.

But goddamn, would all of that be used as fodder for my own future self-gratification. Seeing Avery's face twist up in pleasure like that was incredible, even more so because *I'd* been the one to cause it in the first place.

He'd tasted amazing on my tongue, his weight solid in my hand and thick enough to wrap my fingers around him comfortably. Each twitch of his hips, or flickering of his lashes over his eyes had driven me to keep going, to keep touching and tasting him until he was exploding in my mouth and making a mess out of the both of us.

I'd touched myself to the memory while driving home, coming in my own hand in a humiliating fashion as soon as I'd pulled into my own driveway and parked my truck.

I'd sat there after the fact for a long while, contemplating my life choices and wondering what the hell I was supposed to do now.

How was I supposed to look Avery in the eyes when I'd had his entire cock in my fucking mouth and drank down his cum like it was water found in the Sahara desert?

Scrubbing a hand over my face, I dropped my pen back down onto the desk and sighed heavily.

The problem was that it was too good not to want to do it again. The other problem was that Avery was very much straight and even if this was for some strange reason a moment of weakness or curiosity for him, that didn't guarantee that he'd want to go for a second round.

It was healthy to want to explore yourself. Hell, I never minded showing newbies the ropes once they were comfortable enough to crawl into bed with me and teach them the proper ways to take care of someone else.

Why gatekeep the experience?

This was entirely different, though, and had me wondering if Avery was somehow questioning his sexuality.

If so, how long had that been going on?

Surely, before he'd come back to Ellington Heights.

Pushing back from my desk, I climbed to my feet and headed out of my office toward the back of the shop. I pushed the glass door open to enter the garage. Music was blaring on the speaker closest to Vance's station, some classic rock song that was vaguely familiar but too loud to actually make out of the words over the ridiculous amount of bass.

He was working on the black Bel Air while the Ford Coupe was up on the risers at Charlie's station. No one else besides Vance was back here, which meant that they'd all probably gone on lunch already.

When he turned to grab a socket wrench, he spotted me and waved. "Hey, boss!"

I flicked down the volume on the speaker to less of a dull roar and to something that wasn't threatening to blow my eardrums out. "Everyone else gone?"

"Yup. Just me and you."

Glancing over at the clock, I said, "You want to take off? I've got things until the others come back."

He propped his safety glasses up onto the top of his head, tugging off his gloves in the process. "You sure? We've got that two o'clock coming in soon."

"I think I can manage a valve check."

He grinned. "She *thinks* it's one of the valves because her husband looked it up on Youtube. I'd bet twenty bucks it's actually the timing belt."

A true death blow for an old '92. "Let's hope it's just a valve." Because I really wasn't in the mood to be dealing with a cranky old retiree arguing with me about what her hobbyist husband drilled into her head before she'd brought her car in to us for maintenance.

I never minded people coming in well informed about their issues but sometimes the Internet wasn't the best place to try and replicate a mechanic's decades worth of knowledge.

Vance clapped me on the shoulder. "Twenty bucks."

I shook my head at that.

He tossed his gloves onto his station before grabbing his keys and taking off out the back door that led to our private lot behind the building. Stretching my arms above my head, I let out a soft sigh.

Having the shop to myself for a bit would give me the chance to clear my head. I needed to purge myself by doing something else outside of cooping myself up in that office while pretending that the best way to forget about last night was through paperwork.

I was much better with using my hands anyway. I found comfort in picking things apart and then putting them back together again.

Heading over to my own station, I grabbed a few of the tools out of my belt and laid them out on a rolling table, bringing it over to the Bel Air that was parked closest to me with the hood already propped open.

Peeking at the inside of it, I could see what Tony was already halfway through tuning up before he'd left, and picked up my own tools to finish what he'd started.

Out of the four of Avery's cars, this one needed the least amount of work, which meant that by the end of the week, it'd be set to roll out of here and road ready for whatever buyer ended up taking it off of Avery's hands.

Which reminded me... I still needed to get him that list.

"Wow, you've really got them working on them all at once?"

Startled, I whipped around to where the door leading to the front of the shop was propped open and Avery was standing with one foot already past the threshold. He was wearing a business suit that hugged his fit frame nicely, making him look rather out of place next to the wall of tools right beside him.

His hair was swept back from his face and there was a plastic bag hooked over his arm that swayed when he let go of the door. "Bit of a slave driver, aren't you?"

I ignored the way my body flushed with heat as he drew closer, busying myself with turning back to the Bel Air and leaning over the lip of it to tighten one of the valves. "Weren't you the one bragging about how you'd pay my shop to work exclusively on these for you as long as it got done correctly?"

He chuckled, his footsteps growing quiet right behind me. "I'm kidding, Brandon."

His playful teasing was throwing me off, not at all what I was expecting to be faced with after last night.

Anger?

Absolutely.

Disgust and maybe a little bit of embarrassment?

Definitely.

But this?

It only further confused me.

The sound of the plastic bag being set down caught my attention and then the feeling of something looming over me had me lifting back from where I was bent over the car. Avery's hand came around on my right side to cup the edge of the car, leaning over my shoulder to get a better look at what I was doing.

"How's it looking?" The question was said right into my ear, his voice smooth and slightly gravelly.

I fought the urge to shiver.

Fuck me.

I was pinned against the car. The subtle shift of his hips brushing up against my ass, along with the hand that was anchored to the car, left me little room to side step him. Having him this close to me was making me dizzy. Whatever cologne he was wearing made the urge to turn around and bury my face in his chest nearly impossible.

"Uh..." I swallowed thickly. "Good. Just needed to replace a few valve caps and flush out the engine and replace it with new fluid. This one's the cleanest out of the four."

He hummed softly. "That sounds promising."

I hoped it wasn't obvious that my hand was shaking while I leaned back over to fit the wrench over the last valve cap. "Should be out of here soon. I'll get you that list."

"And I'll have a check sent over to you for the work."

"Thanks."

Not that I really cared about the money, but I was glad he was taking this seriously and wasn't trying to haggle me on prices. Avery could absolutely afford whatever number I threw at him, even if I went out of my way to name it something ridiculous. I simply appreciated that he had enough integrity not to make the process a drag and fight me for an itemized list.

Fixing cars like this was half labor costs and half having the knowledge on how to diagnose and implement whatever needed to be done. A lot of people that came through my shop neglected to take that into consideration whenever the bill came around.

"I brought you something," he said, finally stepping back to give me space to breathe.

When I turned back around, he was already lifting the plastic bag off of the ground and fishing through it to pull something out. What was in his hands was a plastic lunch container with the sections separated, jam packed with food.

"I figured you hadn't eaten yet," he explained, offering it to me. "Hazel made it with love."

I couldn't help but smile at that. "You didn't need to bring me anything."

"I wanted to."

The *after last night* was an obvious unspoken end to that sentence.

Taking the container from him, I noted it was hot to the touch, with slight condensation underneath the clear top. I *was* hungry now that food was being placed in front of me. With my head so preoccupied, I'd neglected to grab leftovers from my fridge and bring them with me this morning. I figured I could live off of the snacks I'd had stashed in my office, but this was way more appetizing.

I traced my thumb along the sharp edge of the top, letting it pinch at my skin to try and draw me out of my already spiraling thoughts.

What did any of this mean?

Where did we go from here?

"Avery... last night—"

"Don't," he said, shutting me up instantly. "Whatever it is... don't overthink it. Please."

I clutched the container tight in my hands when he crowded me against the car once again. An unsteady hand was raised toward my face, faintly moving along my cheek while his expression twisted into something that looked close to pain.

"Please," he repeated.

"What..." I wasn't even sure how to ask, or *what*.

How could I go about encompassing a decade's worth of confusion surrounding my attraction to him that was now seemingly being crashed into by Avery's own unexpected brand of surprise?

I swallowed again. I needed to know. "Did you hate it?"

His eyes widened briefly and then narrowed. "No. Did you?"

Fucking hell.

My heart stumbled over the quickness of his words. "No."

He blew out a breath. "Good... good."

Relieved?

Exasperated?

I couldn't tell.

Needing the subject change, I said, "Tell me why you're in a suit."

He glanced down at himself and then said, "I have a meeting with my lawyer. And with that woman who's contesting the will. I was supposed to go over there earlier this morning but I got a little sidetracked."

I wondered with what. Though judging by how fresh this food was, I was going to wager a guess that when he'd approached Hazel about making this for me, she'd forced him an apron on him, too. That was usually how she worked when asked for favors. A 'you want it done, you're helping', type deal.

"I hope it goes well."

He flashed me a brief smile. "Yeah, me too."

Dancing around the subject like this was

painful but of my own doing. Confronting whatever the fuck was going on with Avery felt like too much right now, even though I was dying to know what was going on inside of his head.

But the problem was that I wanted more. Last night wasn't enough to satisfy that deep rooted craving in me that had always wanted him.

In fact, it seemed to have only made it all worse. I had hoped, years and years ago, that by exposing myself to as much of Avery as possible that it'd somehow get my brain to wean off of him, force me to get bored of him until all that I had left was general apathy in what used to be my feelings for him.

The reality, of course, was much different. All it'd done was make me want to drop to my knees right here in the middle of my shop and get him back in my mouth again. Just to see that blissful expression once more while he came.

Avery surprised me out of my thoughts by cupping my jaw in his hand, holding me firmly in place. His thumb grazed over my cheek, sending a spiderweb of pinpricks radiating across my skin.

"Have dinner with me tonight."

It was a bad idea. But him apparently not regretting last night was what my mind was getting stuck on.

If that was true, then what else was Avery hiding from me?

Or himself, for that matter?

How much farther could this line be pushed between us until a chasm inevitably opened up and swallowed us both whole?

Oh my god, I'm so screwed.

"Okay."

Dinner I could do. That was simple.

There didn't need to be any strings attached to dinner.

Avery smiled. "I'll pick you up at seven."

CHAPTER 18

AVERY

NOTHING COULD BRING me down from that high of getting Brandon to agree to grab dinner with me tonight.

Not the horrible traffic coming back into Ellington Heights, or the guy who cut me off at the red light pulling into Ted's office, and not even the Russian model that was more than likely going to try and fight me for my inheritance waiting inside said office.

All right, maybe that last one was a little more annoying than the rest.

But right at this moment, though, I hardly cared outside of a mild flash of feelings.

I had nothing actually planned for tonight, however, as soon as I got out of this meeting, I'd get to calling around to the high-end restaurants in the area to see which ones were open to taking reservations and plan from there.

Tonight needed to be special. I needed to show Brandon that last night wasn't some fluke in my judgment and that I was open to exploring whatever insane chemistry that was brewing between us further.

I'd put my own personal reservations about my sexuality on the back burner for the time being, knowing that if I got too caught up in the label of things, it was only going to cause me to make a fool out of myself in front of him.

Leaning into my desires in an uninhibited manner was allowing me to stretch my wings in ways I never thought possible. Giving into the temptations instead of forcing myself to behave and move on felt more freeing than I had been in years.

I wasn't about to go psychoanalyzing myself just yet. Not when I'd just started to erase the distance between Brandon and I.

Popping open the door to my car, I climbed out into the afternoon sun and felt the tension bleed back into my body almost immediately. Going into this meeting, I was preparing for the worst. Without having any background as to who this woman was, there were only a few realms of possibility that I could see this moving in.

Was it fair of me to judge someone I hadn't met yet based solely on who I knew my father used to surround himself with?

Of course not.

But the unfortunate truth was that my father's habit in picking out the worst kind of people to entertain himself extended to this circumstance, too.

Why else would this woman being coming out of the woodwork?

Heading inside, I slipped my sunglasses off of my face and tucked them into the inside pocket of my suit jacket.

Ivy, Ted's secretary, lifted herself from her chair, greeting me with a wide smile. "Good afternoon, Mr. McAllister. I can take you back. They're all waiting for you."

While she scooted around the desk, I lifted

my arm to check my watch. There were still over ten minutes before our meeting was supposed to start. How interesting that this woman and her lawyer were already trying to establish dominance by beating me here.

Ivy's clipped footsteps against the tiled floor led me down the hall to one of the larger conference rooms at the back of the building. The blinds were drawn over the glass wall, giving the room a nice amount of privacy that we'd absolutely need.

After knocking twice, Ivy swung the door open and stuck her head in. "Mr. Evans? Avery McAllister is here for you."

She stepped to the side and swept her hand into the conference room, flashing me a brief smile.

"Ah! Mr. McAllister. Good afternoon," Ted greeted, waving me over to a seat next to him.

The top of his head was shiny and bald with dark curly hair wrapping around the rest of his head. He wore a pair of wire-rimmed glasses with the center nosepiece a black plastic compared to the steel of the rest of the frame. He was on the thinner side but had long limbs that gave him his height.

Across from him was another man with sliver hair that was coiffed back from his face and deep wrinkles that were etched into his skin. He was a little on the heavier side but carried it well, making him appear more muscular than overweight.

Alexander Steele, no doubt.

As I grabbed my seat, my gaze pinned right onto the woman sitting next to Steele.

She was around my age and had that kind of beauty that was classic. No overly done lip filler or face injections, no over the top makeup or lash extensions. Just a sweetheart shaped face, high cheekbones that were dusted with a faint sheen of blush, full, pouty lips, and platinum blonde hair that looked well taken care of despite it definitely not being her natural color.

Honestly, she was exactly my type.

Which was a disturbing thought considering she'd been entangled with my father.

I didn't want to think about what the two of us shared in common when it came to our taste in women. As the saying went, the apple didn't fall far from the tree, but in all respects, I really fucking wished it did.

"Thank you for joining us." Ted fanned out

the files in front of him, sliding them across the way for both Ana and her lawyer to look through. "As you know, we're coming to the table with an offer already set. Whatever else you're interested in will need to be negotiated."

Alexander Steele flipped his folder open, flipping through the top few pages with a quick flick of his wrist. "I take it that the expert you contacted to look at the marriage license came back?"

Ted nodded, slipping something my way as he continued to speak. "Yes. Thank you for sending that over. Since the license was determined to be authentic, we're going to go ahead and put that offer I was talking about on the table."

Glancing down at the paper in front of me, I realized it was a copy of the marriage license in question with annotations on it stating that it was verified to be legitimate. For some reason, out of any of this, that fact bothered me the most.

While my father was never a *faithful* man, I'd romanticized the idea that his marriage to my mother was the only one he'd ever have. Not for any particular reason outside of some strange sense of pride that *we* were the only things in his past he couldn't exactly erase, no matter how hard he'd tried to do so.

His life would always intrinsically be tied to my mother in some capacity, and obviously, mine by bloodline.

But with this, that idea began to sour. Somehow tainted by this woman my age who had apparently been successful in convincing the man that after twenty-six years of running around as a single man it was time to tie the knot once again.

Leaning back into my chair, I folded my arms across my chest while both our lawyers spoke.

She was already watching me, a carefully neutral expression on her face. There was some-thing about her that was setting me off outside of this being the kind of encounter I never wanted to have. Meeting my father's flavor-of-the-weeks had stopped quite a long time ago, only rearing its ugly head once at my wedding and I subse-quently banned it from ever happening again right then and there.

My father's messes never truly ended. No

matter how much time and energy had been put into trying to avoid this very scenario before all of this.

Now that we were here, though, I hoped she was smart and just took the money and never looked back on whatever shit my father and her got up to while they were together. It would be easier on all of us that way.

"So, Mrs. McAllister, formally Ms. Liapovich, is requesting an additional few things on top of the money that's been offered." Steele slid two packets across the table at us. "One, she'd like access to the estate."

I snatched the packet up.

Absolutely fucking not.

"Two," Steele went on. "She's requesting compensation for moving to the States while she searches for a sponsor for citizenship."

Unfuckingbelievable.

"Why not stay in your country? Why come here? Is there family over here?"

She shook her head, her accent thick as she spoke. "No. No family. All back in Russia."

Looking over to Ted, I said, "She's not getting past the front gate."

"We're willing to negotiate which portion of the estate she's interested in," Steele said.

I turned to look at him next. "I don't care if she's looking to simply take over the garage for an art studio. It's not happening. She can find herself an apartment with the money that's being put on the table."

Ted slapped a hand down on my shoulder, silencing me with a tight squeeze. "What Mr. McAllister is trying to say, is that there's no reason for Ms. Liapovich to move into the estate when there are plenty of other accommodations in Ellington Heights that are just as nice. The estate is a *family* home."

"Yes. Family," Ana stated, placing a hand over her stomach that I hadn't noticed was swollen until this very moment. "It's perfect for the baby."

The entire room fell dead silent.

Ana's attention flitted between all of us, her brows growing more furrowed the longer none of us talked.

"I'm sorry," Ted let out a strained laugh. "Baby?"

Steele cleared his throat, pulling out another set of papers from his stack and passed it over to us. "Yes, my client is just under six months pregnant."

I didn't need to look down at the paper in front of me to know that it was a medical form reiterating what the fuck just came out of this woman's mouth. Or that at the top of it would be her first name with my last name attached to it.

My chest squeezed with anger, barely contained while I hung on by a thread. She was watching me again with that carefully guarded expression, her hand curling protectively over her belly.

He was supposed to be sniped. He'd bragged about it weeks before my mother's untimely death and had practically celebrated the opportunity to jet set around the world on an international sexcapade.

Reversing it after twenty-six years... was that even possible?

"I want a paternity test."

She frowned at me. "It is his."

My jaw ached from how hard I was clenching my teeth. "I *want* a paternity test."

There was no way I was going to be forced to accept this baby as my sibling. *I* was my father's only child. *I* was the sole beneficiary to his entire estate and legacy. I'd been put through the fucking gauntlet and come out the other side a better man than my father ever was.

This woman was lying and I was going to prove it.

A sibling at the ripe age of thirty-four. No fucking way.

"I'm not willing to negotiate anything else until a test is done," I said, shoving my chair back from the table.

"We can wait until after the baby is born," Steele suggested.

"Then we'll be putting all of this on the back burner until then. There are plenty of tests that are non-invasive if you don't wish to go down that road. But like I said, I'm not negotiating further until this is proven to be my father's child."

Because if, god forbid, Ana *was* carrying my sibling, then we'd be forced to stop all of this anyway and reevaluate the will altogether. Maybe even having to get a judge involved if it came down to Ana fighting me on every little thing she wanted her baby to be entitled to.

The unfortunate part about my father's will

was that the language had been ambiguous enough to allow for loopholes like this. Stating all of his 'naturally born children' were to receive the inheritance with no language stating *how* it was supposed to be split up in the end.

As his only child for the better part of three fucking decades, none of it was supposed to be this complicated. In fact, being an only child was the kind of cut-and-dry type scenario that any lawyer in Ted's shoes had wet dreams over.

How much easier could it get?

Everything was to go to me and that was final.

This added complication was only going to fuck everything up at an astronomical level that even I struggled to comprehend. Some things I'd already had my hands in, like the cars and getting them fixed up to sell.

Would I be forced to compensate for that too in the eyes of the law?

How much of this would be left in a stagnant state until this child grew up to be old enough to make decisions based on what *they* wanted?

How long was I supposed to be kept in limbo until it was deemed unfair to me?

Fuck.

I wanted to scream.

My hatred for my father ran deep, but this was on a whole other level.

Pointing at Ana, I said. "Listen to me. Get the paternity test and then we'll talk."

Her lips remained fused together while her hand worked overtime in rubbing her belly.

Ted pushed back from the table, too, standing while gathering his papers together and shoving them back into his folder. "We'll be in touch."

Steele merely sighed. "All right. Ted, I'll be in touch."

Both he and Ana stood up from the table, the latter far more pregnant than I'd realized when I'd first seen her with the way the table had covered up the lower half of her body from view. My stomach churned in an uncomfortable way.

The possibility of this being some kind of scam was incredibly high. High enough that I shouldn't be this sick to my stomach with anxiety. Sure, my father could've reversed his vasectomy and gotten this woman pregnant, but doing so after *twenty-six years*?

He got married after twenty-six years, too.

Fuck.

Fuck, fuck, fuck.

Steele bid us a goodbye and stuck close to Ana's side while she exited the conference room. The door was left open for us, both of them disappearing from view quite quickly. My legs felt boneless, wanting badly to settle back down into my chair and fold my head into my hands while the entirety of life was contemplated.

"We'll get this figured out, Avery." Ted grabbed my shoulder again, shaking me slightly. "Don't you worry."

But I *was* worrying.

Hadn't I been waiting for the third shoe to drop?

It seemed like the universe hadn't wanted to keep me waiting long.

All this time, I thought it would be something to do with Brandon or work. Never did I expect *this* dumpster fire of a mess.

God, what the fuck.

"Go home," Ted instructed. "Give yourself the day. If she refuses the paternity test, there's nothing to move forward with."

That wasn't the part that I was concerned with.

If she took the paternity test and it turned out that the baby's DNA matched with mine...

Then what?

"Go on." Ted shoved me toward the door. "I'll be in touch."

I stumbled out into the hallway, blearily making my way back to the main lobby where Ivy was waiting for me. She said something that I couldn't quite catch due to the roaring of blood in my ears.

Passing her by, I waved and headed back out into the afternoon heat, greedily sucking in the fresh air while my body shook from pent up rage.

Across the parking lot, Alexander Steele was holding the door to a corvette that was parked backward open for Ana, his back turned toward me. She came around the front of the car, slipping past him to slide into the passenger seat.

Once the door was shut behind her, Steele moved around to the back of the car to pop open the trunk, swinging his bag of documents around to toss inside. Through the windshield, Ana stared directly at me, her face falling into a slight frown that could've easily been mistaken for that flat face she'd worn during our meeting if

I wasn't already paying such close attention to her.

Suddenly, I had the urge to lift my hand up, four of my fingers folding back until only one was facing her. Childish, of course, to flip her off. But at this point, I didn't give a single fuck.

Fuck her and fuck my father.

Her eyes widened for a single second, and then she smirked.

CHAPTER 19

BRANDON

I COULD TELL something was off the moment I climbed into the passenger seat of Avery's car—an unexplainable hunch that whatever happened after he'd left my shop, wasn't good.

His energy seemed controlled, hampered in a strange way that I hadn't been expecting when he'd pulled up to my house an hour after I'd gotten home, freshly showered and shaved—not that I was expecting anything to happen tonight, despite my traitorous dick thinking otherwise—and dressed in a new set of clothes I'd picked up after work.

The tendons in Avery's hands flexed while he gripped the steering wheel, his gaze tracking me as I pulled the seatbelt over my chest and hooked it into the mechanism. We sat there for a long moment, both of us filling the awkward silence with nothing but the sound of our own labored breathing.

Was it wrong of me to want to touch him in some way?

Bridge that gap between us like we had back in his bedroom and earlier today at the shop?

I never thought I'd be the kind of person to be touch-starved. Yet, the second Avery had left my shop, my body had grown cold, no longer warmed without him by my side.

I'd had these moments of flare-ups back in high school. That longing and wanting practically choked me with how badly I needed to be with Avery in any capacity. Those impulses had been so easy to ignore with how much time we'd spent together, only really growing frustrating once I was back at home and in my own bed while I stared up at the ceiling all night.

Now with this weird... *thing* between us, I had no idea how to relieve myself. Clearly going out with Max had done nothing. Only served to slap me across the face with how obviously *not over* Avery I was.

The problem with trying to move on with my life while said person that I'd had such deep affections for was still around was that *he was still around.*

How the hell was I supposed to get a grip on reality when Avery was drowning out all of my sanity?

And last night.

God, last night.

I was getting hard just thinking about it.

Leaning back in my seat while subtly trying to readjust myself, I asked, "So, where to?"

Avery blinked hard, seeming to come back to reality. "I'm bringing you over the bridge."

To Ellington?

I guess that wasn't a surprise. There were places to go in Edgewood, but not the kind that were sit-down worthy. More pizza joints and corner store Chinese takeout places than actual restaurants with a laminated menu and music to set the ambiance.

I'd been trying to reconcile with myself for the entire afternoon, leading into evening, that this *wasn't* a date and Avery was simply taking me out to reconnect. Or something of that nature. Getting my hopes up was only asking to be disappointed.

He could be intending to thank me for the blowjob for all I knew. That's the kind of guy he was.

Avery looked good, though.

Really good.

Dressed in a white button-up that was tucked into tailored slacks, a belt wrapped around his waist with a gold buckle. His matching gold Rolex was the only accessory he wore, yet it made him look more refined than if he'd simply gone without it. His hair was still slicked back from earlier, though a few pieces had come down to curl against his forehead to half frame his face.

Me?

I was in something simple. A dark-colored, cotton quarter-sleeve shirt and dark blue jeans that still had the slight folded crease marks running along my thighs from the department store I'd picked them up from two hours prior.

My stomach churned. Nerves spiking instantly.

This wasn't a date. Just a casual dinner

between friends. Avery was always one to dress up. He took pride in his appearance and tonight was no different. Getting all up in my head about something so simple was just going to make this awkward.

I blew out a slow breath, forcing a smile onto my face. "Cool."

He nodded at that and then turned back to face forward, grabbing the gearshift and maneuvering the car back out onto the road.

For the most part, the trip was silent, save only for the soft music playing on the radio that was barely above a whisper. My fingers twitched in my lap from the effort of forcing myself not to reach over and crank it, to give myself something to focus on other than the sound of Avery's soft breathing.

I rolled my tongue around the roof of my mouth, my saliva thick and hard to swallow while the memories of wrapping my lips around Avery's cock equally teased and tortured me. I wanted to lick up the length of him again and bury him deep down into my throat until my nose was pressed against his body.

The way he'd stretched my throat, I still felt the slight tingles waking up this morning.

Fuck, and the way he came—

"So, my meeting with my dad's widow went to shit."

His words instantly snapped me out of my thoughts. Shit, I forgot he'd gone to that after visiting me. "Wait, did you just say 'widow'?"

He nodded. "She claimed to have a valid marriage license a week ago. My lawyer sent it in and it was found to be authentic. So she's at least entitled to some of the estate."

"Jesus, I'm sorry, Avery." What a way to find out your dad had secretly married someone behind your back. "Tell me she was his age at least?"

"Nope. Around ours, actually."

That was even worse, though it wasn't that much of a surprise. As superficial as he was materialistic, Kurt McAllister dating a woman half his age—or rather marrying her—was definitely something that I wouldn't put past him. He'd been in tabloids before for partying it up with young models on his yacht countless times when he was still alive.

Though, I was surprised he actually went through with marrying someone. He used to brag about being a perpetual bachelor on the rare occasions he was back in Ellington Heights pretending to be a good father.

Blowing out another breath, I said, "That's ridiculous. I hope she's only interested in the money, then?"

Avery was silent for a long beat, his eyes focused on the stoplight when we came to a crawl and paused. The red reflection of it cast an eerily glow on his skin, his eyes carrying a slight sheen to them.

"She's pregnant. Claims it's his," was what he finally murmured just as the light turned green.

I was stunned.

Avery flicked at the turn signal, merging into the lane next to us. "I told her that she needs to get a paternity test or else I'm not cooperating and she can kiss my ass. The problem is that if she really is pregnant with his child, she has legitimate claims to everything. Or, the child does. The will stated 'any natural born children.'"

"Fuck," I mumbled, letting my body sink back into my seat.

What a complicated mess. As was Kurt McAllister's entire life. Him fucking things up for Avery from beyond the grave, unfortunately, tracked just as much as the other ridiculous stuff he'd forced his son to put up with his entire life on this Earth.

To think that Avery might have a sibling soon...

"Did you verify if she was actually pregnant? She could be faking it," I suggested.

He let out a strained laugh. "Oh, she was very obviously pregnant during the meeting. Had documentation proving it, too, that she handed over. Unless the paternity test comes back false, I'm going to have to re-negotiate the entire will with her. At the very least, half of everything will be put into a trust until the kid's old enough to access it."

What a mess.

The worst part about all of this was how willing Avery was with handing over any amount of cash this woman could possibly dream of asking for. The monetary value wasn't the issue here, it was the fact that at the very least, personal possessions belonging to him, his mother, and his childhood would then have to be sorted through and assessed on whether or not it could be split, kept with Avery, or given to this new child.

For someone like Avery, that was a worst-case

scenario. He was a private person to a fault. Opening up and allowing people to come in and dissect him on a deep level, along with his family issues, was probably the worst thing that could ever possibly happen to him.

Not to mention, he didn't know either this woman or the kid.

Would he feel obligated in helping raise his sibling?

What would being a part of their life look like?

Avery had never planned on sticking around in Ellington Heights to begin with.

Would this woman expect to occupy the mansion while he went back to the city?

Would she be entitled to it and whatever came with being a McAllister?

None of this was supposed to be Avery's problem. He'd come back from the city to deal with his father's estate and then call it a day. Wiping his hands clean of everything would've been the ultimate relief once it was all said and done.

But now, with more shit added to his plate, who knew when he'd get to go back to his normal life.

A selfish part of me was happy to have him around a little longer, guilt soon swallowing that up while I was reminded of the fact that Avery never asked for any of this. He had a life and a job to get back to in the city.

The goal was never to be stuck here with the rest of us.

"Look, if you need me to pause work on the cars—"

He shook his head. "Don't. Keep working on them. If nothing else, I can store them back in that garage once you're done."

I glanced his way again. His face was set in a hard frown, his hands flexing on the steering wheel again.

"Please don't quit on me." His voice was barely above a whisper.

My gut squeezed tight. "I won't. I never would."

The corner of his mouth tugged up at that, relieving some of the tension that had settled in my body instantly. I hated seeing Avery under pressure like this. He handled it well, of course, as would be expected of someone like him. While I wasn't sure what exactly his job title was, there was no doubt in my mind that it was something high up on the echelon.

Avery let out a soft chuckle.

To my surprise, he moved his hand away from the gearshift and settled it down onto my thigh, his long fingers curling around me with a tight enough grip that there would be no mistaking it for something else. My heart leaped in my chest at the contact, and how close he was to where I had my dick tucked.

"You always know what to say to make me feel better," he said, squeezing my thigh once.

I swallowed, my voice gruff as I spoke. "Chalk it up to knowing you for decades."

His thumb smoothed along the inner hem of my jeans—killing me. "True. Neither of us have really changed that much, huh."

My head was fuzzy with need, barely able to hear him over the roaring of blood flowing through my eardrums. If he moved his hand an inch up, he'd be touching me where I really needed him. I was glad that these jeans were tight enough to not make much of a difference no matter how hard I was getting.

Sure, it fucking pinched like a bitch, but at least my arousal wasn't *that* obvious.

"Don't know about that." It felt like there were marbles rolling around in my mouth as I spoke. "Don't even know your job."

"Oh. Yeah, I guess I haven't really talked about that. It's nothing special. Just a CEO position at a tech company in the city."

The nonchalant-ness in his tone had me snorting. As if being a CEO was equivalent to a stock manager down at the local mini-mart and that his paychecks weren't a staggering few cool million a year. Hell, probably more than that given the notoriety of the McAllister last name.

"*Just*," I echoed back to him.

He laughed again, squeezing my thigh once more and then trailing his hand down to where my knee was. "Oh stop. You know what I mean."

Holy fuck.

If I came in my fucking pants right here on the way to the restaurant, I was going to be so pissed. And embarrassed. But most of all, pissed.

The fact that I was getting this turned on by such a simple semblance of contact that could be explained away as innocent was wholly ridiculous. But here I was, subtly spreading my legs apart in the hope that Avery somehow took the hint and wandered his hand back up north.

"I've got an apartment in the city that's not too far away from my office," he continued to talk. "Took over the company during a merger and then acquired all the assets when the board wanted to sell in order to cut their losses. I saw potential in the staff and decided to stay on. Now we're in the Fortune 500."

"Impressive," I mumbled, holding back a moan.

It was. Truly.

I just really wished we were having this conversation at any other fucking time than right now.

Maybe this was Avery's sick way of torturing me with what I couldn't have. The blowjob had been a fluke, a one-time thing. Now, he was dangling himself in front of me like a fucking carrot on a stick.

'Sorry, I'm straight and you can't have me'.

"You like running your own place?" he asked.

I did.

Funny enough, everything that I'd been warned about when taking over the shop and completely revamping it into my own were the parts I liked the most. The background of owning a shop wasn't exactly a mechanic's paradise, however, it always had me feeling like a real business owner when I got back to balancing the books and keeping the place running on the clerical side of things.

Would I prefer to be working on cars any day of the week?

Sure, absolutely. But the other stuff wasn't nearly as bad as some made it out to be."

"Mmm, it's nice. No boss to answer to," I said.

"True. I guess I still have people to answer to, in a sense."

"Employees?" I asked.

"That and a board of investors. Annoying stuff." He ran his thumb along the shape of my knee. "Don't ever get into the corporate world."

"Thanks for the tip." My eyes were starting to flutter closed. I was so close to grabbing his wrist and forcing him to put his hand right where I needed it.

I was hanging on to my self-control by a thread, much like I had yesterday before Avery had looked at me with those *eyes*. I'd caved instantly, pushed him on the bed and crawled on top of him like I'd been doing it for ages now.

Finally getting my hands around that monster in his pants was only the tip of the iceberg when it came to quenching my thirst for him. I needed more. The blowjob wasn't enough. That was only a mere appetizer to what I could be having if given the chance.

Fuck, listen to me. Trying to play this off like he'd actually be open to something like that.

But wasn't he?

Wasn't last night indicative to something *more*?

He wasn't avoiding me—actively sought me out, in fact. Invited me *to dinner*. That had to say something about whatever the fuck this was.

Right?

God, I was going crazy. *This* was making me crazy.

"Avery..." I croaked.

He jammed on the brakes instantly, his head whipping around.

My hand latched onto his wrist. "Pull over."

There was no hesitation. He was instantly flicking on his turn signal and merging out of traffic, finding a curb to pull up to and parallel park us at. My leg grew cold when he took his hand away momentarily to slam the gearshift up, causing me to grit my teeth from calling out.

I kept a hold of him, the tendons at his wrist moving against my palm. He settled his hand back over my knee, turning in his seat to fully face me. "You okay?"

No, I wanted to snap.

What kind of question was that, anyway?

How could he have no idea what the hell he was doing to me?

To be that goddamn oblivious to how fucked up I was even sitting next to him in this cramped luxury car with the smell of these leather seats and his cologne overwhelming me—

He grabbed at my chin, forcing me to look over.

"Brandon," he said, his face mere inches from mine. "Do you not want to do this? Dinner?"

My tongue was tied, my mind too busy focusing on the thumb that absentmindedly trailed circles along my cheek and down to my jaw. I was getting dizzy from the attention—the affection—that I'd been starved of for so long.

Hookups here and there were only a means to an end. To blow off some pent-up frustration and then go about life like it never happened. Rarely did I ever hit up anyone twice, and if I did, it was because we were both stumbling out of the bar at the same time and paying for two taxi fares was stupid.

There were never any lingering touches or caresses that were filled with anything but hard lust, soon stamped out the moment either of us climaxed.

I never considered myself to be one to want this kind of attention. But now that I had it, I *needed* it.

I needed *more*.

What was I going to do when he eventually left me?

Starve again?

"You keep touching me," was what finally came out.

He stilled for a moment, then asked, "You want me to stop?'

"No," I blurted out.

Avery blinked at me, his lips parting in surprise.

I forced myself not to follow the movement with my own eyes, keeping my gaze level with his.

Before he could say anything, I followed up with, "What is this? What are we doing?"

He hesitated, his thumb moving along my cheek and jaw again. "I don't know."

That wasn't good enough.

Not this time.

"You need to figure it out."

His brows knitted together. He tightened his hold on me when I tried to pull away, keeping us locked in a staring contest that I had no choice but to compete in. Avery's lips parted again, his tongue darting out to wet them with a quick swipe that caught my attention immediately.

I wanted to lean over and press mine there instead, slide my tongue between his lips and play with his until we were both squirming in our seats.

What kind of sounds would I drag out of him if I played with his tongue the way I had with his cock?

A soft moan tumbled out of me at the thought.

"Jesus," he breathed out.

He pushed me against the back of the seat, keeping me there by the hold on my jaw and lifted himself up over the center console just enough to untuck his legs from where they were trapped under the steering wheel.

There was already a prominent bulge between his legs, mirroring my own trapped one. His slacks were much more forgiving, though, giving me a front and center look to how turned on he was also getting from this.

Something in me clicked, then.

If I was going to do this—actually let Avery explore whatever he needed to with me—then I needed to get out of my own head and ride this wave for however long it lasted. Turning him away because of my own insecurities and the fear that he'd leave me eventually was only going to make me regret not letting this happen in the end.

Would I survive the inevitable heartbreak?

Who fucking knew.

But what I *did* know was that if I got to have Avery—*all* of him—for this short amount of time, then I needed to jump on the opportunity.

He was clearly willing and ready.

"I need you to touch me," I said, my voice firm.

His eyes widened for a split second and then grew serious. Without a word, he shifted his hold on my jaw, switching hands in order to reach over my body and down to a button on the side of my seat.

The back of my seat slowly lowered at an agonizing pace, until I was finally flat on my back. Before he could lean back, I grabbed the front of his shirt, keeping him close to me. His cologne clogged my senses in the best way, intoxicating me.

"Show me," he murmured.

I followed the line of his arm down to his free hand, taking it and placing it over my aching hard on. The second he made contact, my eyes fluttered shut, another moan leaving me. I heard him suck in a short gasp, his fingers tightening instantly.

"Right here," was all I said.

Fuck, that felt good.

My legs parted further, taking up as much room as possible until I had both my knees knocking against the door and the console. It wasn't enough by any means, but at least spread like this, I got a little relief from how cramped in my jeans I was.

Avery's hand moved in a slow circle, kneading my balls through the material of my jeans in a way that had my cock twitching and squeezing out a little precum. The motion was slow and torturous, with not enough friction to really satisfy me but forced me to hold on for dear life nonetheless.

The urge to meet his hand half way and grind up into it had me gritting my teeth together.

I needed to take this slow. Scaring Avery off was the last thing I wanted to end up doing.

I snapped my eyes open again. Avery's own staring back at me were dark in the dim lighting from the cars passing by, his pupils dilated and his mouth dropped open just enough that I could see his tongue pushing at the back of his teeth. He was so close that all it would take was one shove up and our mouths would be smashed together.

"More," I breathed out.

He paused and then moved his hand up to where the button of my jeans was, his fingers twisting around the front of it until it finally popped open.

I shoved the fly apart along with my jeans and underwear, needing to free myself or else I was going to burst. My cock was rigid, popping out to smack against my stomach with a hard slap that had my balls squeezing tightly.

I heard Avery gasp, his hand coming down to ghost over the line of my cock almost instantly.

"*Fuck,*" I ground out, causing him to pause.

Oh, no you don't.

Grabbing his wrist again, I guided him right to where the line of my jeans ended. His fingers spread for me, curling around and cupping me in his hand. He didn't move or so much as squeeze tight enough to give me any kind of relief.

Instead, he simply stared.

"Jesus, you're pretty," he murmured.

What the hell?

"I don't know if I..." He trailed off, licking his lips again.

Honestly, I really didn't care what he did so long as he did something. For now, we could start easy. Use this to get him familiar with someone else's junk other than his own. Lucky for him, I was an excellent teacher.

"Like this," I said, tightening my hold on his wrist and then guiding him once more.

He followed the motion, dragging his hand up the length of my cock until we reached the head. Simply seeing his hand on me had me leaking more, the erotic view turning me on way more than I thought it ever could.

To think that I'd had wet dreams about this very thing over ten years ago, fantasized about it more times than I ever cared to admit, and now we were here doing this.

There'd been times when we'd driven around in his car with just the two of us after school, freshly licensed and without any other cares in the world but getting as far away from our high school as humanly possible, that I'd had these same wild thoughts.

Wondering what would happen if I just reached across the distance between us and put my hand in his lap while he was driving down the highway.

How fast could he push his dad's luxury car to go while I had my lips wrapped around his cock? Till he was fisting his hand in my air and pulling me up before he came.

Fifteen years was all it took for the fantasy to become a reality.

This was so much better than sitting in a stuffy restaurant while we argued over the dinner rolls and butter that would be the only thing to hold us over during the forty-five minute wait it took us to get our entrees.

The tendons in his hand flexed while he tightened his grip on me, causing my balls to squeeze again and drool more precum.

"Shit," Avery mumbled, dragging his hand up over the head to collect the slick accumulated there and then moving back down my shaft again. "You like that, hmm?"

I arched my back, folded my body back into the seat. "Yeah…"

I liked this. Him keeping a hold of my jaw—practically pinning me against the headrest—while he moved his hand. I felt safe like this, trapped in the best way possible. I had nowhere else to go, nothing else to focus on but his hands on me.

"Up here." I grabbed at his wrist again, pulling him back up to circle around the head and then drawing it back down, slicking my skin with my own fluids. "That's it. Little faster."

His hand curled around me, measured strokes pulling another moan out of me that had him cursing softly under his breath. I could feel the quick bursts of his breathing as he panted against my cheek, and gave into the need to pull him closer.

Avery's forehead was hot against my own slightly clammy one. His audible swallow was not lost on me and neither was the way he tilted his head, almost like he wanted to kiss me. I fucking wanted him to but I needed this more—needed him right here with me and watching as I came undone from his touch.

"Fuck. I'm close," I ground out.

He swallowed again, his voice rough. "Yeah?"

"Keep going. Just like that." My entire body throbbed, the need to come so overwhelming that it was getting hard to focus on anything else.

Avery, despite his rather amateur knowledge in how to give another man a hand job, was doing fucking fantastic. He'd always been a quick learner, picking things up pretty much straight away when he actually tried.

This was no exception, apparently.

He was a goddamn natural.

What else was he capable of doing with those perfect hands of his?

His fist drew up to my head again, keeping it there while he stroked quickly in rapid bursts. The sensations sent shockwaves rolling down my spine, my body pitching back to arch out of my seat, still held down partially by his other hand that kept me from going anywhere.

The moan that left my lips was tortured sounding—caught between a plea and a demand.

"*Avery,*" was all that I could manage to choke out before exploding in his hand.

He moved his hand down me again, using long strokes that had me spilling all over his knuckles and making a total mess of us both.

I came for what felt like ages, until my body was empty, and then I slumped back into the seat behind me with a dazed feeling washing over me.

He buried his face in my neck, pressing his mouth against the column of my skin in a way that almost had me believing he was kissing the spot over and over again. My post orgasm bliss was apparently making me delirious.

Was it fucked up of me to like that he still had his hand wrapped tight around my dick?

I was already getting soft, however the firm hold he had me in was comforting in a weird way. Just like his hand on my face.

God, that was fucking good.

I wanted to stay like this forever. Damned our responsibilities and whatever else we'd have to go back to once we both sobered up and pulled apart from each other. This close intimacy felt so right and so damn good.

I was afraid for what reality would eventually bring. What regrets would follow once we could no longer ignore the fact that last night, and now tonight, weren't just flukes—minute lapses in judgment that could easily be explained away by some haphazard excuse.

Something chimed in Avery's car, causing the lights on his dashboard to flash. He slowly lifted his head to crane his neck back around to look at whatever notification popped up, a frown suddenly crossing his features.

"What?" I asked.

"Phone call."

I was disappointed when he pulled away completely, letting me go in order to sit up and tap at the notification. His hand was still coated in me, glossy looking in the dim lighting of his car's console.

When he retrieved his phone from the slot next to the cup holder, his eyes widened.

"Shit," he muttered. "I gotta take this. She never calls this late."

I was still fuzzy from the orgasm, my mind

half gone while the other half was running on fumes. "She?"

"Carrie."

"Who's Carrie?" I said blearily.

"My ex-wife," he clarified, and then pushed the door open to step outside and take the phone call. "Give me one sec."

CHAPTER 20

As soon as I picked up the other line, I could tell something was very wrong.

Hell, I could tell that by how late I was receiving this phone call and with no warning text to let me know she'd be calling ahead of time. Carrie wasn't one for idle chitchat and the humdrum of keeping up with the daily lives of those she knew.

Me, being her ex, even less so.

So when I heard that small sniffle on the other end of the line, I prepared myself for the worse. "Hey, what's going on?"

She let out a short sigh, but it didn't at all sound like she was frustrated or tired. It was the kind of sound that you'd make when trying to calm down before an absolute breakdown hit. "I'm sorry... I didn't know who else to call."

Immediately, that put me on edge. "Everything okay?"

"Ryan's out of town for the week on some business thing and I can't get a hold of him and his parents aren't answering either—"

"Carrie." My voice held firm. Her spiraling wasn't helping anyone, least of all me when she'd clearly called me for a reason. "Tell me what happened."

"Eva's sick. I had to bring her to the hospital because her fever wasn't going down. They admitted her and now no one's telling me anything. I heard one of the nurses talking about an infection in her brain and now I'm freaking out—"

"I'll be right there," came my instant response.

No way was I going to leave her to deal with all of that by herself. She may be my ex-wife but that didn't diminish the care that I still held for her. And for Eva.

Ryan could get over himself if this ended up pissing him off. If I were in his shoes, I'd be grateful to have someone keeping my fiancée company while their daughter was laid up in a hospital bed, most likely unconscious and hooked up to a bunch of machines.

"I'm so sorry," she said."

"Don't be. It'll take me about an hour to get into the city. Text me what hospital you're at, okay?"

She let out a relieved breath, sounding a little more settled than when I'd first picked up her call. Her voice was still small as she spoke, but no longer had that tiny tremor to it. "Thank you, Avery. I'll see you soon."

"Of course."

Ending the call, I flipped over to my text thread with her and waited for her pinned location to pop up. The skin around my knuckles was tight for some reason, causing me to glance over at my hand—

Fuck. Brandon.

Whipping around, I yanked the driver's side door open to peer into the cab. He was already sitting up with his chair upright, cleaned up and tucked back into his pants like the last fifteen minutes had never happened. His hair was combed back from his face, looking artfully messy like it always did.

The only remnants of what we'd done was now crusting over on my hand.

"I'm sorry," I blurted out.

He was already shaking his head, though, reaching for the seat belt to pull it across his body. "Don't be. You can drop me off at the shop since it's closer. I have some paperwork to get through anyway."

I tightened my hand around my phone hard enough that it was going to leave an impression against my palm. It vibrated twice with Carrie's incoming text.

Fuck, this was *not* how I wanted any of this to end. Blowing him off like this after we just...

I swallowed. "Bran."

"We're all good, Avery. Emergencies happen." But he wasn't even looking at me while he was saying it, doing everything in his power to avoid making eye contact with me while fiddling with his belt and then the strap that went across his chest.

"Yeah."

I was so fucking torn.

Carrie needed me. She wouldn't have called otherwise if I wasn't a last resort. If there was going to be bad news delivered to her about Eva, she needed someone there. And I wanted to be there for it, too. Eva wasn't my kid but I still loved her. She was a sweet little girl and would always, in a weird way, be like my baby niece.

She was the reason I even came to the conclusion that having a family one day *would* be something I looked forward to and wasn't some far off obligation that I was staving off.

The worst part about all of this was that I was leaving Brandon behind once again to run back to my other life. Back to my other obligations and responsibilities that would eventually force us to part ways in the end.

I could stay, tell Carrie that something came up. The only downside was that the guilt would eat me alive.

"We should get going." His voice was soft as he spoke.

My heart lurched in my chest.

Sliding back into my seat, I slotted my phone back into the compartment, the screen automatically connecting to my car's console and pulling up Carrie's location. Brandon said nothing while

I got buckled in, nor when I pulled back out onto the main street and headed back toward his house instead of the shop like he'd requested.

I doubted he actually had anything to get done at the shop—he was simply trying to make himself as non-inconvenient as possible, despite it being *me* who was the one bailing on us tonight. Out of the corner of my eye, I caught the way his fingers twisted together in his lap while he stared out the passenger window.

There was so much I wanted to say, to explain, but nothing was coming out. No matter how hard I was trying to force my mouth to work out some kind of sentence to apologize again.

What *could* I even say to make any of this not awkward as hell, though?

I'd felt kind of lost and confused when he'd left me last night after blowing me and now here I was returning the favor.

I'd tried not to read too much into him leaving as anything other than a spontaneous response to what the hell we'd gotten up to. The tentative approach to seeking him out at the shop to test the waters again, to see if he was going to avoid me at all costs or if he'd just been surprised by the turn of events, had been nerve wracking.

Finding out it was the latter was more of a fucking relief than getting that phone call about my father's death.

And now I was fucking it all up.

When I pulled up to his house, he barely let me put the car in park before he was unhooking himself out of his seat and popping the door open.

My knee-jerk reaction was to snatch his arm and yank him back into his seat so that we could talk but again, what could I say?

He paused, grabbing the side of my door before shutting it, ducking down to look at me to say, "I hope, um... whatever's going on turns out okay."

My smile was tense. "Thank you. I'll call you?"

His expression faltered—flickering between uncertain and pained. "Yeah. Sure."

When he slammed the door shut, the entire car rattled from the force. His steps were quick going up to his front door, unlocking it and disappearing inside without a wave or anything to say goodbye.

I slammed my head back against my seat, groaning.

I'd make it up to him later.

Somehow.

As much as I hated to ruin our plans like this, for now I needed to be there for Carrie and Eva.

CHAPTER 21

B RANDON

I SUPPOSE I should've seen it coming.

A man like Avery McAllister wasn't meant to stay single, no matter how hard he'd preached about doing so when we were kids. Heirs of billionaires, no matter the estrangement, would always eventually find their way back to the roots that their families had laid out for them—a carefully crafted plan that ensured that the money stayed within the family system and would continue to be reinvested for the next generations to come.

Assets were contingent on the legacy to

continue. Letting it die with an unkept heir and redistributed to the government would never be allowed, no matter how much of a fight said heir could theoretically put up.

That's just how that world worked.

And Avery was no exception to it.

Ex-wife.

That word echoed in my head for so long that now it felt like my mind had been permanently branded with it.

I wondered if he'd left behind a family in the city. He'd never mentioned children before this but then again he never mentioned having an ex-wife, either.

How much did I actually know about this man that I'd allowed to get me off in the front seat of his Audi?

Hardly anything, now that I thought about it.

Ex-wife.

He'd jumped out of the car at her phone call, which meant that whatever happened was serious. Avery wasn't one to leave unless necessary, and definitely not when we were in the middle of what we were doing.

That meant she mattered. She wasn't some

fluke—a small blip in his radar that he'd soon forgotten the second the ink dried on their divorce papers. He cared enough to run to her, despite them no longer being together. She'd called and the second he'd picked up, he'd left.

My stomach ached so damn bad. Like a fist had been slammed into my body and it was taking everything in me not to double over and vomit.

Having a life after me was inevitable. Something I'd been expecting to find out eventually when it came down to us actually sitting together and talking about everything. I'd expected to hear about past relationships and the sordid tales of lovers gone by.

This wasn't one of those things. A marriage meant something. He'd walked down the aisle, promised her a comfortable life, and legally bound himself to her. For how long, I really couldn't speculate. It wasn't like I'd been looking at his ring finger searching for a damn tan line.

Kids were another thing.

I had a hard time believing Avery's willingness to leave a child behind, even if it was to come sort out his father's affairs. A custody arrangement could be in place, or the kid could not exist at all.

Both were very real possibilities. Especially with Avery only mentioning himself when it came to fighting his father's widow for the estate.

At this point, though, anything was possible.

And that was the part that was killing me.

I'd allowed my fantasies to pull me from reality. To fool me into thinking that anything that I built with Avery now could somehow be permanent and change his mind from leaving again. Our 'date' had been a stark reminder that I needed to get my head on straight and to focus on what really needed to take priority: moving on.

Come the next morning, and with no word from Avery at all, I decided that instead of wallowing in my own self-pity party, I'd be proactive with actually getting the ball rolling on this whole Max thing.

If anyone had the potential to turn my attention elsewhere, I hoped to God it was him.

Max: Hey! Good to hear from you :) Yeah, I'd love to grab dinner. How's tonight sound?

Me: Sounds perfect. Want to meet somewhere?

Max: How about I pick you up?

I blew out a breath at the offer.

Obviously, it was a way for him to have the excuse of dropping me off back home himself and potentially being invited in for something more. An idea that I didn't exactly hate.

The only problem was, would I be into it?

Would I have Avery off my mind long enough to focus on a new partner and not let that man swarm my thoughts like usual?

I could still feel his hands on me, gripping my face and cock even now almost twelve hours later. Maybe another set of hands could over-write his. Marking me in the same way his had.

Or maybe it was all a damn pipedream.

Me: Yeah, that sounds good to me. I'll send you my address. How does 8 sound?

Max: Perfect! Can't wait to see you :)

"So, this is your second date, then?" my sister asked.

I moved the phone away from my ear to put it on speaker and set it down on my dresser. "Technically, yeah."

Fishing out a pair of jeans from my dresser

and slipping them on, I moved to my closet and swung back the hangers to reach the nicer shirts I had hidden away in the back. Grabbing two of them, I turned to hold them both up to my chest in the mirror.

"What's with the *technically*?" she said.

"Well, the last time we went out, we got interrupted so it ended early." Not finding either of them flattering, I tossed both hangers onto the bed and grabbed two more shirts out, doing the same to them in the mirror.

How sad was it that I was stressing out this badly about my date?

The first time I'd gone out with Max, my head had been too preoccupied to really care what the hell was happening. I'd met him straight from work and had figured if he still liked what he saw with my minimal effort, then maybe that made him soulmate material.

Which was a stupid way of viewing it.

The man deserved effort, so that's what I was going to give him. If I could go out of my way to look nice for Avery, then I damned as hell needed to step up my game for Max. That was the only way I was going to force myself to take this seriously.

"Oh? Interrupted by what? Don't tell me you scared him off, Bran."

"No, nothing like that. I just—" I clamped my lips together before I could finish the sentence.

I'd been adamant not to mention anything related to Avery to any of my siblings up until now. Lila would have no idea who I was talking about, but that didn't mean one of my brothers wouldn't clue her in after she recounted the story to them.

All eight of us were close, despite us being a large family. Coming together had been tough at first but slowly we'd made our own way, relying on each other as if we'd always been a part of each other's life since the beginning.

I loved my big family, even if they drove me completely nuts sometimes.

"Uh oh," she teased. "I sense you're trying to hide something from me."

"Am not." But even to my own ears, I sounded like a damn liar.

Lila being Lila immediately picked up on it. "Tell me what happened. I need to know if this guy that I got you set up with is a total sleazebag!"

I wanted to sigh to both her and myself.

Fuck me. Seriously

"It had nothing to do with Max."

"Okay? Then what?" she said.

"It's..." A soft grunt tumbled from my mouth. "I ran into someone from my childhood. That's all. And... well, we got to talking and wanted to catch up."

Lila was silent on the other line for a long while—enough that I had to pick up my phone to check and make sure she was still connected on the other end of our call.

When she finally spoke, her tone was slow. "So... you ditched your date... to go hang out with an old friend?"

"Yeah. Essentially. It wasn't planned." Especially, what happened afterward...

"Huh." She was silent for another pause. "I guess I never would've expected that out of you. To... ditch a date to catch up with a friend."

I winced at the subtle accusation: *this isn't you.*

I was supposed to be the levelheaded one, not the flighty type that had barely any regard for things outside of my own personal bubble of reality. If anything, I was painfully aware of social situations to the point of bending over backward just to accommodate everyone around me.

Lila had stressed how hard she'd worked with her matchmaker to find Max—as she'd described it, like searching for a pearl amongst sand grains —and to hear that I'd completely ditched him for someone else was no doubt strange coming from me.

"It's complicated," was all I could think to say. Because it really fucking was.

With still no word from Avery about anything since he left to go back to the city, I was being forced to face the uncomfortable truth of not being a priority in his life, just like I should've known all along.

It hurt. No matter how much of it was the truth being served to me plain and simple.

Ex-wife.

A whole life away from here.

Avery belonged back in the city. Not fucking around in bum-fuck nowhere with me.

"Complicated, as in *feelings* complicated?" Lila asked.

"No." I lied. "Just catching up. It was nothing. I wanted to make it up to Max for being an ass, hence tonight."

"Oh good." I could hear the smile in her voice. "Well, tell me how it goes! I really hope you guys get along. On paper, he seemed perfect for you."

My stomach twisted into a tight knot. Lila meant well, as she always did.

The pressure to get this right was a little overwhelming, considering my failure would ultimately reflect back onto her, no matter what way this got spun. Hopefully, it didn't come to that, though. Whatever money she invested in this, I'd get a good return for her.

It was the least I could do.

"I will. I'll talk to you soon."

Ending the call, I wandered back over to my bed and face-planted down onto it. I had about a half hour to get ready and meet Max at my door, and so far, I was running majorly behind. Outside of dinner, there were no real plans either of us had come up with.

And assuming that dinner went well and we got along, he'd be coming back here to... well, get more familiar with me.

I let my hand wander down to the fly of my jeans, cupping myself over the fabric and giving a firm squeeze. I suppose it was fucked up of me to consider anything about my body Avery's, no matter how hard it's been trying to get his damn touch out of my head. I'd never had something like that happen before—where I'd felt claimed in a way.

Sex was simply a release for me as it always had been since I'd started hooking up with guys at sixteen. I'd never had any lingering feelings outside of that and certainly not after a fucking handjob.

I squeezed myself again.

But...

Oh, fuck me.

My phone's ringtone went off again, Lila most likely calling back to pep talk me up about this date. No matter how enthused I tried to sound on the phone when she'd first called, she probably saw right through my bullshit.

That was the problem with having sisters. They were too good at calling things out that my brothers would've simply left alone.

Dragging myself up from my bed with

another sigh, I shuffled over to my dresser to retrieve my phone. The number that flashed across the screen wasn't my sister's however, and was some random one that I didn't have saved in my phone.

Curiously, I answered. "Hello?"

"Hey." *Avery.*

My heart jumped. "Hey..."

"Sorry, I got your phone number from the shop after they told me you went home early. Hope that was okay."

"No, no. It's fine. Everything okay?"

"Uh." There was some noise in the background, the sounds of voices and something like a pager going off that passed by rather quickly. "Yes and no."

Was it my place to ask?

I'd had this man's cock shoved down my throat not even two days ago—didn't that award me some kind of privilege?

Fuck it.

"What happened? Where are you?"

"The hospital. My ex-wife's daughter had a really bad fever that wouldn't break, so she brought her in. She's hooked up to a bunch of machines right now that are helping her breathe. They think it's RSV."

My eyes widened. "Jesus. That's rough."

"Yeah. She's being a little trooper, though."

I could hear the pride in his voice, sending another dagger through my chest. I tried to ignore it, knowing that having a sick kid far outweighed my own insecurities at the moment. I could dwell on my own feelings later when I wasn't listening to the sounds of a hospital in the background.

"Glad to hear it. You with her mom right now?"

"Yeah, we—" Some kind of alarm went off near him, causing him to curse softly under his breath. "Hold on."

As the other line went silent, I found myself wandering back over to my bed and sitting down on the edge of it. It was only a few more long seconds that passed by before the other end clicked and I could hear Avery's soft breathing again.

"Sorry about that," he said. The background sounded much quieter, his voice mirroring it. "This place is a madhouse today."

Such was city life. There was no rest for anyone, let alone the medical staff at a hospital.

Avery running off without a second thought to be with his ex and her (their?) kid showed the type of man he was. And as much as it pained me to think about, those were the markings of a great father. That little girl was lucky, as was his ex.

"Hey, I'm sorry about all of this," he said, surprising me. "I didn't—I wasn't planning on leaving you like that."

"No worries," was all I could think to say to that. I wanted desperately to read between the lines, but refused myself from going any further than what was at face value. "I'm glad you're there to support them."

He scoffed. "Yeah, well the fiancé's not. He had all sorts of things to say to my ex this morning when she called to update him. He's a good guy, don't get me wrong, but he has a tendency to get jealous whenever I'm in the picture."

I wondered why that was. Perhaps there was still obvious chemistry between Avery and his ex that the fiancé was constantly picking up on. Or maybe their shared child was a cause for tension between the ex and her fiancé.

"Which is ridiculous," Avery continued. "Because I'm not even in the picture. Carrie and I remained friends because there was no animosity between us when we divorced. Hell, I even sent them a damn night nurse after Carrie gave birth as a pushing gift."

Not his kid.

Oh my god, I could fucking cry.

"That was nice of you," I barely choked out before my voice cracked.

"I guess. What else was I supposed to get her? They'd already gotten plenty of diapers and outfits."

I let out a soft snort.

Leave it to a billionaire to think of grand gestures as small acts of service. Such a typical Avery thing to do, though. He'd never once begged for a thank you after enacting a good deed, and half the time was surprised when he got one in the first place.

That was the charming thing about him. Helping people was second nature and not once did he ever expect anything in return. He was a good man—far better than me or anyone else I knew for that matter.

"Anyway," he cleared his throat. "How, uh, how are you?"

"Is that code for something?"

He cleared his throat again. "I meant—fuck. Last night, Bran. How... are you okay?"

What a loaded question.

To be honest, I was fucking messed up in the head with no discernable way of fixing that, short of putting my damn brain inside of a tub of bleach and hoping for a damn miracle. It was safe to say that getting entangled with Avery was as I'd predicted the second he'd walked into my shop looking like a lost puppy: going to be my downfall.

Here was the problem, though. I didn't know how to *care* about that. All I could focus on were these damn butterflies in my stomach that refused to calm down since the second he'd said that the child in question wasn't his and that his ex had a damn fiancé.

Did that give me hope for something to bud between us?

Yes, of fucking course it did. No matter how much I tried to stamp these damn feelings down, nothing was stopping them from cracking through the concrete and blooming all the same.

"How are you?" I shot back instead of answering him.

"Don't do this to me. Please." The fear in his voice was not lost on me at all. "Did we—tell me if I fucked up."

I couldn't help it, I burst out laughing.

Only Avery would think that after giving me a mind blowing orgasm and sending me to cloud fucking nine would count as him 'fucking up'. Honestly, most men would be walking around with their heads held high and a kick in their step if they were in his shoes.

It never occurred to me how Avery was perceiving any of this. How he'd been worried about *me* when I'd be doing the same thing for him.

"I'm good," I said.

"Brandon."

Smiling, I said, "Avery. It was good."

He was quiet on the other end for a long moment. "Really?"

"Yes. It was great." Being bold like this sent a hot flash through my body. At this point, though, I didn't care. He asked, so he'd get an honest answer. Even if it made me look like a damn fool.

"Bran, I..." He pulled in a sharp inhale. "I liked touching you. Like that."

I pitched backward, hitting my mattress hard enough to bounce my body. I gnawed on my bottom lip a little while cupping myself through my jeans again, giving my rapidly hardening cock a good squeeze.

Imagining it as his hands was only making me hornier—needier.

"How much?" I asked.

"A lot."

Aching to be let free, I yanked at the front button and shoved my jeans down just enough to get a hand wrapped around my cock. It throbbed against my palm, his confession causing a little bit of precum to bead at the tip.

"I did, too." Admitting it out loud was risky, even with his own confession having just been made.

I wasn't used to playing all of my cards like this, putting my raw wants and desires out on the table for the person that I wanted most to see and examine, to pick apart and potentially reject me over. Perhaps my horny brain was giving me less fucks to give, or Avery's own words were fueling me to being completely transparent.

On the other end of the line, his breathing became labored. "Fuck..."

"You know what else I liked?" I waited for his response and then said, "I liked you watching me."

"You were... you looked *so* fucking good, Brandon."

I gave my cock a long stroke, curling my palm up around the wet head and dragging it back down toward my balls. Who knew getting off to being this honest was a thing? A week ago I would've been mortified at the thought of Avery ever suspecting I was attracted to him. Now I had my fucking hand wrapped around my cock, getting off to him telling me how much he liked watching me come.

"Avery..." I darted my tongue out to wet my lips. "Where are you?"

"Um. I'm hiding out in an empty bathroom. One of those family ones."

"You're alone?"

"Yeah."

Perfect. "How hard are you?"

The strangled sound was music to my fucking ears. "Jesus Christ."

"I want you to touch yourself with me."

"With you?"

I hummed in response, flexing my fingers around the base of my cock and then giving myself a few quick strokes to force more precum to leak out. I smeared it from the tip and down again, getting myself slick enough not to be uncomfortable.

On the other end of the line, there was some rustling and then the sound of a toilet seat slamming down. Getting him to do this in a hospital was risky and even more so with him taking up a family bathroom with the sole purpose of getting him off.

I wasn't about to regret a damn thing, though. Not when I knew the second he had himself in his hand by the way he groaned into the phone.

"Shit," he muttered.

My horny brain was screaming at me to tell him to take a picture and send it over—an impulse that was damn hard to ignore over the rushing of blood in my ears that was soon traveling down to my crotch.

Damn, what I wouldn't give to add a photo like that to my own personal spank bank collection. He'd be the first one in that folder. Maybe even the only.

"You were a natural," I told him. "Could've sworn you'd given someone a handjob before."

"Just you."

The fluttering in my stomach kicked up again. I doubted he meant for his words to be so flattering, but damn if that didn't make me feel special. Obviously, Avery hadn't changed his preferences all that much since leaving at seventeen. And whatever fluke this was of him finding an interest in experimenting with me, I'd give him the best damn crash course I had to offer.

The last thing I'd let this man walk away with was regrets and shame. There would be none of that when it was just us.

"You know what I liked the most? Your cock in my mouth."

He groaned again. "You've got a talented fucking mouth."

"Wish I was there with you. Kneeling on the floor at your feet. Your cock in my mouth. I could suck on it all day, Avery."

"Oh my god," he wheezed. "You're killing me…"

My hips kicked up at that, fucking myself right into my fist just like I imagined I'd do with him. Him fucking me, me fucking him, I literally didn't care. Both were erotic as fuck to fantasize about and both had my balls tightening to the point of it being painful.

"I'd run my tongue along that thick vein you have. Trace it all the way up to your cock head where I know there'd be cum waiting for me to taste."

"So much," he mumbled.

"You'd let me take you in my throat again, wouldn't you? Tell me what you'd do once you had my mouth around you."

Avery sucked down another sharp inhale. "Wanna grab you by the hair, force you to deep throat me."

"Mmm." My cock twitched against my palm. "Then what?"

"I'd fuck your mouth. Make you choke on me."

My eyes rolled into the back of my head. "Fuck yeah."

I could picture it now: Avery's hand in my

hair, keeping me in place while I was on my knees, his pants shoved halfway down his thighs to reveal that giant monster cock of his that he'd force past my lips with a single thrust. My throat would tighten around the intrusion until there were tears in my eyes. He'd pull his hips back and then thrust forward, shoving his cock down my throat until I gagged.

Being at the complete mercy of him like that was so hot that I nearly came.

"You like the sound of that, Brandon?" Avery's voice was growing husky and more guttural. "You want to choke on my cock?"

"Yes." The confession was so easy, tumbling right out of my mouth without another thought.

Avery answered back with a deep laugh, one that had my gut clenching with lust. "I like the sound of that."

"Next time I see you." I moved my hand rapidly, my cheeks beginning to burn. "I'll get on my knees for you."

And that was a damn promise.

Avery answered me in the form of him gritting out a short *"oh fuck"* and then gasping. While I couldn't see what was happening on the other end of the line, I knew that familiar sound of him coming, spilling all over his own hand with that pinched expression etched into his handsome features.

Slamming my hips up twice more, I groaned back, shooting cum all down my hand and across my bare chest. I collapsed into the mattress, the buzzing inside of my head finally stilling.

Avery was panting into the speaker, the soft bursts of air causing my stomach to twist again.

"Wow," was all he had to say.

I hummed again, letting my hand relax and fall from where I'd been death gripping myself. "Send me a picture."

He choked. "Of the cum on my hand?"

"And covering your dick."

"Jesus Christ, Brandon."

I grinned, quickly ending the call before he could try to talk his way out of it.

If he didn't end up sending me anything, that was fine. I'd live off of the sound of him coming to my words for the next ten years at this point. Hell, maybe even the rest of my damn life. Nothing could top what just happened or the shit he'd said to me that had me wanting to drive to the fucking city and drag him out to my truck so we could fool around again.

Even though I'd said it in the heat of the moment, I meant my promise. If he was still eager to explore the chemistry between us, I'd get on my knees for him and let him fuck my throat raw. Getting Avery back into that position had my balls squeezing and my limp cock giving a very pathetic twitch.

But damn if that mental image wasn't hot.

Sitting up slowly, I sighed at the mess I made of myself. What the hell time was it anyway?

My phone vibrated next to me, a text from Avery's number incoming.

Grabbing it with a pounding heart, I opened it, my mouth falling to the damn floor instantly.

There, framed against the white tiles of the hospital bathroom and the slight view of the sink across the way, was Avery's hand and his dick resting in it. He looked like as much of a mess as I did, cum still wetting his tip with some of it smeared down his hand and shaft.

The text under the picture read: *'got some on the floor too'.*

"Fuck me." Throwing my phone back onto my bed, I leaned forward and used my clean hand to rest my head against it.

There was no going back from this. He was

actually going to be the death of me. Trying to pretend like we could would only be setting us both up for failure—one where we crashed and burned in a spectacular fashion.

That could still happen obviously, but perhaps if we leaned into this, we could at least enjoy getting each other off until that time came.

Where he'd eventually have to leave.

Grabbing my phone again, I quickly saved the photo into the secure folder on my phone. I jumped when another phone call came in, this time from Max.

Shit. I can't believe I'd gotten distracted for that long.

"Hello?"

"Hey," he said. "I'm just pulling up to your house."

Fuck. I wanted to groan, only barely holding it in at the last second. "Okay, great. I'll be right out. Just give me five."

"Take your time."

Quickly ending the call, I slid off the bed and headed to the bathroom to clean myself up, ignoring the guilt that going on a date right after I'd had phone sex with another man made me look real fucking bad no matter how you spun it.

Canceling on Max wasn't an option, not with him literally pulling up to take me out. Playing sick would only get him guilting me into letting him in in order to nurse me back to health. Which would *not* be happening now that I was certifiably insane for Avery.

Ignoring my reflection in the mirror, I grabbed a washcloth to wet it and swipe up the cum coating my stomach.

This was going to be the longest date in history.

CHAPTER 22

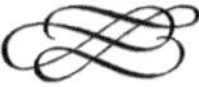

Avery

"You look sweaty," Carrie commented the second I flopped down into one of the chairs across from Eva's bed. "You okay?"

I hadn't looked at myself in the mirror after cleaning up, but I could feel how flushed my face still was and knew it showed as clear as day. Which no doubt wasn't helping my case in looking innocent after taking that phone call.

I was still buzzing from it—my skin still tingling from the aftereffects.

Under any other normal circumstances, Carrie wouldn't give two shits about who the hell I was getting involved with romantically. At this point, she'd probably encourage it and tell me it was about damn time.

Being at the hospital while her daughter was undergoing breathing treatments and getting pumped full of antibiotics, however, wasn't exactly the best place to be admitting to having phone sex and getting myself off in the damn bathroom while she'd needed my emotional support.

In fact, she'd probably call me a pervert and ban me from ever seeing her or Eva again.

So, lying it was.

Rubbing my hands over my thighs a few times, drying them of the excess water from the tap in the bathroom, I forced a quick smile. "All good. Hear anything yet?"

She gave me another cursory glance before nodding. "One of the nurses swung by and checked her vitals. Said she should be waking up anytime now. I wanted to run down to the gift shop and grab her something. A stuffed animal to have with her while she's got all these wires on her."

The poor thing looked so tiny in her bed, wrapped in a thin sheet while there was a mask over her face, feeding her humidified oxygen, and an IV taped at the crook of her arm that was pumping her system full of antivirals.

She had a heart monitor patch on her chest that was tucked under her hospital gown, and another set of wires that I really couldn't tell what they were for laid out on the opposite side of her body, two of which were clamped around her small fingers.

Eva's long, sandy blonde hair was tucked back away from her face, the front fringes tangled between Carrie's fingers while she stroked through the strands every so often. She'd been out of it since arriving, her fever finally breaking a little under an hour ago after another round of drugs.

This entire situation was scary beyond belief. I didn't know how Carrie was holding it together so well because if it were me sitting in that chair, holding onto my daughter while she struggled to breathe, I'd be a mess begging for any medical staff walking by to do something.

Rolling to my feet, I nodded. "Let me. You stay here."

Carrie hesitated, looking back and forth between Eva and me.

I knew how torn she was over this, wanting to stay by Eva's side in case she woke up but also not wanting to put me out by asking me to do things that her fiancé should be here doing instead.

While I was plenty grateful for her including me, I wasn't a fool to not know that all of this had been done out of desperation. Ryan being a seven hour flight away had made it impossible for him to get back to the city quickly, leaving Carrie to do all of the heavy lifting when it came to medical decisions for their daughter.

He'd been upset after hearing I'd come to keep Carrie company while she waited on answers, only really calming down after I'd snatched the phone from her and told him to get a grip—now was not the time to let the raging jealousy take hold of any rational decision making.

None of that would help how stressful any of this was.

I wasn't interested in trying to step into his shoes anyway. I'd had that with Carrie years before he ever came into the picture and had decided pretty early on that it wasn't for me. Hell, it would've been easier on both of us if we'd sucked it up and popped out a few kids to please both of our family's expectations.

The thing was that people changed. What I thought I'd wanted with Carrie—an easy life with a beautiful and successful wife, a few kids and maybe a dog that we crammed together into a penthouse in one of the upper east high rises a few blocks from my office building—wasn't the future that I ended up being the happiest living.

My happiest was driving to that damn body shop and sneaking into the back and surprising my best friend with a hot meal and reveling in the warm smile that crept across his face, and the slight color that rose to his cheeks.

"I'll get her something cute," I promised. "Stay, Carrie. She'll want you first thing when she wakes up."

She sighed softly, her shoulders slowly relaxing while she nodded. "Okay. Hurry back."

Turning on my heel, I headed out in the hallway and down to the main floor of the hospital.

I wasn't kidding when I told Brandon that this place was packed, patients and doctors all moving at a breakneck speed that was hard to keep up with when I exited the elevator and nearly collided with two medical staff pushing their way in with a stretcher.

Being back in the city after spending the past two weeks away felt strange in a way, like I'd distanced myself from the very place I'd called home for the past decade.

I never thought I'd somehow grow unaccustomed to life here, reverting back to liking the placid lifestyle of Edgewood and Ellington Heights over all of this in such a short amount of time away.

I wondered what that said about me. How much I'd changed after finding myself back in Ellington Heights and how much of the 'real' me was slowly starting to unthaw from the frigid bitterness I'd held onto all of these years.

Coming back to the States two degrees heavier and with a determination to make something out of myself that surpassed the McAllister name I'd been born into, I'd settled on sinking my roots down in an unfamiliar city an hour and a half away from my hometown and never once thought about looking back.

Why would I when all that awaited me back there were painful memories?

Until seeing Brandon again had ended up completely rewiring my brain entirely.

Now I was second-guessing everything.

The gift shop was stationed right as the lobby to the hospital opened up past the security desk, with a spinning rack of overpriced cards right outside of the glass doors as the first thing to welcome me inside.

Stepping through the doorway, I felt my shoulders slowly relax, no longer tense from the heavy atmosphere of a very active hospital. I wasn't afraid of coming to places like this where miracles and death were commonplace—I'd spent enough time as it was when I was a kid with a strangely sick mother that never seemed to get better no matter what treatment the doctors put her on.

But I never quite could ever get over the stress that seeing such things put on me, more than a boardroom full of angry investors ever could.

Thankfully, stepping inside of the gift shop was a nice break from all of that, allowing me to breathe a bit better while the tranquil elevator music seeped in from the speakers overhead.

The place was small, jam-packed with stuff

that ranged from hospital branded sweatshirts and sweatpants, to small knick-knack trinkets that looked at least a few years old given how faded the coating of paint on them were.

Finding my way toward the back of the store, I spotted a shelf full of stuffed animals easily enough. Eva was the type of little girl to like the unconventional stuff, not the run-of-the-mill horses and cats that any typical three year old would gravitate toward, giving most people a run for their money when gifting her things.

But to me, I found it too charming not to encourage.

After all, who could resist her begging for a pet pigeon when most kids wanted a dog or cat?

Rummaging through the plushies until I reached the back of the shelf, I grazed my hand over a plump one in the back that felt too soft to the touch not to drag out from the dusty and dark corner it'd been pushed back into. Grabbing a hold of it, I scooted it out until I could get a better look at it and then ended up laughing softly to myself when I realized it was actually *perfect*.

It was a chubby-looking pill bug sewn in a blue fabric that shimmered on the underside of the stitched thorax. Squeezing it a few times in my hands, I decided it definitely felt soft enough for Eva to cuddle with when she eventually needed to sleep again. Hopefully, on the way home once she was finally discharged.

As much as it pained me to see her hooked up to all of those machines, she was in the best place she could be at the moment. Having a sick kid wasn't for the faint of heart, and that I didn't envy Carrie over at all.

How in the world would I ever be able to handle any of this shit if, or when, hopefully, I ever had one of my own... Actually, I didn't even want to dwell on the absolute fucking wreck I'd be.

Tucking the stuffed bug under my arm, I grabbed a few snacks for Carrie on the way up to the register and set everything down on the counter, flashing a polite smile at the older woman working the counter.

As much as I appreciated being involved in all of this, I had it in me to be wary of growing closer to Carrie, and subsequently, Eva, through a tough situation like this one. It hurt the first time I'd been forced to distance myself in order to help her save her relationship, and I wasn't sure how I'd feel the second time around when it inevitably came once Ryan was back in the state.

Truthfully, I had every right to be annoyed with the guy for assuming things but at the same time, how would it feel if we were in the reverse roles?

If this was Brandon and I was coming back from a long flight to find his ex-spouse comforting and taking care of him and our child together?

Fuck, I'd lose it.

"Here you go, dear." The cashier handed me a paper bag with my purchases in it. "Have a nice day."

Shaking myself out of the thoughts, I took the bag and thanked her before heading out of the shop and back over to the elevators.

Brandon had been my wild card. An unexpected wrench in the gears that was my boring life here in the city.

Being surrounded by my childhood, and by him, had gotten me to reevaluate a lot of things. Had me thinking that maybe staying in Ellington Heights wasn't so bad of an idea after all.

What was holding me in this city aside from avoiding my father who was now dead?

Outside of the drama with Ana Liapovich, I had the freedom to do whatever the hell I wanted now. Live wherever I wanted, including my childhood home back in Ellington Heights where I didn't fear my father showing up just to fuck with me.

Could I live in Ellington Heights again?

At the very least, I'd have to quit my job.

There'd be no way of moving a company that size to a small town like Ellington Heights without some major economic pitfalls and tanking all of my employees' hard work. Selling it off was an idea, along with turning it over to my VP, who'd been one of my best performers and confidants when cycling through our various board of directors until we'd finally settled on our current one.

An early retirement didn't sound so bad. I had the McAllister property to call home and enough money to live more than comfortably for the next few centuries even if I never picked up a damn pen ever again.

Would Brandon want me to?

My stomach churned at the question.

I wanted him to want me to—stupid as that

was. Me, a grown man, searching for the approval of another.

But wouldn't he be the entire reason I'd be leaving my life here and picking up and moving back to Ellington Heights?

I had no other reason to. It wasn't like my father's, or rather, *my* estate couldn't run itself as long as the bills were paid.

Hell, I bet Hazel loved having the entire place to herself and the staff. They could do whatever they wanted so long as the upkeep on it was maintained.

"Avery!"

Turning to the sound of my name, I spotted a man pushing his way through the security line, having just been checked, while he slung a bag over his shoulder and jogged over to me.

His dark hair was shaggy and pulled back from his face in a half-updo, his beard, which was usually well-groomed, looked messy and slightly greasy, like he'd been running his fingers through it nervously over the past few hours. He was tall, probably around Brandon's height, but had a much more slender build.

Ryan.

He was panting heavily, probably having just

run all the way from the parking garage to get over here. When he reached me, he bent over at his waist and rested his hands on his knees.

My lips thinned. I had half a mind to chastise him—but for what, I wasn't really sure. We'd always had a bit of friction between us, so it was hard not to automatically fall right into that, even when there was nothing to argue about. "Your flight get in okay?"

He nodded, swallowing back a rough breath before straightening up again. "Yeah... long as hell. But I made it."

The elevator dinged, the doors parting for a small group of people to leave before we climbed in ourselves. I jammed my finger against the button for Eva's floor and settled myself back against the wall behind us. Ryan let the bag slip from his shoulder—an overnight duffle—while doing the same.

"How is she?" he asked.

"She isn't awake yet. Still has an IV and an oxygen mask on, but the doctors are confident she's going to be okay."

He visibly sagged in relief. "Good. That's... That's good."

All right, maybe it was the softie in me who

had recently been seeing the light of day more often now that I had Brandon back, that gave me the half a mind to reach over and clap the man on the shoulder. Ryan wasn't a bad man by any means, clearly caring very deeply about his daughter and soon-to-be wife.

Whatever beef existed was between us and didn't need to affect anything else.

Holding up the bag, I pulled out the stuffed plush. "Found this in the gift store for Eva. Figured she'd like it."

When I handed it over to him, he snorted. "That's... definitely something she'd be into."

"I had a feeling."

He squeezed it a few times in his hands, a frown slowly creeping over his face.

I opened the bag up for him to drop it inside, then offered it to him. "You should give it to her."

While his brow quirked, he took the bag anyway. "Not wanting to play hero today?"

I *almost* rolled my eyes. "That's not what I came here to do, Ryan."

He looked like he was about to argue with me, most likely to accuse me of whatever ridiculous bullshit he'd been cooking up in his head the entire flight over here, but then stopped himself at the last moment.

If this were any other time and I wasn't just coming off of a mind-blowing, and frankly, life-altering, phone sex call that had me actually contemplating imploding my entire life and moving back to my hometown at the mere possibility of my childhood best friend being interested in taking things to the next level, I'd probably be telling this man off before we got up to Eva's floor.

That being said, it was also quite obvious that Ryan was under a lot of stress at the moment. It wasn't like it was fun news to get in the middle of a work trip that his daughter was sick enough to be brought to the hospital and was currently hooked up to a bunch of machines that were five times the size of her.

"Sorry," he finally mumbled. And then he sighed. "I'm sorry. I know you're here to—I'm being an asshole."

At least you're finally admitting it.

"I'm not here to steal your place, Ryan. I came because she called and you weren't answering your phone."

His lips pressed together. "I know."

When the elevator slowed and the doors chimed open, I pulled myself away from the wall and stepped out into the hallway. He followed after me, tugging his bag back up onto his shoulder and hooking the one I'd given him around his wrist.

"Listen," he said, moving away from the doors. "What I said on the phone to you. It was wrong. I know you're only here to support Carrie because she asked you to. I know neither of you would do anything behind my back."

"No offense, Ryan, but if I wanted to keep her, I would have. We had a good life together."

"Then why didn't you?"

I paused before answering.

It was a genuine question, not one asked out of malice of contempt. If I were in his shoes, I'd be curious, too. Carrie was an incredible woman; beautiful, highly accomplished, and came from a long line of wealth that would make most people's jaws drop.

She was a total catch and Ryan was damn lucky to be marrying her, as was I at the time.

Being comfortable in a marriage wasn't the same as being passionate. Loving her like a companion wasn't the same as loving her like a partner. Keeping us both trapped in a marriage while trying to justify my very surface level feelings wasn't fair. Not when I knew she could be with someone better, more affectionate and doting.

Just like she deserved.

And that wasn't me. No matter how hard I tried.

At the end of the day, us splitting up meant we could both move on. Her with Ryan and me with...

Well.

I grabbed Ryan's shoulder and squeezed it. "She was meant to be with you. I loved her but not in the way she deserved. You make her happy. That's all I care about."

His mouth opened as he clearly meant to say something, only to slowly close once more.

"Listen. As long as you're good to her and Eva, we have no animosity between us," I said.

He gave me a slow nod, exhaling through his nose. "All right."

Letting him go, I gestured down the hallway. "They're in room 405."

"You're not coming?"

I shook my head, catching the doors to the elevator before they closed again. "I think you've got it from here. Let Carrie know I had something that came up. Have her text me when she can once Eva wakes up."

"I will. And... thank you, Avery."

Slipping back into the elevator, I gave Ryan a quick nod before punching the door close button a few times. I felt a little bad for ditching so suddenly, but honestly, now was not the time to be intruding on a family moment like that.

There was no doubt in my mind that Carrie would be grateful for me being there for her, but at the end of the day, she'd wanted her soon-to-be-husband by her side, not her ex. I was fine with that—more than fine, actually, since it meant I got to go home to see Brandon again.

We needed to talk. We needed to sort out where we were going and what we wanted going forward. If this was just a sexual thing, fine, I could handle that. He didn't seem to mind me fumbling through things like an inexperienced virgin.

If it was *more* than that?

My stomach tightened with butterflies.

We needed to figure it out. *I* needed to figure it out like he'd asked me to in the car.

I owed him that much.

CHAPTER 23

BRANDON

"YOU LOOK REALLY NICE," Max commented when I slid into the passenger seat of his sedan.

I had half a mind to flip down the visor and check myself one last time for any stray signs of what I'd been doing ten minutes earlier, but stopped myself at the last moment, and instead, grabbed a hold of my seatbelt and wrenched it across my chest.

I felt bad about going into this date already eager to get it over with.

Max was a nice guy and had a great personality. Charismatic, smart, was easy on the eyes and had a subtle way of flirting that wasn't overly sexual like a lot of past hookups I'd had. He was the kind of man that I wouldn't mind bringing back to meet my family and would probably charm the pants off of all of them once we sat down together for family dinner.

I knew if given the chance, they'd end up loving him.

Why wouldn't they when he was everything that a man like me would want?

If I wasn't wound up from hooking up with Avery in the car and felt like it was a do-or-die situation to force myself to move on from it, maybe I would've given it another day before I contacted Max and saved us both this headache in getting him to take me out right before I'd gotten that call from Avery.

I'd been too impatient, too ready to move on and bury my feelings for Avery and the chokehold that our sexual chemistry had on me. Instead of waiting another day, I'd jumped the gun, and now I was paying the price.

Or rather, *Max* was paying the price for my fuck up. Getting his hopes up under a false promise that I had no intention of following through with. Not when Avery had made it damn clear that he wasn't backing down from exploring himself with me.

"You okay?" Max's voice was gentle.

Shaking my head to clear my thoughts, I gave him a firm nod. "Just, uh... a little nervous."

He laughed. "Why don't we stick to something low key? Since I haven't had much time to spend in Edgewood, you should show me some of the local hangouts you like to go to."

That had me raising a brow. "You sure? They're a little... quaint."

"I want to get to know *you*, Brandon. Where you come from. What life is like in Edgewood. Who knows, maybe I'll end up settling down here once my contract is up in a few months."

My stomach tightened at the thought, but not in the good way. Not in the way I'd fantasized about Avery doing the same thing.

Don't get me wrong, Edgewood was a nice place, as was Ellington Heights right across the bridge and even Palmerston, where our high school had been, right down the road. They all had their charms and quirks, as did the people who lived there.

It wouldn't be right of me to discourage anyone from setting down roots here, even Max, who probably had much better prospects to look forward to on the horizon than chasing me around when I clearly had nothing to give outside of little white lies and the ever-dwindling hope that something would come between us.

This thing with Avery could all come crashing down at any moment, sending us both into a fiery blaze that neither of us would probably ever recover from. I wouldn't be the same afterward, and yet, that still wasn't a deterrent at all.

In fact, it only made me want to do it more.

I felt Max watching me closely, his patience practically slapping me in the face with guilt. "Yeah, we can go to Crossroads. It's a bar down on the strip. Pretty popular with the locals."

"Great." He shifted the car into drive. "I think I passed that on the way over here."

"If you saw the big bull out front with its left horn missing, then that was the one."

Max laughed. "Quite the hometown landmark."

"The owner won it at a state fair about twenty years back. That thing hasn't moved from the front sidewalk since. The paint's so worn on it because it's like a family tradition to take your kids over there and get a photo with them riding it."

"What an interesting piece of history. You know, I kind of miss that about small towns."

I glanced over at him. "You ever have anything like that back in East City?"

He shrugged, flicking on his turn signal and pulling out onto the main drag. "Not really. It's not as huge as the city up north, but it's pretty decent sized. It's mostly a commuter city, so not many opportunities to make solid connections with anyone. I was out of there by the time I turned twenty."

"You like traveling around?"

He grinned. "Yeah. It gives you a sense of freedom, don't you think?"

I wished I could relate.

The farthest I'd ever been was Palmerston when I went to school. While Edgewood was a small town, it had at least one of everything you could ever imagine, making it rather hard to want to leave for some place unfamiliar and farther away from where you grew up.

I'd never thought about traveling before, figuring I'd live and die in Edgewood and that was fine by me.

"Guess I never really thought about it," I said.

"Do you ever..." His words were slow. "Think about leaving Edgewood?"

I could lie and say that I had—that it was my big dream to get out of this town and forge my own path on the road ahead.

What would really stop me other than the lengthy process of selling my business?

Other than it being a total pain in the ass?

Even then, I had a feeling one of the guys would end up taking it off my hands, wanting to keep it 'in the family' as they'd call it.

I wouldn't mind if the place was passed that way. At least then I knew it'd be in good hands.

Edgewood was my home, though, for more reasons than just the shop. I had so many memories here, along with Ellington Heights, that it would be hard for me to part with and start fresh. I was sentimental to a fault and craved having the familiarity of the roads, the people, and everything in between.

"No," I finally said.

He hummed in response, pulling into the parking lot of Crossroads and parking on the right side of the lot, facing the building. There were a few cars already here. The door to the bar was propped open with a large tin, music from the jukebox inside playing loudly.

"You weren't kidding about the bull," he said, nodding through the windshield.

I kicked open my door and climbed out, pulling in a lungful of air while shoving my hands into my pockets to check for both my wallet and phone for the nth time. Max slid out of the driver's side and shut his door, coming around to my side to do the same for me and only missing by a split second as I hip-checked it closed.

"Oh—"

"Sorry," he apologized.

Ugh, this was already turning into a total disaster.

How many points would I wrack up with karma if I were to pretend to get an emergency phone call and have to rush home?

Canceling this date felt rude as hell, especially when *I* was the one who'd contacted him about it in the first place and not the other way around. But the alternative, I feared, was that this weird energy was only the beginning to a date that was already looking like it was spiraling into a complete mess from here.

I had a feeling that I was being punished for not being patient. That this was some cosmic force giving me the proverbial finger wag while chastising me with that old *'good things come to those who wait'* saying that my mother loved beating me over the head with as a kid.

Of course, I never listened. I was always too damn stubborn to learn anything without actually finding myself bulldozing my way head first through the problem instead.

How else was I going to learn but doing it myself the hard way?

I supposed that was a symptom of growing up as the youngest male sibling and always seeing my brothers' mistakes and finding the exact opposite solution, even if it was still wrong in the end.

Two fingers came up to stroke along my cheek, ripping me back into the present.

I froze against the side of the car, my eyes going wide while Max leaned forward, his eyes growing heavy. The worst part about all of this was the way he cupped my face—almost identical to how Avery did—but instead of my skin burning at the touch, it just felt off.

Wrong.

I steeled myself for the inevitable press of his lips against mine, prepared to give him the best kiss I could muster up. To my surprise, he frowned and then leaned back, giving me room to breathe again.

"You're kind of wincing," he muttered.

Fuck.

"S-Sorry."

He took a full step back, ran his hand through his hair. "Is it me? Is there—are you not attracted to…"

"No, no." Jesus, how was I even supposed to go about salvaging this for both of our dignity's sake. "It's not that, Max."

"Is there someone else, then? I've got to be honest, I'm kind of stumped here."

"You're a perfectly good guy, trust me."

His frown deepened. "That definitely sounds like you're trying to let me down easy. Look, I get it, Brandon, if you aren't feeling it—"

"It's not you. I swear. It's a me thing." It was *all* a me thing. Max was perfect and I was the dumb idiot for leading him on in the first place.

The first taste of Avery should've been my red flag to cut Max loose and let him go find a guy that was one hundred percent invested in him.

Not someone like me who was clearly ready to get his heart crushed again.

I sighed. "It's not you, trust me. If I could, I'd date you in a heartbeat. You're literally every guy's wet dream when it comes to a partner."

Even though my words were flattering, he didn't look happy to hear them at all. He stared at me for a long moment, causing me to squirm against the car out of discomfort. It felt like he was trying to dissect me—see past my layers to the truly fucked up loser I was underneath all of this.

"Is it that guy?" he asked. "The one we ran into at the festival?"

My jaw practically hit the parking lot.

How the *hell* did he guess that?

Max shook his head, sighing. "I had a feeling, but I didn't want to jump to conclusions. You two seemed... *close*."

"He's just a friend. From my childhood," I tried to defend.

"Looked like you wanted more."

The words weren't at all accusatory but for

some reason my protective instincts flared. It took a lot to reel them in and not lash out at Max because I was feeling vulnerable. None of this was his fault, and him pointing out the damn obvious was the least of what I needed to face the music about.

"Okay." Admitting it out loud had bile rising in my throat. "Yes. I do. I never meant to drag you into this."

"Then why text me earlier? Is this some kind of rebound?"

Can't really be a 'rebound' if nothing ever started.

"Not exactly..." The words were mumbled.

He sighed once more, digging two of his fingers into his eyes. "I'm trying to be understanding here, Brandon. I'm just a little confused. If you and your 'friend' are together, why did your sister sign you up for a dating service?"

"Well, she doesn't exactly know about my friend. No one really does."

Max dropped his hand to his side. "Don't tell me he's some serial killer."

With a snort, I said, "No. Nothing like that. Just a lot of past history, that's all."

I felt awful. This entire situation was awful.

If I were a better man, I would've never let my sister bully me into signing me up with a matchmaker in the first place and would've just dealt with her endless whining until her wedding day where she'd inevitably forget all about it.

Though to be fair, at the time Avery hadn't come back into my life, so I supposed in that aspect I had a good excuse. However, the second he'd waltzed into my shop, I should've cut it off with Max right then and there.

I knew myself better than that, to have hope that I'd be able to move on from that man, even before he'd showed me an ounce of interest.

"I'm sorry," I said. "Really, really sorry. For wasting both of our time."

"Yeah. Me too."

It hurt my heart to see him looking that upset.

While I didn't know Max too well, he was generally an understanding guy and seemed like he wasn't one to take things to heart too deeply. But with this, I could tell I hurt him, even if it was unintentional.

His gaze wandered over to the bar. "I think it's time we head inside for a drink."

"Actually, I think it's probably a better idea if I head home."

He nodded, avoiding meeting my eyes with his while he fished his keys out of his pocket. "I'll bring you back."

"You're good." Stepping away from the car, I held my hands up. "I'm fine walking home. Go have a drink. Tell Sam to put it on my tab."

"Brandon."

"You're good, Max. Seriously. I'll text you when I get back so you know I didn't get kidnapped."

He looked at war with himself, gaze darting from me to the door of the bar and back again. If this was anywhere else but Edgewood, I'd take him up on his offer to drive me home and get me safely tucked inside my house.

With a population of barely 1800, it wasn't like these streets were crawling with criminals. I'd be lucky to run into anyone at this hour, let alone someone looking to mug me.

"I promise," I said, digging my phone out of my pocket and holding it up.

Clearly this conversation had worn him out because all he said in return was, "Get home safe," before heading to the bar and disappearing inside.

Blowing out a breath, I turned on my heel and started down the sidewalk.

Jesus, what a fucking mess.

Out of any way I'd wanted to break that kind of news to him, *that* was definitely not the one.

Sitting down at a restaurant and holding his hand while I told him I was in love with someone else?

Sure, a good option.

Pulling him inside to sit on my couch to tell him instead of bringing him out into public where there was a high chance he'd feel humiliated?

Also a good option.

Hell, even breaking the news to him in my grease-stained uniform, bent over the hood of one of Avery's car's would've been better than what the hell just happened.

I was such an asshole.

Tomorrow, I'd try to call him or something and apologize once more. The man deserved better than whatever mess I had going on. Once he got over this, he'd come to realize that, too. As did everyone aside from Avery, who I already considered crazy.

The walk back home took less than half an hour and gave me time to clear my head while settling my own nerves.

This was all for the best. I was sure once my sister found out, I'd get an earful but it was better than continuing to lead the poor man on when he was better off getting matched with someone way more stable than me.

And who knew what they fucking wanted.

Finally rounding the corner to my street, the last thing I expected to find in my driveway when I got there was a familiar Audi and an even more familiar figure sitting on my doorstep waiting for me.

CHAPTER 24

AVERY

SHOWING up on Brandon's doorstep was probably an impulsive decision on my part—which tracked for how this whole thing started between us anyway.

I'd driven straight from the hospital to here, stepping on the gas to an obscenely dangerous speed that I was lucky I hadn't gotten pulled over for. I was chalking that up as a sign from the universe that coming over here to see him was what I was meant to do.

And who was I to ignore an approval from up top like that?

Seeing Brandon walking down the street alone with just the flash on his phone guiding him had me stumbling to my feet, startling him into stopping right at the bottom of his driveway. I couldn't see his expression from here but judging by the way his chest moved, he was preparing himself before coming up the rest of the way toward me.

I didn't want to take that as a sign that bad things were to come. That I was potentially walking into a situation where I was going to go back to my family's property with my heart shattered and Brandon's words of regret ringing in my ears.

All of it was a very valid fear and one that I hadn't exactly prepared myself to face when leaving the hospital. But so much could change in a matter of hours. Regrets could start worming their way in. Hell, sensibility could, too.

None of this was thought out in the slightest. Brandon and I were riding this damn rollercoaster by the seat of our pants and hoping like fuck we didn't go careening off the ride on the way.

I stayed rooted to my spot as he drew near,

stopping right at the start of the steps leading up to the stoop. He tilted his head back to look at me, slightly shadowed from the light he pointed at his feet.

"Hey... how did it go?" he asked.

My fingers itched to reach out and grab at him, pull him into my arms and bury my face in his hair. Fisting my hands at my sides was the only way to stop myself from doing that and being sensible for once in my life.

"Good. Carrie texted me on the way home that her daughter is awake and alert. The doctors said her vitals are looking really good. She came down with RSV."

Brandon's face morphed from shocked to sympathetic. "Oh. That's a terrible thing for a kid to go through. I'm glad she's feeling better, though."

I nodded. "I left as soon as her dad showed up. Didn't want to intrude."

He smiled a little. "I'm sure they were all glad you could be there for as long as you were."

I hoped so.

I wasn't exactly looking for some grand '*thank you*' or anything like that. But just some kind of memo that I hadn't overstepped any boundaries and gotten myself in the middle of their family. That was the last thing I wanted to come across as doing.

In the future, I hoped Ryan grew to be less paranoid around me, because in a perfect world we'd all get along and could stand being in the same room together without some weird tension brewing between us.

"Where were you coming from?" I asked.

"Oh." His brows pulled together. "It's… a long story. Want to come in?"

Fuck yes, I did.

Not trusting myself to not make a fool out of me, I simply nodded and stepped back as Brandon fished his house keys out of his pocket and jammed them into the door to open it. A warm aroma greeted us as we both stepped inside, enveloping me like a gentle hug.

Brandon swung the door shut and locked it, eyeing me as he slipped off his shoes and hooked his keys back on the hook next to the door. I did the same, minus the keys, and watched him carefully. I'd never felt so needy in my life, wanting to touch another person.

Perhaps this was all remnants of our phone sex, or maybe I was becoming addicted to him in general. Either way, it felt fucking unhealthy and way too intoxicating not to lean into.

"I missed you," I mumbled.

I hadn't meant to say that, not so soon into him inviting me in, but the words were practically burning my tongue.

Brandon's eyes widened slightly and then grew soft. "I missed you, too, Avery."

Oh fuck it.

I reached out and cupped his face with my hands, used the leverage to back him up against the wall where I pinned him with my body. A soft sound escaped past his lips, drawing me in until all I could do to fight the urge to kiss him was to stop short of pressing my mouth to his.

Brandon bridged the gap between us anyway, tilting his head forward in my hold to slot his lips over mine in a chaste kiss. It was fucking perfect and not enough all at the same time. I'd been wanting this for so long and yet, now that he was right here with me, his mouth against mine, I needed it all.

My grip on his jaw tightened while I tilted his head back further to deepen our kiss. His lips parted with a short gasp, giving me the perfect opportunity to slip my tongue past and dive into his mouth.

He tasted slightly of something sweet and a bit bitter—coffee that he'd brewed right before he came home from the shop, most likely. I swiped my tongue against his, tasting more of that bitter flavor that had me rocking my hips into his.

Brandon jolted against me, his hands coming out to grab at my shirt—the one I was still wearing from our sort-of-date—and held it tightly in his hands. He drew me in closer until we were practically melded together. Our chests rising and falling in sync while I kept my hips locked against his.

My cock was growing so hard that it ached. With just a simple kiss I was ready to explode.

What the hell was Brandon doing to me?

I just about groaned when our kiss was ended entirely too quickly in my opinion. He wretched his head back from me with a soft 'pop' of our lips, a trail of spit lingering between us that I swiped my tongue at to break.

His throat bobbed twice before he said, "Bedroom."

There was no hesitation in his voice. No

sense of shy or bashfulness that I'd grown accustomed to associating with Brandon. He was taking charge and I was going to let him. I'd follow his lead to wherever the hell he was taking us and I wouldn't complain one bit.

With one hand still fisted in my shirt, he dragged me down the hallway and to his bedroom—a room I blearily remembered from him taking me back here the night I'd showed up wasted at his shop. When he let go of me, he moved across the room to where there was a pile of clothes thrown over the bed and a few pairs of pants haphazardly stacked next to them.

He gathered them quickly, tossing everything onto the floor in a heap at the foot of his bed.

I couldn't help it, I laughed. "Bit of a wardrobe mishap?"

He shot me a look over his shoulder. "I'm not one for fashion. But I think we both knew that."

That was a charming quirk about him. Brandon never much cared for looking like he stepped out of a magazine. He preferred to be comfortable and functional, two traits that I'd associate with him on any given day.

Me?

I unfortunately had an image to uphold most days. So, I'd gotten used to looking put together.

My footsteps were slow as I strode over to him. "How do you want to do this?"

For the first time since we stepped inside of his house, he looked uncertain. "That depends. How do *you* want to do this?"

I shook my head. "I want whatever you'll give me, Bran."

He blew out a short breath, his cheeks growing red. "Wow. Okay."

"You lead us. I trust you."

He nodded slowly, his gaze darting around his room again. "I think I should bottom tonight. Since I've done it before. We'll work you up to it."

My stomach clenched pleasantly. He was planning on this happening again.

Fuck, I loved the sound of that.

I meant what I said—I'd take anything he'd give me. I'd get on my knees or get off of them, whatever suited his fancy.

When he looked back at me, he asked. "I was tested a few months ago but nothing too recent. I'm also on PrEP."

Oh. Right.

"Uh."

Brandon frowned. "Avery, don't tell me you don't get tested regularly."

This time, it was my turn to feel bashful. "Actually... I haven't slept with anyone in a long time."

"How long?'

"Like... since my divorce. Which was almost five years ago."

His mouth dropped open. I could tell he was trying to search for the words to say something, but nothing was exactly coming out. Nothing coherent at least. Which wasn't exactly helping my self-esteem here.

"Is... that a turn off?" I asked.

His mouth snapped shut. "No, not at all. I'm just surprised. You were so active in high school."

I rolled my eyes. "Really? You're comparing me to my horny teenage self who'd just discovered boobs for the first time?"

He shrugged at me. "So, no tests since then?"

"Is that a deal breaker?"

"No. I've got condoms. It's fine. But we're going to the clinic tomorrow."

While I wasn't exactly a fan of him having what seemed to be a healthy supply of condoms at the ready—my jealousy rearing its ugly head—I was glad that he was conscious about his health and taking care of himself. You never knew nowadays, and neither did anyone else for that matter.

The world was a scary place at times.

"On the bed," he instructed.

The déjà vu sent a shiver down my spine that ended up going straight to the ache between my legs.

Falling back onto his bed, I watched him move about the room, shedding the shirt he'd been wearing and unhooking the button above his fly but not parting the flaps at all. He opened his dresser next to his bed and rummaged around the top drawer for something, pulling out a large, clear bottle and a box of condoms—that I hoped to fuck were still full and not already half used.

Before coming back over to me, he turned and headed through another doorway right next to his closet, flicking on the light inside for a moment and then emerging with a small hand towel.

"I have a feeling we're going to get messy," he said, smiling.

Yeah, I fucking hoped so.

He tossed the towel and the bottle on the bed next to me and then ripped into the condom box, yanking off one from the sleeve with his teeth, which was the single hottest thing I'd ever seen him do.

Coming back over to me, he pulled the foil wrapper out from between his teeth and tossed it with the other supplies.

"You okay?" he asked.

"You keep doing shit like that and you're going to make me come before you even touch me."

Brandon blinked twice and then laughed.

My body grew hot as he slowly lowered himself onto my lap, straddling me. Both of his hands trailed down my chest, teasing the buttons that held my shirt closed. It was such a small gesture, one that shouldn't be turning me on this badly, but with Brandon in control of all of this and me along for the ride, I couldn't help the small moan that was pulled from my throat.

"I love that sound," he mumbled, tugging one of the buttons free.

"I love your hands on me," I countered back.

"Good thing I can't stop touching you."

I swallowed at the admission, so similar to my own.

There was always a bit of an obsession between us, a mutual feeling that we'd pretended was nothing more than the tight bonds of friendship. Looking back on it now, it was wild to believe that I was so naive to pretend that even something as simple as an arm graze wasn't able to send a shock of pleasure racing through my system.

How I hadn't seen it until twenty years later, I'd never know.

But at least I had time to make up for all of it

Upon getting the final button undone, Brandon slid my shirt off of my shoulders and tossed it onto the floor where the rest of his pile was.

"Do you trust me?" he asked.

I didn't need to think twice about my response. "Of course I do."

Both of his hands pressed down against my pecs, nudging me back until I was flat against the mattress. He scooted back in my lap until he was truly straddling me, his ass lined up with my crotch that he slowly lowered himself down on top of.

I moaned instantly, the friction and the pressure feeling fucking phenomenal. I'd been so damn starved since leaving him to go to the city, our phone call only holding me over until this very moment.

Brandon rocked against me a few times, sending more spikes of bliss rushing through my bloodstream. "I know you're going to feel so good," he murmured. "I can't wait."

I'd do anything to please him—to pleasure him. Whatever he asked, it was his.

I held back a whine when he lifted himself off of me and stood, the tent in his pants prominent. He made quick work of my fly and helped me slide my pants down my legs and over my feet, tossing them to the side as well.

My cock was so swollen that it looked and felt painful. I was tempted to reach out and touch it to relieve some of the pressure but was beaten to it by Brandon doing it for me instead.

"Look at you," he whispered. "You think *I'm* pretty..."

"You are," I shot back, not caring at all how fucking delirious I was probably sounding.

Sure, it wasn't like I'd had my fair share of experiences with other cocks, but his was perfect.

It was shaped nicely, was thick but not too much to hurt if it slipped inside something, and was long enough to impress but not enough to be concerning for the other party having to figure out where the fuck something like that was going to go.

Brandon simply laughed and shook his head, stroking his hand up the length of my cock and squeezing just below the head.

He let go of me for a second to strip himself and toss his pants, leaning over the side of the bed to grab the bottle of lube and draw it closer.

"You tell me if things get overwhelming, okay, Avery?"

I nodded, my eyes already threatening to slide shut.

"Maybe we should have a safe word..." he mumbled, wrapping his hand around my dick again.

"I'm good, Bran. I trust you." I arched my body, needing more so badly. "I'm okay."

In fact, I was more than okay. This was the best sex I'd ever had and we hadn't even gotten to the finale yet.

Brandon snapped the cap of the bottle up, settling himself down onto the floor in between my legs, and squeezed some of the liquid—lube, now that I thought about it—onto his fingers to wet them. I watched, fascinated as he rubbed the digits together, wondering where the hell that was going to go.

Around me, I guess?

I didn't get an answer, only the fucking fantastic sensation of Brandon tilting my cock back and wrapping his mouth around it.

"Oh, *fuck*."

I slammed my eyes shut instantly.

Obviously, he was way more experienced than me in this department, but it still impressed me nonetheless. He bobbed up and down my cock, taking me in deeper each time he swallowed until I had no idea how the fuck he wasn't suffocating.

He moaned around me, keeping a tight grip around my base as he moved.

His tongue flicked along the underside, teasing me in a way that was both infuriating and tantalizing—both of which I couldn't decide which one was winning. He was taunting me with each pass of his tongue over my leaking head, languid in the way he drew me back down his throat and held me there.

Oh my God.

Fuck.

I could die like this.

My balls were drawn up tight with how badly I needed to come, and only through sheer willpower was I forcing myself not to. Exploding in his mouth like I did last time was an option—a very sexy one that I wouldn't at all mind a repeat of—however I wanted all of this. I wanted to see where he was going to take us by the end of the night.

Brandon's mouth popped off of my dick with a wet sound, his hand stroking my throbbing hardness in quick bursts that had my hips snapping up to meet his hand.

"Good?"

"So fucking good," I slurred.

He squeezed me. "Good."

Working my eyes back open, I lifted myself up onto my elbows to watch him. He had his face close to the base of me where he was sliding his tongue up halfway, not quite getting where I wanted him to.

I quickly realized his arm was twisted around behind him, and he was moving it slowly, completely capturing my attention.

He was prepping himself.

My throat tightened at the promise of him leisurely sinking himself down onto my cock bit by bit until he seated himself fully. Of getting me shoved so deep inside of him that it had him gasping for breath, begging for mercy.

Oh, I wanted that so fucking much.

When Brandon finally pulled back from me, I was panting from the effort not to give in to the screaming desire of coming. He lifted himself off of the floor, his arm coming back around to his front and his fingers slightly glossy.

Brandon crawled on top of me again. "It's going to be a tight fit."

There was a second delay before my brain caught up with what he was referring to.

"We don't have to—" I was starting to say, cutting off quickly with him shaking his head.

"I want to. I just need a bit more prep or else I'm going to probably be making some unpleasant faces."

All right, maybe I was being a bit of a prick to be proud that he really thought *that highly* of my cock, enough that he was worried it'd rip him in half or something—which was ridiculous because I wasn't *that* big. And... okay, maybe I was also a prick for wanting to ask him if it was the biggest he'd ever had.

Which didn't matter. Obviously.

All that was important was him enjoying himself.

And me, too.

Obviously.

"Avery?" My attention snapped back to him. "Hand me that."

He gestured to the bottle of lube he'd tossed closer toward me, holding out his hand for it. When I grabbed it, though, I held it in my hand, rolling it slightly to test the weight.

Would I be overstepping here if I asked to help?

I was probably over-thinking things. Getting into my head about all of this when he, quite literally, just had my dick in his mouth and was planning on shoving it into his ass here soon enough.

My cock twitched at the thought.

"Avery?"

Glancing at him, I said, "Let me."

CHAPTER 25

Brandon

My heart stuttered in my chest as my mind caught up to what he was saying—what he was subtly getting at when one of his arms snaked around my waist to pull me flat against his body. He was warm under me, his skin slightly dewy from sweat and flushed a light rosy shade.

I liked seeing him like this. His eyes practically black with how dilated his pupils were, the slight stumbling of his breathing when I dragged my hand along his jaw, tracing the hard line underneath. His tongue darting out to wet his lips, slightly swollen from how hard he'd kissed me.

He was the picture perfect of undone. And *I'd* done that.

"Please," was all he said when he trailed his fingers along my spine, moving down to the small of my back.

I felt my face heat up, but not from embarrassment—quite the opposite, in fact. My hips bucked up on their own at his plea, grinding against him in the process. Both of us let out soft moans, mingling with each other's labored breathing.

At the end of this, I was going to be wrecked.

Avery's fingers ghosted over my left ass cheek, dipping down the crack to circle around my already lubed up hole. He pressed along the outer rim gently, his eyes searching mine for an answer.

The funny thing was that he didn't even need to ask. He could flip me over onto my stomach and hold me down while having his way with me and all I'd do was beg for more.

He had no idea how many times I'd fantasized about this very thing, how many years I'd spent touching myself to an ambiguous figure that rocked my world, only for the last few seconds before I spilled into my own hand to reveal that it was Avery that I'd been imagining all along.

How ironic that none of those ever lived up to the real thing. To *this.*

His hair was soft between my fingers as I stroked through the long blond lengths. I kept a tight hold on the ends while I wiggled my hips back, bearing down onto his fingers while both digits speared inside me.

"Fuck." I sucked in a hissing breath.

His cock twitched under me.

It was an awkward angle do be doing this, half spread out over his lap like some kind of weighted blanket while I fucked myself back on his fingers. At this point, my mind was already too far gone. I was too lost in the high of Avery touching me and feeling him respond to me in a similar way to even care about the back ache I was signing myself up for come tomorrow.

My ass was still loose from when I'd prepped myself, Avery's fingers gliding inside of me easily but somehow still feeling exponentially better than my own by margins. A third finger soon joined, pressing against my entrance and slowing the rolling of my hips while Avery's arm around my waist stilled me.

His brows were pinched together in concentration—an adorable expression given the kind of situation we were in right now. All concentration and taking this seriously.

What else did I expect from this man?

I appreciated the care, though. A lot of men that I'd slept with couldn't give two shits about prep. They were all about shoving me face down into the mattress and then sticking it in like we were both going to die or something if it took longer than fifteen seconds to get our clothes off.

And god forbid if *I* wanted to top.

Here, we had all the time in the world. There was nothing stopping Avery from fingering me until my balls were practically bursting with the need to come. There was nothing stopping me from sitting back and grabbing a hold of Avery to edge him until he had tears in his eyes.

There were no rules here. No decorum that we had to follow. Just me and him.

I fucking loved that.

Leaning forward, I tangled our mouths together as his third finger slowly slipped inside of me, burning a bit when he curled them all together and moved them deeper.

This felt good. It felt right.

Why the hell hadn't we done this fifteen years ago?

What had stopped us other than my incessant need to hide my true feelings?

Avery had never been the type of person to preach prejudice. He'd been happy for me when I came out. Was supportive in more ways than I ever thought possible.

I should've bit the bullet and stopped being such a fucking coward back then. Told him how I felt and saw where it went from there. Who knows where we would've ended up. How many years we could've saved ourselves from wasting by staying apart.

Rejection could've been inevitable. But so could've *this*.

"Bran," he whispered.

"I need you." I practically choked on the words, the deep vulnerability in them not lost on either of us.

Something flashed in his eyes, and before I knew it, he was slipping his fingers out of me and rolling us over. He flattened me on my back against the mattress, worming his body in between my legs until we were practically molded together again.

When he kissed me, I felt that familiar lick of fire burning in my belly. The dire need to get him inside of me steadily encouraged my hand to wander between us and grip him again while my other slapped against the bed to blindly search for the lube and condom I'd carelessly tossed there.

Avery rolled his tongue against mine in a sinful way. It was too good. Too fucking much for him to never have thought about doing this with me beforehand.

What if he had? What if I wasn't the only one fighting my feelings back then?

Wishful thinking, of course. But at this point, anything was possible.

By the time I got a hold of the condom, Avery had moved his lips away from mine and was now meandering a path across my cheek and over to the spot right under my ear. My body jolted the second his teeth grazed over it, forcing my poor aching cock to leak all over him and my own belly.

"Fucking *shit*." I squeezed my hand around

him, drawing out his own set of curses. "You're going to end this before we can get to the good part."

He laughed against my neck. "I can't help it."

The second he dragged his tongue along my pulse point, I turned my head to tuck the condom between my teeth and then pushed against his shoulder. He sat back easily and with no sense of hesitation in his body language, his eyes pinning right on me with a slight worried pull to his brows.

Between us, I'd left a visible mess. Both of our stomachs coated with the slight sheen of precum. I couldn't believe he almost made me come just by teasing me like that. He was so damn lucky he was charming and I had more discipline.

As soon as I popped open the cap of the lube bottle once more, Avery's expression softened. He leaned forward just enough to snag the condom from between my lips, a playful smile stretching his mouth wide.

"I'll take that," he said, his voice gravelly.

My hyperfixation with the tendons in his hand working to open the wrapper was definitely not something I'd ever thought I'd be into. Nor so focused on them moving under his skin as he ripped the wrapper and rolled the condom over his impressive length.

"Come here," I curled my fingers at him.

Avery leaned forward instantly once more, his hands planting on either side of my body in order to lower until his lips hovered over mine again. The ghost of his breath had me wanting to catch his mouth against mine, taste him in every way that I could while he was still this close to me.

I laughed softly as I squirted lube into my palm. "That's not what I meant." But hey, it would do the job nonetheless.

"I want to see you." His voice was low and husky as he said it. "Up close."

My stomach clenched. How could he say such incredibly sexy things in a way that made them sound endearing and sickeningly sweet?

But that was the way Avery had always been. Charming and honest. A stoic outside with a soft inside that rarely anyone ever got to see. I was privileged to have gotten him to open up to me twice now. Both had given me an inflated ego.

Who else could claim something like that?

His cock jumped in my hand when I

wrapped my fingers around it, coating him generously while he kept his eyes locked onto mine. This kind of intimacy was nothing like I'd ever experienced before, and yet, I didn't at all want to shy away from it.

In fact, I wanted more.

Other men were far too quick to get off and get on with their lives. Whereas here with Avery, it felt like we had all the time left in the world.

I liked that.

Loved it, actually.

Once he was coated from tip to base, I guided him back slightly with a hand on his hip and pressed the tip of him right against my hole. Lifting one of my legs to hook around his hip, I settled back against the mattress, nodding at him.

"Ready?" he asked, his eyes only flitting down briefly before snapping back to mine again.

Oh, I was so fucking ready, he had no idea. All I could give him was a tight nod and an encouraging squeeze at his hip, a moan cutting at the back of my throat the moment he teased himself at my rim.

My body was tense with need making it hard to think straight.

The second the head of his cock slipped

inside, my toes were curling. At this rate, I'd be lucky if I lasted all of two fucking pumps before I was making another mess again. Forcing myself not to arch my back off of the bed and drive him in deeper was difficult, nearly impossible, really.

I wanted this to be good for him, too. Rushing into things without letting him get himself comfortable was the last thing I wanted. Not when we were finally doing this.

Avery regretting this in the morning—or hell, right after we were done—would kill me. So whatever he needed to ease into sex, I'd give him without any questions.

A hand squeezed my jaw, causing me to snap my eyes open, which I hadn't even realized I'd closed.

"Eyes on me, Brandon," he whispered.

Jesus fuck, if that's not the hottest thing a man's ever said to me.

My desperate exhale seemed to only further encourage him as he slid in deeper, my channel burning as his cock stretched me full. It was good —*too* fucking good—to be fucked like this.

How the hell had I been missing out on this for so long?

"Bran." My name was gritted through his teeth, his expression straining. "*Shit...*"

Using my hand on his hip, I guided him into rocking in and out of me in shallow thrusts, kicking up my heart rate each time he came close to nudging against my prostate. Clenching down on him and giving him a test squeeze had all sorts of other curses tumbling out of his mouth, and his hand tightening on my jaw.

"That's—" He grunted again. "Not fair."

I wanted to laugh. Maybe to tease him if I could actually concentrate past those sparks of pleasure coursing through me. Any other time, I would try, but at the moment my brain was short-circuiting on how fucking good it felt to have my best friend's dick buried in my ass. To feel that sharp burn fade into the familiar sparks of pleasure that soon had my jaw going slack.

I couldn't help it when I slid my eyes shut again, keeping my hold on his hip as he continued to rock into me. "Keep—just like that..."

Holy fuck.

The pressure was overwhelming, swallowing me whole until all I could focus on was the passing of Avery's cock over my prostate, hitting me perfectly like he fucking knew what he was doing. I don't know how the hell he was so good at getting me off, because at some point it was turning from sheer dumb luck to something else entirely.

"That good for you?" he asked. When his forehead pressed against mine, he shifted his hand away from my face, soon wrapping it around my aching cock. "You like someone fucking you like this, don't you. How long have you been waiting?"

So fucking long.

My nails dug into his hip. I could only let out a strained groan in response to his question.

He ground his hips into my ass, clearly reading it for what it was. "I'll make sure you forget all about them. Everyone else who touched you before me."

I loved the possessive tone in his voice. Needed more of it, actually. I hoped that was a fucking promise he was willing to follow through on. Because at this rate, I'd be lucky to remember how to fucking breathe.

I let my leg fall back from his hip and replaced it with my hand, slapping my other one on his ass cheek and digging my nails in deep. He groaned at that, pistoning his hips back and then slamming into me.

The momentum of it pulled a strangled gasp from my lungs, all other thoughts but Avery's cock pounding into me erased from my mind.

"*Right there—*" was all I could get out before my tongue got tangled on the words.

He swirled his hips slightly, nailing my prostate over and over again in time with the hand stroking my cock. It was like a race to see which was going to get me to come first: his hand or his cock. Fuck, probably *both*.

Was that even possible? My eyes snapped open.

Without warning, my balls squeezed, and soon, I was coming all over his hand and my belly. Waves of it dripped down his knuckles, coating them in a milky sheen that was fucking hot to look at.

Ripping my hand away from him, I hooked my leg up around his hip once more and locked it there. "Keep going. I want you filling up that condom."

I needed to see him come again. I needed that twisted up expression to be ingrained into my mind as he emptied himself inside of me and replaced all of the fantasy versions I'd cooked up over the years.

Nothing would compare to the original, and I was ready to be proven wrong as to how I'd imagined it.

His thrusts were erratic. That tight control he usually had over himself was nowhere to be found while he lost what little he had left in the pleasure of my body.

I loved it.

I loved *him*.

"Oh fuck. *Bran*—" He was done for.

"That's it, baby," I babbled. "You feel so fucking good. You're gonna make my ass yours, right?"

His expression pinched. Eyes flickering with unhindered want. "Already is."

Yes. I slapped his ass cheek and dug my nails in again. "Show me."

With an arched back, Avery rolled his hips once more before locking us together, fusing himself against my ass while he hissed and exploded inside of me. His moan came deep from his chest, vibrating slightly against my own when his body settled against mine.

My arms came around him instantly, curling

tight to keep him tucked into my body while we both panted. I smoothed my fingers through his hair, brushing the slightly damp strands away from his forehead.

That was... wow.

He trailed lazy kisses along my jaw until he lifted his head in order to reach my lips again.

I could get used to the press of his lips against mine. Hell, I could get used to *all* of this.

Laying bed together. Letting our bodies slowly relax until our heartbeats were in sync again. Feeling the way his arms tightened around me and held me close like I was something precious to him.

"Come home with me in the morning." Avery's voice was soft as he spoke. "Hazel will cook us breakfast."

I loved the sound of that. It was so domestic, so goddamn safe sounding. "Only if you talk her into making us those hazelnut pancakes."

He chuckled softly, tucking his face back into my neck. "Deal."

THERE HAD BEEN times in my life where I'd often dreamed up moments back in time where I'd find myself being driven up to the McAllister mansion and passing through those wrought iron gates, the radio playing softly and Avery humming to it in the driver's seat, one hand on the steering wheel and the other wrapped around mine.

He'd squeeze my fingers every so often, reminding me just how vivid fantasies could be when you weren't paying close enough attention to the outliers or the details that never quite added up the closer you looked.

But in those moments, I never cared. I'd let myself dream and pretend like it was all real until my alarm became my untimely tolling of the bell. Waking up tangled in my bed sheets with nothing but those familiar touches that had once been impressed into my skin now slowly fading into nothingness.

This morning had felt like that—being woken up by the morning light coming in through my uncovered windows, coiled around Avery with one hand woven into his hair and the other pressed against his sternum. His heartbeat was steady under my palm, thrumming along in time with mine as I laid in the quietness of the early morning.

I prayed that none of it was some fucked up delusion my brain had cooked up to torture me. To tease me with the possibility that last night had been real. That *we'd* been real.

My sore limbs were, thankfully, a stark reminder. One that stung my eyes with relief as I slowly slid out of bed to head to the bathroom to shower while Avery buried his face into my pillow.

I wasn't sure where we went from here, or if it was even the time to be having some kind of conversation about our futures with Avery's own being so up in the air right now.

What I knew for certain, while staring into the eyes of my own reflection while I brushed my teeth, was that I was never going back to the way things were before all of this. I couldn't. My own sanity wouldn't be able to handle it.

I couldn't simply move on and chalk all of this up to a one-time thing. Not when my literal heart was on the line here. Avery wouldn't hurt me intentionally, even if all of this was far more new to him than it was to me.

Last night had given me confidence that

whatever happened, he wouldn't be shattering me to a million pieces by cutting loose and running back to the city where it was safe to deny things. He had far too much integrity than that, and above all else, respected me too much to do something that heinous.

He was a good man. Far better than most I knew.

As I bent to spit out my toothpaste and to dip my hand under the running water to cup and use to rinse my mouth out, the door to the bathroom was slowly pushed open, and soon, a pair of arms encircled around my waist.

Popping my head up from the sink, the mess of Avery's blond hair was all that I saw in the mirror before he buried his face into my neck and pulled me back against his chest until we were practically molded together. He let out a soft sigh, his naked chest hot against my back.

I stared at his figure in the mirror, my chest blooming with affection at the carelessly sweet gesture. Slowly, I lifted my hand up to graze through the tangled lengths of his hair that leaned over my shoulder.

"You okay?" I asked.

"Mmm," was all he grunted out, his voice still hoarse from sleep.

It had me smiling. "Don't tell me I wore you out."

He puffed out a laugh against my neck. "Funny."

The second his lips smoothed over my skin up near my ear, warmth pooled into my gut.

Not mad. Not avoiding me.

Quite the opposite, in fact.

"You're coming over to the estate," he said. Not a question, just simply stating a fact.

I liked that.

"You did promise me breakfast," I teased.

When he lifted his head, a small smile played on his lips. He brought his hand up to cup my jaw, pulling me back into a soft kiss. He held me there, keeping his mouth pressed against mine in a chaste way but still somehow managed to make my body flush with heat.

The fact that this man could do something so simple and still get me all hot and bothered was ridiculous. Charming, sure, but ridiculous nonetheless.

And I lapped that shit right up.

He traced his thumb along my chin and jaw

when he finally pulled away, leaving only a hair's breadth between us. All of this sudden affection was dizzying. "Are *you* okay?"

What a question.

As if anything could be answered so simply. Yet, I'd asked him the same damn thing only moments ago. There was so much to say and yet no words that I could come up with to properly express any of what was circling around in my head came out.

What I did know was that this feeling of contentment—of rightness—was exactly what I'd been searching for over the last decade. The pieces of the puzzle had finally fallen into place like they'd been there all along and I'd simply needed to look elsewhere to find them.

"Yes," I murmured.

He smiled again, his shoulders falling from their slightly tensed up position that I hadn't noticed they were frozen in before. With another kiss, he then said, "Good."

"Go shower," I said, shoving him toward the drawn curtain. "Hazel will whip me with that dishrag if I let you go over there smelling like sex."

He snatched my wrist up into a firm hold. "Only if you're joining me."

I looked down at the towel wrapped around my waist, barely a second's worth of hesitation between me looking back at him again and using my free hand to tug at the knot pressed against my hip. The towel pooled at my feet.

Avery laughed and tugged me with him. "Come here."

CHAPTER 26

AVERY

I COULDN'T BELIEVE how fucking blind I'd been.

My whole life, I'd always felt like a stranger wading through the small twinges of envy that had constantly prickled at the back of my mind from being surrounded by couples and their happy endings while my own seemed to be nowhere in sight.

No matter how hard I'd tried to look for my soulmate in the faces of those around me, or believing the lies I told myself of it one day happening when I least expected it. I'd soon become resigned to swallowing the harsh pill of reality that my father had fucked me up too much—that I was too far gone in the bitterness he'd instilled in me—to believe in trusting and opening myself up to someone like that ever again.

I'd never been the type to believe in divine intervention or whatever it was that Hallmark loved to peddle to the hapless romantics of the generation before mine.

It was too cheesy for me to buy into. Too convenient of an excuse to hypothetically find myself going back to the same small hometown I grew up in, only to realize that my soulmate was there the entire time and life had thrown so many curveballs that it was impossible to tell until it was far too late.

Funny that in reality, I was actually just too stupid to realize I'd been my own worst enemy the entire time. That my apathetic nature when it came to all of my past relationships wasn't some by-product of being raised by a covert narcissist and, in reality, I'd been denying myself the inevitable.

I wished I could remember why I ever stopped writing to Brandon. Why I cut off contact and decided it was best for both of us to move on with our lives when all I'd felt since then was an impending sense of doom and melancholy.

Chalking up my indifference toward my life to finally shedding the shackles of my father had given me the excuse to float through life without caring about anything outside of the remedial pleasure that came with climbing up the corporate ladder and making an obscene amount of money in the process.

I'd detached myself, pulled on an aloof mask that only Marlow and Silas could see through. All for it to be fucking shattered the moment I stepped into Brandon's body shop and was reminded that I actually did have a beating heart still left in my chest.

One that was sickeningly in tune with my former best friend and that longed to have him back in my life like I was dependent on it.

What did it mean other than the obvious?

Was I alone in this, or was Brandon also willing to drudge through the unknown with me?

Sex with Brandon last night had been eye opening. Way more than I thought it would be when he'd first invited me inside and had looked at me with that cautious gaze right before yanking me down into that first kiss.

Now that he was in my veins, I was sure that there would be no end to this. I'd always feel like I was starving until I had him back in that bed with the both of us naked and panting.

I was growing hard again, even reminiscing about it now.

We'd left his place to come back to mine right after we'd showered and gotten dressed. Him in his shop's uniform and me in the sweat suit set I'd bought day two at the hospital after finally giving in to needing a fresh set of clothes that weren't wrinkled with the remnants of sweat and other things from our almost-date.

Upon pulling up to the circular driveway outside of my family's home, I threw the Audi into park and killed the ignition.

Brandon slipped his hand down between the console and his seat to unhook his seatbelt, turning slightly toward me as he did so. As soon as the belt moved across his chest to retract back into the door, my knee-jerk reaction was to bridge the small gap between us and cup his face in my hand like I'd been doing so often lately in order to bring his mouth to meet mine.

I couldn't get enough of him. Of touching him and tasting him. Of the little gasp he made every time I pulled him closer to me. Of when that subtle shiver rolled through his body whenever my hand wandered.

I fucking needed him so badly.

Would there ever be a time when I got used to any of this? That my need to invade his bubble with my touches and caresses until there was no telling where he ended and I began would ever fade?

My intuition was telling me no. Screaming it, rather.

I'd lived so long with feeling numb, and now I was dying to keep that fire within me burning bright. Stoking it with whatever kindling Brandon was willing to give me.

His lips were soft and tasted like mint against my tongue. They pursed slightly and then parted to let me in, his tongue meeting mine in the same kind of fervor that we'd shared when he'd invited me into his house.

How fucked would we be if I dragged him across the center console and into my lap and threw back my seat while trying to work my hands down into his jeans?

The estate had cameras out here facing the driveway, yet there was a part of me that was willing to test out just how good my Audi's tint was.

I brushed my hand down between the door and my own seat, feeling for the control button on the side of it to start the decline. The second my finger brushed over it and pressed it, Brandon grabbed my arm.

He pulled his mouth away from mine and huffed out an amused, "Behave."

I tightened my hand on his face. "No."

He laughed when I tugged him down into another kiss, tilting my head to deepen it while he slapped at my arm again. As we were lowered together, his torso was practically hanging over the center console and into my lap from the awkward angle.

Brandon could protest all he wanted but the ironic part about it was him kissing me with the same amount of animalistic lust that had me lowering the goddamn seat in the first place.

"Avery." He laughed again, tilting his head to

the side and away from me the second my seat was flat.

I leaned up to nip at the skin along his jaw. Keeping my hands and mouth off of him was impossible with my head swimming with this much lust.

"We're not fucking in your car." He had a more serious tone this time, but I knew if I grabbed the hair at the nape of his neck and tugged him back around, I'd see a delighted smile on his face that was completely at odds with it.

"I'll turn around and face us away from the house," I offered.

He slapped my chest, turning back to glare at me. "Knock it off, you horndog."

Can you blame me?

I got a taste of fucking paradise.

How the hell was I supposed to properly behave after that?

I needed to hear those incredible sounds tumbling out of Brandon's mouth again—the sooner the better.

Unfortunately, he shoved himself off of me too fast for me to catch and shimmied back into his own seat still wearing that amused smile.

"Come on. Feed me and then we'll think about sneaking up to your room after."

That had me kicking my door open almost instantly. Music to my fucking ears.

Before I had Brandon pinned against my bed again, I'd need to tell him that this wasn't some kind of hookup situation where I was looking to blow off steam and he was simply an available party. Sure, I was new to this entire part of life with no experience whatsoever and no prior curiosities, either.

However, that wasn't about to mean I'd be using Brandon to do a little soul searching. Whatever emotions were coming to the surface because I was allowing myself to be open to them were the real deal. Not some kind of passing interest that would soon fade once I got this all 'out of my system'.

Something that I doubted would be happening anytime soon, if at all.

I had to tell him before he got up in his head again. He had to know I wasn't going to leave him to pick up the pieces of the aftermath.

I slammed my own door shut and came around to the other side of the car while Brandon did the same. He flashed me a quick smile and then headed up to the front steps, a single pace ahead of me. As we both reached the top landing, I snagged his hand and wrapped my fingers tightly around his, causing him to whip around and regard me with the beautiful eyes of his that were slightly wide.

His mouth pursed together as if to form a question, only to be interrupted when the front door was kicked open.

"Morning," I chimed to Jonas, whose brow was raised rather high as I slipped through the crack of the doors with Brandon in tow. "Hazel up yet?"

"Yes," he said slowly, nodding and then closed the doors behind us with a firm push. "We weren't expecting to see you, or Mr. Anders, back so early. So forgive us for being ill-prepared for breakfast this morning."

"Um, it's Carmichael now. Sir," Brandon corrected. His fingers tightened around mine, twisting slightly as I felt a slight, nervous jitter in his hand. "And that's okay. We figured if we came early enough we could make a special request."

Jonas glanced down at our hands, causing me to slightly move myself between him and Brandon protectively. If there was going to be anything said about this, even as an off-hand comment, I wasn't going to have it. It'd break my heart to fire any of the staff that had been here for most of my life, but intolerance of any kind wasn't going to fly.

No matter whose mouth it was coming from.

Jonas's brow simply rose further but he said nothing else on the matter. Instead, he gestured with his chin down the hall to the kitchen while saying, "Better go let Hazel know now before she starts putting something elaborate together. You know how she gets."

His casual words had me relaxing a bit. Behind me, I adjusted my hold on Brandon's hand, running my thumb over the top of his palm in a soothing way and nodded to Jonas. "Some special occasion coming up?"

"Not that I'm aware of. But last week, she made a whole quiche, so anything's possible."

I breathed out a laugh. "Got it."

"Thanks, Jonas," Brandon said, moving from behind me.

The second his eyes met mine, a small smile crawled across his lips, melting my heart. It seemed that all time stood still. Here, with Brandon, in the foyer of my childhood home, memories rushed through my head. Of us standing in this exact spot a million lifetimes ago and saying goodbye for the last time.

It killed me to leave him behind. Even more so when we lost contact.

This time around, I wasn't going to mess this up. Not when I finally felt alive for the first time in ten years.

I started for the hallway leading down to the kitchen, Brandon following along while keeping in time with my footsteps. After breakfast was done, I was going to take him up to my room and lock the door behind us so that I could finally bare all of my feelings to him without anyone else interrupting us before I could get everything out.

Behind us, the door's bell chimed, the sound of it echoing against the empty space of the marbled floors and grand ceiling.

I stopped and turned to the sound, confusion bubbling up inside of me.

Who would be visiting at this hour? Moreover, who the hell had gotten past the gate?

No one had been following me and not close enough that they'd be able to sneak in right behind me without being noticed in the rearview. I wasn't expecting any guests.

A visitor for one of the staff, then?

It wouldn't be completely unheard of, though at this hour, it was rather strange.

I felt Brandon's curious gaze fall on me—clearly wondering the same thing as me—before he, too, faced the front doors.

With a sharp heave, Jonas grabbed and parted the left one from the frame, sticking his head out into the morning air.

"Is there something I can help you with?" he asked.

A man's voice answered. "Yes. We're here to assess the property."

What the hell?

Nothing was supposed to be touched with the litigations between my and Steele's law offices still ongoing. At least, not without proper documentation and a fucking meeting first.

Letting go of Brandon's hand, I stormed over to the door just as the other one was pushed open. The sound of heels clicking against the stone steps was the first thing I heard, even before seeing whoever it was on the other side push their way through and step into my foyer.

Blonde hair caught my attention first, the thick waves of it cascading down over her narrow shoulders. Her large sunglasses covered up half of her face and were dark enough that I couldn't see her eyes through them. Her lips were painted a cherry red, eye-catching against her pale skin and a stark contrast against her dark clothing.

One of her hands came up to rub at her protruding baby bump that was pulling at the tight fabric of her dress.

My feet instantly stilled as she turned to me, red hot anger igniting inside of my chest.

Ana Liapovich.

"Get out of my house." The words were gritted through my teeth.

Showing up here was a bold move on her part and an act of war on mine. I'd warned her not to do anything drastic before getting that test, yet here she was trying to pull a fast one and invade my home like she already owned the place.

It wouldn't surprise me if this was some sort of shake-down technique. Playing on the sympathies as a poor, widowed pregnant woman to my staff while giving me the middle finger in the process in a hope to gain some sort of loyalty. If she had any hope that she could turn my own staff against me just because she'd been married to my father, she was out of her mind and league.

The smile on Ana's face was brief before it was quickly smothered by the flat expression that replaced it. She continued to rub her belly at me, while behind her, Alexander Steele pushed his way past Jonas with a piece of paper pinched between his fingers.

"Mr. McAllister," he greeted with a nod. "We have this to present to you."

The second it was within reach, I snatched the paper out of his hand.

The header was from a local health clinic right outside of Ellington Heights, Ana's name listed under the 'party' line, along with mine and the child's.

Below that was a table with DNA markers that were checked, all accounting for different percentages of the DNA and whatever else had been tested with the small sample I'd gladly sent over the second I'd been requested to do so a few days ago.

Down at the bottom, right above the signature line of the clinic's director, was a line that stated the DNA of the child had a 50% match to mine.

"As you can see," Steele said. "The child is biologically related to you."

No...

"It's a boy," Ana stated. Just to drive the knife in deeper.

How? How had this happened so long after he'd proudly gotten a vasectomy? How the fuck had she even talked him into it in the first place?

My father was the most stubborn man on this planet. He'd barely raised me, what sense did it make to have another that he'd soon abandon, too, once things got too tough?

Fear of his legacy? The impending pendulum of morality finally catching up to him?

I couldn't wrap my head around it. No matter how many ways I tried to.

Without warning, my body swayed, the solid weight of two hands coming up to press against my back being the only things that kept me upright while my vision began to shift from red to seeing spots of black instead. I was holding the piece of paper so tightly in my hands that the edges of it were wrinkling.

What the *fuck*.

"Since we'll need to negotiate the trust with this new information coming to light, my client requested access to the property to properly assess it and see what things she may want to negotiate for when we come to the table again." Steele's voice was quick and to the point. Something I'd normally appreciate in a lawyer if it wasn't for the fact that my entire fucking life was falling apart at the moment.

This process was going to take much longer than a few sessions in Ted's office while we argued over who got the family's cast iron set and who got the titled sports cars in the attached garage. I'd have to wait for this child—*my sibling*—to grow up and divide everything fairly then.

Even as his mother, Ana had no claims to anything. She was merely the surrogate mouthpiece until his son was old enough to speak for himself. Until the *courts* decided he was old enough to make these decisions on his own.

A little less than twenty years would be spent sitting with my thumb up my ass. Everything would be frozen. Untouchable.

My eyes locked on Ana again. "Just take the money. Whatever amount you want. Just take it."

Her mouth twitched slightly. "No. I want the house."

"Just *take the money*." I felt Brandon's hands fisting in my shirt as I tried to step forward, keeping me from moving any further than the spot my feet had been planted in. "You could buy another damn mansion with it. Just take the fucking money, Ana."

"No. I want my son to grow up here. With his father's things."

"He's *dead*," I spat out. "It's not going to bring him back. Your son's not going to learn jack shit about that man while living under this roof. Take the money and move on."

She gave me a firm shake of her head. "No. We stay here."

"Avery," Brandon mumbled softly to me while hooking an arm around my waist.

He kept me locked tight against his chest, not letting me advance on her or Steele. I'd never hit a woman before, never would either, but that wouldn't stop me from dragging her and her fucking lawyer outside by whatever I could grab onto and throw them out of the house and slam the door shut behind them.

God, what the *fuck*.

"My client has expressed what her desires are, so we'll be taking a look around and an inventory as we do so." Steele went on, completely ignoring how devastating of a bombshell that had been to drop on me. "You're welcome to join us but I suggest that it's best for both your sake and my client's to let us handle this process privately."

Jonas cleared his throat. "Mr. McAllister... I can notify you when they leave."

None of this felt real.

I had to be in some terrible dream. I had to still be in bed, with Brandon tucked against me while we slept the morning away, completely oblivious to the world around us.

"Avery," Brandon said again, this time using his arm to pivot me backward. "Let's go upstairs."

I was shaking my head, even as he was guiding me to the staircase and up the first few steps. I couldn't let these strangers roam around my home. Not with these walls still seeped in such agony.

"Jonas..." My voice was tight.

He seemed to understand, even as my words failed me. "I'll show them around and will let you know as soon as they leave."

I wished those words would've given me some kind of relief, but all they did was harden the pit of dread that had long since settled in my stomach. I stumbled back into Brandon when we reached the top landing, my heels digging into the thick carpet the moment we were stationary.

None of that deterred my best friend from lurching me backward, forcing us both to take the corner that led down to my room.

And with that, both Steele and Ana disappeared from my view.

CHAPTER 27

AVERY

"I CAN FOLLOW up with the clinic she used, but if the director signed off on it, there's a very low chance of fraud, Mr. McAllister. Not many people would risk their careers for a patient they have no connection to."

My heart sank once more as I clutched my phone in my hand, Ted's voice coming in through the speaker loud and clear.

Foolishly, I'd had hope we could make a case for proving Ana's claims as illegitimate. Somehow backtracking through Google that she'd paid for a fake test and slapped my and her names on it to try and pass it off in order to gain access to my house.

There were plenty of documented cases of false paternities before this. Why not hope that this one was among those statistics?

While Ted was typically one to entertain my delusions, this one was clearly not one of them. Even as I begged him to dig deeper, he sounded hesitant. I'd pay him a handsome salary to do whatever was necessary, yet clearly his ethics were keeping him from making audacious claims.

"Is there any history of fraud with the clinic?" I asked.

"Again, I can look into it, but I haven't heard anything."

I fisted my hand in my hair and bent over to rest my elbow against my knee, balancing the phone on my other one. I was so damn tired of this—of getting screwed over at the last minute when I was finally finding myself on steadier ground.

When would it end? When would I finally be able to live my life peacefully without someone or something coming in to bulldoze it all down and force me to start over?

"I know this is disappointing," Ted went on.

"Right now all we can do is wait to see what the other party is requesting. It could be a few simple things and some money."

"She wants the house," I argued.

"If that's the case, then they're going to need to be willing to negotiate. You're currently residing and paying the bills. That gives you more claim over the property as of right now."

'As of right now' wasn't exactly guaranteeing me forever. Not to mention everything that was *inside* of the property. My skin crawled at the thought of Ana rooting around my family's personal property, looking for anything of value that would be worth her while in fighting me on.

What's to say I kept this thing going for the next decade? Fighting her on every choice she made until she gave up and cut loose? Was that possible or would the courts force me to negotiate despite my wishes?

I found it ironic that, eventually, a baby would have the same amount of rights as me to claim property. Hell, it could probably be argued he had rights now if Steele found his client the right judge with an equally bleeding heart.

"I want my family's assets left alone," I mumbled into the phone.

"I know you do, but unfortunately, we're past that point. I can call you when I get the reports sent over with what they're interested in. After that happens, we'll go from there."

Dismissed. He was done dealing with me. We'd lost and Ted was cutting himself loose.

He'd gone into this thinking it'd be a cut and dry case with no frills, a little bit of paperwork to sift through and a hefty paycheck at the end. Taking me on as a client hadn't come with a posted warning that he'd be getting more than he bargained for after signing our contract.

And now he was pulling out.

I couldn't blame him.

If I had that option, I would, too.

"Sure," was all I said before ending the call and tossing my phone onto the bed next to me.

I leaned the weight of my head against both palms, threading a hand through my hair and gripping the strands in my fist, a long sigh escaping me. If it wasn't for Brandon currently blocking my bedroom door with his body, I'd march downstairs and try to scare Ana and her lawyer into fleeing the premises, damned if the cops were called on me afterward.

Who cared at this point? Maybe being

thrown in jail for the weekend would help clear my head. Maybe I could even get some jailhouse legal advice. The kind where I'd be paying someone under the table to find out where Ana was currently staying and scare her into getting the fuck back on a plane and heading home to Russia.

Cruel? Sure, but I was well past giving a fuck at this point.

"Avery," Brandon said, his soft footsteps coming over to me.

Through the strands of hair falling over my eyes, I watched him sink to his knees in front of me and reach out to wrap both hands around my wrists. He gave them a gentle tug, clearly trying to peel them away from my scalp where I was holding onto the roots hard enough to hurt.

The pain was helping clear my head, though, breaking through the noise of my mind that was slowly devolving into a chaotic mess.

"Hey," he tried again. "Look at me."

I didn't want to. I couldn't. If I did, he'd see the tears brimming in my eyes. Looking weak in front of Brandon was the last thing I wanted. Not right now, at least, when I should've been keeping things together.

Running into snags and fixing them was a part of my job. Yet the second it had anything to do with my personal life, I was crumbling.

The second he was able to force me into dropping my hands, I fell forward until my forehead rested against his shoulder. He let go to wrap his arms around me, practically cradling me in a tight, comforting hold.

"What do I do?" I whispered.

"I don't know." He dragged his fingers lazily through my hair, trying to comfort me with the simple touch. "But I'm here with you. No matter what you decide to do."

"Help me get rid of her."

"You asking me to help you hide the body?"

Despite my horribly plummeting mood, I laughed. "Would you?"

He was quiet for a while, simply continuing the motion of his hand running through my hair. The gesture was soothing on more levels than I thought possible and exactly what I needed at the moment, regardless of how tough I wanted to pretend to be.

What good would it do trying to postulate in front of Brandon when he knew me inside and out? He could see right through me with hardly any effort and would call me out in record time if I kept it up.

That was the one thing I'd always liked about him. He knew when to keep it real with me no matter the circumstances.

When Brandon finally spoke again, his words shook me to my core. "I would go to the ends of the Earth for you, Avery."

I pulled back to look at him, surprised to see a set frown on his face. I had half a mind to challenge him on it—to force him to prove his words and put his money where his mouth was.

But wasn't that what he'd been doing this entire time since I'd come back? Proving to me that no matter how long and how far the distance between us had been, we'd snap right back to where we were always meant to be?

I cupped his face in a gentle hold, bringing him closer to me in order to press a couple of soft kisses to his pursed lips. I widened my legs, allowing him to slip in between them, soon getting trapped when I locked my thighs around him.

He let out a soft grunt, both of his hands coming down to rest on my thighs and give each a small squeeze.

"How did I get so lucky in meeting you," I mumbled between kisses.

"I like to think that time at lunch when you gave me your extra pudding cup after I forgot my lunch bag on the bus was what really sealed the deal."

"Of course I did. Your stomach rumbling could've woken up a dead man."

He let out a soft snort. "I was a growing boy. Sue me."

Smiling, I said, "Yeah. Now I can barely lift you."

His eyes widened when I scooped him up from under his armpits and hauled him off of the floor, dragging him into my lap. Once my arms were better secured around his body, I flopped back down onto my bed, taking him with me and letting us both collapse into a heap.

Brandon's startled grunt was the only sound he made, and aside from the slight adjustment he made in order to shove his hand under my back, he laid still against me.

I liked us like this. Pressed together with nothing but our thin layer of clothing separating us.

I wasn't sure when my mind had made the

switch from not wanting anyone to touch me or touch in reciprocation to exclusively needing to have my hands all over Brandon as much as possible. It'd come on so suddenly and with such a strong sense of conviction that ignoring it was near impossible.

Regardless, it felt right. *This...* This felt right.

"Bran," I mumbled against his temple, glossing my lips along the hard ridge of his forehead.

"What?"

My stomach squeezed, my self-consciousness suddenly kicking in.

He could be humoring me with all of this. It certainly wouldn't be the first time I'd pushed him into doing something he wasn't exactly 100% on board with. Fuck knew, I had plenty of crazy schemes in the past that I'd somehow roped him into without fail by simple batting my eyes at him and promising to give it a rest for a while after the fact.

I wanted to believe this wasn't one of those times. That Brandon was also genuine in the obvious chemistry and budding feelings between us and wasn't simply doing any of this out of a past-filled obligation he thought he owed me.

I wasn't exactly in-tune with who I was becoming, or what path I'd choose at the end, but what I did know was that I wanted Brandon.

I needed him.

Seeing him on that stupid date had done something to me—changed a part of my brain that I was never going to be able to undo, regardless of how hard I tried to ignore the pangs of jealousy that choked me every time I thought about that man's hands on him.

He was *mine*.

"Avery..."

I loosened my arms when he moved to sit up, planting both of his hands on either side of my head while leaning over me.

He had a brow raised. "You got quiet on me."

Smiling slightly, I apologized. "Sorry. In my head."

"I could tell. Penny for your thoughts?"

"You'll end up having to give me many more pennies if you want to know all of them," I countered.

His brows pulled together. "Good or bad?"

I laughed. Leave it to Brandon to always prepare himself for the worst. Here I was contemplating how to tell him that I wasn't about to let him go so he could run off and start dating again while he was worried I'd... what, tell him I was done with this?

Absolutely not. Not when we were this deep.

I lifted a hand to tuck a few strands of his hair behind his ear, letting my fingers linger along the shell of it, and then dragged my digits down to trace his jaw. "All good. No worries," I murmured.

He sighed softly, but looked a little more relieved. "I know you're worried about this Ana thing."

The reminder had me groaning. "I need to figure out how to prove all of this is false."

Brandon tilted his head. "You really think it's fraud?"

"It has to be."

I couldn't ignore the ringing of my intuition that was telling me my father would in no way get his vasectomy reversed, and even if he did, there was no way that after nearly twenty years, he wasn't fucking dry.

The odds were way too severe.

"How are you going to go about proving it?" he asked.

I thought for a moment, tracking the movement of my fingers along his face.

What *could* I do?

Realistically, anything.

I had enough money to do whatever I wanted. I had a trust fund that could buy a small country and that wasn't even counting my own separate bank account from my day job.

Why not put it to good use?

"Let's go down to the clinic and see how far a few thousand can get us in obtaining Ana's records."

Brandon's eyes widened briefly and then a determined look settled on his face. "All right. Let's get going before she tries to steal anything more from you."

CHAPTER 28

BRANDON

THE CLINIC WAS your run-of-the-mill facility
that specialized in family planning and women's
care. It had a cheery sign out front with a
dancing mother and child, declaring an enthusi-
astic welcome.

There was barely anyone in the lobby when
we stepped inside—an elderly woman who very
obviously gave mine and Avery's linked hands a
hard stare as we passed by, and a young couple
with a small child playing quietly on the floor—
and made our way over to the front counter.

I had no idea what to expect during this so-called mission of ours, though I had hope. The thing about having an obscene amount of money like Avery was that it went far. Especially, with getting people to work with you and do favors under the table that they'd otherwise balk at.

There was a budding belief in me that all of this pregnancy thing was still somehow fake and with us coming here to gather the paperwork (or in our case, the lack thereof), Ana would soon be revealed to be the scammer Avery's gut was telling him she was.

As the cynic out of the two of us, it was hard not to give in to the rational side of my brain telling me that we were wasting our time and that even with some amount of proof favoring our side, proving it to a jury or a judge was going to be a hell of a lot harder than either of us knew.

The fact of the matter was that I loathed seeing Avery hurt. If we somehow did manage to get the proof and it only proved Ana's case more, then what? How crushed would Avery be? His entire world would be split in two once again.

He'd still be forced to work with a woman he didn't know and a brother he'd probably never have any kind of relationship with. It wasn't like she was interested in getting to know him while she was married to his father, anyway.

The only logical reason she was rearing her ugly head now was because she knew she had a one-way ticket into the high life. Being married to a billionaire *and* pregnant with his unborn child? That was the kind of plan bathed in gold.

If she played her cards right, which was looking very likely, she and her future family would be set for the rest of forever. That kind of money seldom ever ran dry.

Avery tightened his fingers around mine as the window at the counter opened and a nurse flashed him a polite smile. "Can I help you?"

I couldn't help the sharp churn in my stomach now that we were actually doing this. Nor the tickle of butterflies that were kicking up from holding Avery's hand out in public so blatantly. He'd grabbed it the second he'd come around to my side of the car after parking, lacing our hands together like we'd been doing it for years.

All of this was so damn new that it was throwing me for a loop. But that was Avery for you. Always switching things up when I least expected it.

"Hi, we're here to obtain some records for a patient," Avery said.

The woman's keyboard clacked loudly as she typed on it. "Patient name?"

"Ana McAllister."

My heart pounded in time with her keyboard. How was any of this going to work? Sure, everyone had a price but that didn't mean some random person was going to throw their entire career away for a couple of randoms like us and a pocket full of hundreds.

"Oh, Mr. McAllister," the woman suddenly said, her eyes widened as soon as she seemed to recognize his face. "Yes, uh... your wife?"

I quickly let go of his hand while he gave her a warm looking smile. "Yes. She needs a copy of her medical records and any tests that were performed here at the clinic. For our insurance. Did you need my license?"

Keeping it short and simple. I had to hand it to him, he was still quite the smooth talker.

She nodded, her eyes darting down to her screen. "You'll need to go to the records department. They'll ask for your ID down there and verification that you're on her HIPAA. But once that's all set, they can print you off some copies."

"Thanks. This way?" He gestured to the door on the opposite side of the office.

She shook her head, standing from her chair in order to lean her torso out of the little window to point with her pen at the door next to it. "Go through that one and follow the signs down. I'll let Patty know you're on your way."

Avery grabbed my arm while turning from the counter. "Thanks so much."

Without wasting any more time, and in an effort not to look any more suspicious than I already felt we did, we headed over to the door and slipped on through, letting it slam behind us. The hallway was poorly lit, and thankfully empty, giving us time to pause and collect ourselves.

Breathing out slowly while simultaneously trying to *not* freak out and blow our cover, I leaned back against the wall. Funny that something like this was making me feel like we were trying to bust out of jail when in reality at any point, we could walk away from this cleanly and without anyone knowing.

Avery and I had never been delinquents of any kind, choosing to keep to ourselves while the rest of our peers were off partying and doing whatever they could to pass the time before we all graduated and went our separate ways.

Yet, here we were at the precipice of something way worse than stealing my mom's liquor and sneaking off into the woods to have a small bonfire and down it between the two of us.

This was a damn felony in the making.

"Hey." A hand cupped my face. "We've got this."

Looking up into Avery's deep blue eyes, I had the instinct to argue with him but... couldn't. Not when he brought me peace the second he dragged his thumb across my cheek, settling all of my nervousness instantly. He'd always had that way about him—calming the raging storm inside of me no matter what was going on around us.

I trusted him intrinsically. More than my siblings and my parents combined.

Still, I asked, "What if we get arrested?"

He shook his head. "I won't let that happen. I'd get us bailed out before your ass can warm that bench."

Despite my nerves, I laughed. "What a promise."

"One I intend to keep."

I believed him.

Avery wouldn't make statements like that if he didn't have full confidence in what he was saying. Not to mention if we were going to go down for doing something reckless and stupid like this, at least we'd be doing so together.

What more could I ask for?

Grabbing his hand again, I squeezed it. "All right, let's go commit a crime, then."

Avery laughed.

AS IT TURNED OUT, the price for a record keeper's silence, and for a freshly printed copy of a former Russian model's medical records, was about five thousand dollars wired to a local credit union and an old twenty-five dollar gift card I'd had stuffed in my wallet for a local fast food joint.

I never wanted to get to the point where I thought something like that was getting off easy, but... well...

Not to mention how hot it was watching Avery work his charm on the record keeper.

Picturing him doing the same thing but in a boardroom setting with a bunch of old men with too much money burning in their pockets, and a shotgun cocked to fire the word 'no' at any suggestion brought up that could possibly threaten their bottom line, was hot enough to make my pants grow tight the moment the papers were being passed over to Avery, fresh off the printer.

He always impressed me with how he could navigate a tense situation. In control, confident, and ten steps ahead. His mother would be proud of the man he turned out to be. I know I certainly was.

Once we were safely back in the car and the doors locked behind us, my entire body flopped back against the seat, sagging with relief that we were in the clear.

For now.

"I can't believe that actually worked." Rolling my head to the side, I regarded Avery with a cursory glance. "You think that lady at the front desk is going to follow up with Ana about us obtaining her records?

Avery shoved his key into the ignition, starting the car and then throwing it into reverse. "If she does, I'll slap her with a lawsuit."

Despite his harsh threat, I smiled a little. "Can't really sue her if she's doing her job?"

"Lawsuits scare people into silence."

I snorted. Spoken like a true CEO.

Though, he was right in a sense. If the record keeper was smart and wanted to keep his money, he'd shut down any questions the front desk lady had no matter how morally wrong it felt to do so. Because if anything, he was an accomplice in all of this as well and like hell Avery would show him mercy if he so much as squealed.

If we were going down, that record keeper was coming with us. Maybe even the front desk lady, too, for not verifying Avery's identity.

The McAllisters weren't to be messed with. Everyone in Ellington Heights knew that.

This was all speculation, of course, and my paranoid mind working overtime because I felt guilty for doing something illegal even to help a friend out of a difficult and desperate situation. However, if a woman like Ana was in any way a con artist scamming my best friend, were Avery and I truly hurting anyone innocent?

Gesturing to the papers, I asked. "So, now what?"

As he drove us into traffic, his hand drifted over to rest on my thigh. "We'll bring it to my lawyer. He's going to be pissed with how we obtained them, but I really don't care. He'll figure out how to get it admissible if it turns out we need it for evidence in court."

I felt like I was in some TV drama as the sidekick to a billionaire protagonist and his ragtag team of morally gray assistants. I imagined working for Avery was kind of like that—dangerous in terms of how far he'd be willing to push the envelope at times, and yet garnered fierce loyalty due to his protectiveness over those he deemed his responsibility.

All that to say, looking down at the papers in my lap, and trying to ignore the heat radiating through my pants from where Avery was touching me, I hoped that whatever was in here turned his luck around. I hated seeing him suffer.

His console lit up with a phone call. To my surprise, and relief, the name 'Marlow Knight' appeared.

At least it wasn't his ex...

I still felt bad getting jealous over a woman he clearly had no intentions of getting back together with and who had a whole ass fiancé and child to go home to every night. Unfortunately, my head and my heart loved to be at constant war with each other over getting my emotions settled long enough to remain level-headed when it came to Avery.

Jealousy had never been my forte. Not when I could just as easily remove myself from a potentially toxic situation and move on with my life instead of trying to compete against someone else.

However, every rule I'd ever had for myself was quickly tossed out the window whenever Avery entered the picture.

"Yes?" Avery said upon answering the call.

"I'm beginning to suspect you hate me," the voice on the other line stated.

Glancing over at him to see his reaction to the clearly very dramatic words, I was charmed to see him rolling his eyes in an equally dramatic fashion. "Seriously?"

"First, you ditch our dinner date. Then, you keep avoiding my calls. No texts. Nothing. Just tell me you hate me." The other man's tone was so matter-of-fact that if it wasn't for Avery shaking his head, I would've thought this was a very serious discussion.

"This is the first time you've called me," was all Avery responded with.

"Is that all you heard!" the voice accused.

The responding shit-eating grin, coupled with the squeeze of my thigh, sent butterflies fluttering in my stomach. "Isn't that all you said?"

The man on the other line, Marlow, groaned loudly. "Where are you..."

"Driving."

"Oh, great. So you'll swing by La Roux's for lunch."

Avery popped a brow. "You ever stop and think whether or not I'm busy?"

"With what? The guy fixing up your cars that you wouldn't shut up about the last time we saw you? I know you don't have a job currently, but you've got to stop hanging around there like a lost puppy, Av. Let that man do his job," the other man goaded.

I watched his mouth drop in shock.

Avery's talked about me?

Damn, why was that so flattering?

Obviously, I knew I'd be brought up if the past was ever talked about or used as background fodder for any particular story Avery might've shared—we were a part of each other's lives for so many of those formidable years, I was bound to come up, even if it was an off-handed mention.

But from the way Marlow was speaking, it sounded like I was being brought up in far more than simply the retellings of past days gone by.

"Can you stop." The words were gritted through his teeth, a deep flush coloring his face. "It wasn't like I was chatting your ear off. You were doing plenty of talking yourself. And I still have a job, thank you very much."

"One, that's a lie because Silas and I were doing shots every time you mentioned the guy's name which almost sent us to the hospital to get our stomachs pumped, thank you very much. And two, it's been weeks since you've been back to the city to visit your office. Does the board even remember your name?"

"Seeing as I'm the one that pays their salaries, I'd hope so."

My brain was in overdrive, still trying to wrap itself around Marlow's words. This all could be one massive exaggeration in order to goad Avery into quipping back at his friend who clearly liked the verbal sparring, however I was beginning to lean toward that not exactly being true.

Not with Avery's face still that beautiful rosy

shade that seemed to grow even darker the longer Marlow spouted on.

Feeling like it was my duty to rescue my poor best friend from the persecution, I cleared my throat. "Um, Marlow was it?"

There was a pause, and then, "Oh? Avery didn't tell me he had a friend with him."

Other than the hand gently squeezing my thigh before he took a right turn, he wasn't telling me to stop or not talk to his friend. So I took that as him giving me his blessing and carried on. "Yeah. The one you mentioned, actually."

Marlow let out a hearty laugh. "*Oh*. I see what's going on."

"What's that supposed to mean?" Avery muttered.

He laughed again. "Nothing! Just call me when you're actually free. I think there's some things you need to catch me up on."

"Fine. Let Silas know I said hello."

"Will do. And Brandon?"

I blinked. "Yes?"

"It was nice to put a voice to the name. I hope Avery brings you around soon."

Even though I hardly knew this man, I could

tell he was a good egg and was someone in Avery's corner who clearly cared about him, even with what seemed like the endless teasing. Those were the kinds of people I was hoping Avery had found after being sent to Switzerland. A solid group of friends he could count on when I could no longer be there.

I was happy for him and the life he'd made for himself. And while I wished it hadn't forced us apart, in the end, us finding each other again felt like divine timing.

"I look forward to one day meeting you," I said.

Marlow chuckled. "Don't let that bastard hide you away for *too* long. And if he keeps distracting you at work, I hear chasing him out with a broom works wonders."

Avery scoffed. "Goodbye, Marlow."

Lifting his hand off of my leg briefly to stab his finger against the console's panel to end the call, he shook his head again before clapping it back down again. He traced his thumb along my knee, circling slowly along the joint.

"Pain in my ass," he mumbled.

"Does he... know? About..." I waved a hand between us. Not that it really mattered one way or the other. I wasn't ashamed of what Avery and I had gotten ourselves involved in with each other, or whatever label it was we were sticking to.

I was simply curious because if he *had* told Marlow about us, when the hell did he find the time? When he was on the way back from the hospital? Before that?

Avery shook his head. "No, no. But he's also not an idiot."

My eyes narrowed suspiciously. "*Are* you going to tell him?"

The groan I received in response was incredible—more pained than embarrassed sounding. "Yes. Of course I will. And I'm warning you now, both he and Silas are *gossips*."

It was too good not to continue poking fun at him for. And even more so to know he was open to sharing *us* with his friends, ones that I'd yet to meet but by the sounds of it, were eager to get that ball rolling. "Wow, Avery. Just tell me next time you have a crush instead of it getting to me through the grapevine."

"I wouldn't call it a crush."

"Then?" I prompted.

He was quiet as he rotated the wheel with

one hand, taking us down a side street and away from the busy intersection that seemed to always be jam-packed this time of day. "I *like* you, Brandon. A lot. More than just a friend. *A lot* more."

I swallowed. The air was suddenly growing way too hot.

"If that freaks you out, just tell me." His voice had grown quiet, eyes staring steadily out his windshield.

How ironic for him to sit there and think that *I* wouldn't be receptive to his feelings. Actually, scratch that. That I wouldn't *welcome* his feelings. "You should drive us back to my place."

He darted his tongue out to wet his bottom lip. The hand on my thigh slowly crept up my leg. "Yeah...?"

"Yes." The second I got him into my house, I was tearing off his clothes.

He flicked his turn signal on and quickly merged. "Yeah, definitely. Let's drop this paperwork off first and then we'll head over."

"Perfect." Because after we did that, he was all mine.

CHAPTER 29

Avery

Over the next two weeks, I waited by the phone like a stray dog praying to be let in from the rain.

The anticipation was killing me, as was being kept in the dark from the moment I'd slapped the files down onto Ted's desk. He'd been surprised to see me, and even more so once he'd lifted the top part of the manila folder and spotted Ana's name on the first form's page.

From there, I'd been kept out of the loop with strict orders *not* to discuss this with anyone else. Well, aside from my accomplice.

In the corporate world, silence was never a good thing. It meant parts were moving without approval and decisions were being made behind closed doors that I wasn't privy to. None of which were helping with the nagging urge to know what the hell was going on.

Leaving a task like this to the professionals was obviously in my best interest. After all, why else would I have gone through the trouble of hiring a shark like Ted in the first place if he wasn't up to par with doing his damn job? He was the best of the best for a reason and not simply because of his impeccable track record inside of the courtroom.

His team was well known for their expertise in digging up dirt that the other side of the bench had long since believed to be buried.

All *I* needed to do was be patient.

A virtue I severely lacked these days.

Fortunately, the one thing keeping me sane thus far was Brandon and his brilliant distraction methods—namely in the form of him showing me the beauty of exploring each other in every way possible.

Much like this afternoon when I'd stopped

by to bring him his lunch, only to find myself with his dick down my throat.

"Fuck," Brandon's deep groan had my cock straining in my pants, dying to be let out. "Little more tongue. Right... there."

The hand in my hair tightened as I dragged up along the hard ridge, my lips puckering at the crown of it that was still slick with my spit. I had a hand fisted around the base of him that I used to stroke up to where my mouth was, meeting in the middle from both ends.

Being on my knees for this man in the middle of his shop's office while he lounged back in his chair, pants down and legs spread to give me plenty of room to suck him off was hotter than I'd ever imagined.

While I was still new to all of this, I was eager to learn and get a better handle on how to please and pleasure him. I was eager to know exactly what made Brandon tick—or rather squirm and twitch until he was putty in my hands.

So far, Brandon had been an excellent teacher. Showing me the perfect ways to get us both off.

Using my hair, he guided my mouth back down onto him. I sucked him in greedily, happy to hear that soft hitch in his breathing as he buried his cock deeper down my throat.

The sensation was overwhelming. Having another man's cock tickling the back of my throat wasn't something I ever thought I'd be capable of being into, let alone readily drop to my knees for the second I'd caught sight of Brandon growing hard after I'd locked the door behind me.

But as Brandon's desperate moans pitched higher and higher each time my throat tightened around him as he slowly worked himself in and out of my wet mouth, the more I wanted from him. To suck him dry, fuck him deep, get us both off until we were twitching messes on the floor.

"You look so damn good right now," Brandon mumbled. His face was flushed, eyes half-hooded with desire. I loved him looking at me like that—barely contained and ready to blow at any second.

After unbuttoning my pants and shoving them down partially, I gripped my own aching cock in my hand to stroke it in time with the rolling of Brandon's hips.

Fuck that felt good.

"That's it," he murmured to me. "Keep

touching yourself, baby. I want us to come together."

How the hell did I ever miss this side of Brandon growing up? That he had such a filthy mouth but still said it in the sweetest of ways?

I'd never been into dirty talk before this, or being praised, and yet those words spilling past his lips were fanning the flames inside of me.

I let him take control, fucking my mouth until his ragged breathing grew hoarse.

"Where?" was all he could ground out, hips bucking.

I kept my mouth firmly tight around him, not letting him get the idea to yank me back at the last second and rob me of finally tasting him on my tongue. That was, apparently, all he needed before he choked out a quiet curse and started to come.

The second it splashed against my tongue, I was done for, my own hips bucking while cum spilled all over my hand and dripped down onto the concrete floor under us.

I couldn't believe this was what I'd been missing out on with him. For *years*. We had so much to catch up on.

Brandon loosened his grip on my hair,

slumping back into his chair as the last few spurts leaked from his cock and coated my tongue in the thick mess. It slid easily down my throat, and was only slightly bitter to the taste.

"You did so good," he told me, his cock slick with spit and cum as it slid from my mouth. "So, so good."

My chest was warm from the praise, my head slightly fuzzy from the endorphins still racing through my bloodstream. "Only for you."

He chuckled, cupping my face in both of his hands. "I like the sound of that."

There was no way any other man on this planet would get me to do the things I'd done with Brandon. He was his own special breed that I was desperately attracted to and had no interest in changing anytime soon. If ever.

What did that make me? Straight with a clause? An exception?

Whatever.

As long as Brandon was equally as interested in me—in *this*—I wasn't at all concerned with labeling myself.

What did it matter in the end when all I wanted, and needed, was him?

Lifting up from my heels while ignoring the

pins and needles in my legs, I leaned until I could press my lips against his. Kissing him felt like a drug I needed to survive—a hit that I could barely go twenty minutes without having again.

He stroked his fingers through my scalp to the ends of my hair, gently detangling where he'd been holding it hostage. "You doing okay?"

I smiled, drawing him in for another long and lingering kiss before saying, "Yes."

He sighed softly, shoulders releasing from the tense hold.

"Worried?" I asked.

"I don't want to pressure you into anything."

That had me rolling my eyes. "If anything, I was the one that pressured *you* at the start of all of this."

The puzzled look on his face had me sitting back slightly, though I didn't get very far with the way he was still holding my head. "What are you talking about?'

I ran my tongue along the backs of my teeth. Did I even want to get into this right now? Bring up that faithful morning that had sent me into a fucking spiral that almost had me locking myself away in my family's mansion like some 1820's asylum patient out of shame?

I supposed he deserved a proper explanation for what happened. And a far better apology than what I'd been able to give him at the time.

"The night after I visited your shop drunk." I sighed. "I... when I woke up, I was feeling a little... out of sorts. You were just—you smelled so good and felt like a dream wrapped around me like that. I didn't mean to try and get off on you."

"Get off..." he echoed. "Avery, I—what? I made the moves on *you*."

My brows pulled together. "Brandon, who do you think was the one that started the dry humping?"

His mouth dropped open, an incredulous laugh escaping him. "You're kidding me."

My face flushed hot. "I'm sorry. It was shitty of me. I'd like to blame it on being drunk or hungover but that's no excuse, especially not when it comes to you. I never wanted you to feel like I was using you to get off because you were gay and somehow convenient. And then there was the lack of consent. That was so wrong of me. Disrespectful."

He blew out a short breath. "Wow. Okay. So, I hate to be the bearer of bad news but it seems we were *both* trying to get off that morning. I was in the middle of a... certain dream, when all of that happened."

Dream? What the hell did any of that have to do with us—

Oh.

A smirk slowly crawled across my face. "What were you dreaming about?"

He groaned at me. "Don't."

"Tell me."

"No, you voyeur."

I leaned forward again, catching his bottom lip between my teeth and giving it a sharp nip that had him hissing in response. Letting him go, I said again, "Tell me."

"You already know. Don't make me say it."

Oh, this was too good. Brandon having a wet dream about me? I needed to know all of the dirty details. Was it his first? One of many? If so, how far back did *that* go?

My cock was already growing hard just thinking about the endless possibilities. Would it be fucked up of me to fuck him while he recounted every little detail so that I could give him the real thing?

Actually... that sounded damn fun. We definitely needed to try that when we got to some-place much softer for my knees than this concrete floor.

Brandon grabbed me by my hair again in a tight grip. "I don't like that smirk you're wearing."

I grinned instead. "What smirk?"

Right as he was opening his mouth to retort something, my phone went off. Together, we both sighed.

Honestly at this point, distractions should be expected. I was fucking cursed with the worst timing imaginable.

I pecked his mouth one last time before leaning back from him. "I'm going to get that dream out of you one way or another."

He mumbled something I couldn't quite hear while I rolled to my feet and tucked my half hard dick back into my pants. When he offered a grease-stained rag to clean my hand with, I took it carefully and wiped myself clean before tossing it back to him.

Pulling my phone out, I stared down at the screen.

Ted Evans.

Good news. We were manifesting *good* news.

I swear to god if he was calling to tell me that nothing could be done and that I just needed to suck it up and move on with my life, I was going to lose it.

In fact, I might go nuclear.

"This is Avery."

He wasted no time getting into it. "There's a lot I'm going to tell you. Are you home?"

My heart squeezed. Not even bothering with a formal introduction... that wasn't a good sign. Glancing over at Brandon, I said, "Not at the moment."

"Get in your car and go over there. Now."

"Hold on." Putting him on mute, I grabbed Brandon by the arm and hauled him up to his feet. He didn't question me at all, only tucked himself back into his pants and followed me out as I quickly jogged down the hall and into the main lobby of his shop.

I barely heard him spout off some lie to one of the guys manning the front of the shop before he darted after me, ducking under my arm as I held the door open for him and led him out to my car. The second we were both buckled in and I had my phone hooked up to the bluetooth, I tapped he mute icon again.

"Go ahead, Ted."

On the other end of the phone, he breathed out a short sigh and then his tone grew clipped. "Looked into those files you dropped off about Ana. Something stuck out to me when I was reading through them. The timestamps seemed off. After digging a bit deeper, I discovered the paternity test had been done a week before our meeting and before you requested them from her."

Okay... not exactly abnormal. Ana could've already suspected I'd want something like that from her, especially having never met me before this. Fighting me on it during our meeting could've been her way to test my boundaries—to see how hard set I was in them and to tell where she could possibly skirt the line.

That wasn't screaming guilty.

"So," Ted continued. "I requested the video footage from the clinic of the day she went in for the test. Alexander Steele was with her."

That was weird. Why bring your lawyer to a private and personal matter like that? To prove the legitimacy?

Blinking a few times, I said, "You're sure?"

"It's him."

My hands tightened around my steering wheel. "I'm assuming you're bringing this up for a reason?"

"I don't know who they paid to forge the documents but it's not your father's baby, Avery."

I wanted to believe—I wanted to let myself hope. But what solid proof was there outside of video footage of them at a local clinic? "How do you know?"

"They were seen kissing outside in the parking lot. My team dug into Ana and from what we can gather, she and Steele have been dating for a while."

"For eight months?"

"We're not sure yet. I've requested an emergency hearing with the judge to determine the legitimacy of their claims on the paternity test. The marriage license *was* legitimized, so there's no question that she was married to your father before his death, but that isn't his baby."

It wasn't until I felt Brandon tug on one of my arms to peel my hand away from the steering wheel and wrap his hand around my own that I realized how badly I was shaking. From anger? Adrenaline? I couldn't tell.

She was a fucking scam artist. A talented one at that, getting a lawyer in her pocket and possibly impregnating her while still being married to my father? Diabolical.

How long had this scheme been in the making? Was she targeting my father for long or had he simply stumbled into her web at a convenient time?

Ana struck me as an opportunist to her very core. If Steele was in on this with her, he was just as much of a scumbag.

"Steele called my office this morning and told me his client would be over at your estate later today," Ted said. "I'm not sure for what but I'm guessing they got a judge to sign off on something. The paperwork hasn't come through for us yet. That's why I need you over there."

"Shit," I mumbled. "I'm about twenty minutes out."

"I'll be heading down shortly. Let me know when you get there. We may have to call the authorities to get them off the property."

I squeezed Brandon's hand tightly. I was so glad I decided to swing by to bug him on his lunch break instead of lying around at home all day until he got done with his shift. If he wasn't here with me, I wasn't sure how the hell I'd be able to stay levelheaded. "I'll let you know what I run into when I get there."

"Thank you." Ted let out a soft sigh. "Please be safe. I'll see you soon."

The second the call ended, Brandon squeezed my hand. "We really should have the cops meet us there. It's going to take them a bit to get over the bridge anyway."

True. Not to mention the second we called bullshit on this whole thing, Steele was going to try and throw out some legal jargon to get me to allow them both to stay. Or flash whatever paperwork they'd gotten a judge to sign off on. He also had a lot to lose if he was caught getting twisted up in Ana's schemes.

No amount of funds or whatever else Ana promised him to help her would save his career.

"Why don't you call them, then," I suggested. "We'll have them meet us down at the gate."

He nodded and slipped his phone out of his pocket. "You got it."

My heart was in my throat driving up to my family's property.

As expected, there was already a familiar sports car parked in my driveway, along with a moving truck with the ramp down and two guys loading what looked like a vanity set into the back of it. Anger boiled in me. To be that brazen with stealing my shit was out of this world.

Even if this situation was still somehow legitimate and she was entitled to half of my family's things, I wasn't getting a say in any of what she was currently taking from me—which was exactly what all of us had come to a tentative agreement on weeks ago that this wouldn't fucking happen.

Her arrogance was going to be her downfall.

As soon as I had the car parked, I threw my door open and slipped out into the warm air. The ironic part about today was how nice it was outside despite the deep turmoil that chilled me. This would've been the perfect day to sneak Brandon away from the shop for a little while under the guise of running an errand with me.

Or better yet, a date.

Instead, we were here dealing with this mess and a half.

Coming up the drive behind us were two officers from Palmerston, both of who were eager to swing by with their patrol cars and a possible K9 unit on the way as backup once Brandon had gotten on the phone with dispatch. Normally, I'd consider it overkill, however, there wasn't typically much activity going on in our small towns, so any excuse to bring out the so-called 'big guns' got the local PDs excited.

Fine by me. The more that were on our side, the better.

Leaving Brandon to handle filling in the officers, the sound of my door slamming grabbed the attention of the two movers, their necks jerking toward the noise as they paused halfway up the ramp.

"Afternoon, gentlemen," I called out, my tone clipped.

"Mr. McAllister," one of them said, look like a deer caught in headlights. "We were told you were out of town for the week."

"Is that so."

Figures. If Alexander Steele had one thing going for him, it was the impressive amount of balls he had commandeering not only a moving company but most likely my staff inside, too, to do his bidding for him.

Though how they got my gate code was an entirely different story. One I fully intended to get out of Steele before banning him and his mistress from my property.

Bypassing the two movers, I headed up the stairs and through the open doors of the mansion. In the foyer were already a few pieces of furniture laid out on dust sheets, stacked in a row and ready to be lifted out of the door and into the truck. None of it was furniture that I recognized, so where they were pulling it from was probably one of the guest rooms.

A few of my staff were stiffly milling about, looking lost in the chaos that was slowly turning the once grand entrance into a college move-in day imitation.

Clacking heels brought my attention toward the left of the foyer. The doors to the secondary hallway were propped open, leading down to a few of the guest bedrooms on the first floor. Two voices were heard coming my way, causing my body to tense as they drew near.

The second Ana and Steele moved past the

archway and into the foyer, they stopped short at seeing me.

"Ah, Mr. McAllister." Steele shot me a brief smile. "We were told you'd be out today."

"Really, I wasn't aware I was supposed to be expecting guests."

Ana remained tight-lipped while she stared at me. The sheer fabric of her dress clung to her swollen belly, making it seem much more pronounced than the last time I'd seen her. The stilettos she wore were of an impressive height, making her almost as tall as Steele when she stood next to him.

"I didn't want to bother you," Steele explained.

Popping a brow, I said, "So you hopped my gate instead?"

"No, no." He shook his head. Breaking away from Ana, he moved across the foyer in my direction, unfolding a piece of paper from the inside of his suit jacket as he did so. "We stopped by to take some things back to Ana's guest house. Since it may take a while for us to negotiate what will and will not be going with her, the judge granted us temporary custody over some of the property in order to make her comfortable during our proceedings."

The second he was within reach, I snatched the paper out of his hand.

Judge Matthews. County Court of Forest Hill. An order of compliance and notice of a filing.

The rest of the paragraph, where it explained in a bunch of legal jargon, essentially stated that Ana had full rights to seize temporary custody of any item that was designated as 'unused for more than three years' in order to create a 'safe and comfortable' space for her and her unborn child (the legal heir to the estate) until proceedings could begin.

At the bottom it was signed by the judge and notarized by the Ellington Heights township clerk.

What the fuck.

"We made sure to only grab some of the guest bedroom furniture," Steele explained further. "Your staff let us know it hasn't been used in... a very long time."

The jab wasn't unnoticed. Nor was his professional tone that bordered on condescending.

Again, the man had balls. If we weren't playing for the opposite team, I'd consider hiring him as another one of my personal lawyers. But as it stood, he was public enemy number two.

Folding the paper in half, it was a conscious effort *not* to rip it up in front of him. "I never gave you permission to enter the home."

"You didn't need to. We were given the access code to your gate a few weeks ago."

My eyes rolled over his shoulder to focus on Ana who remained rooted to where she stood right outside of the archway. It hadn't crossed my mind before this but her showing up at my door a few weeks ago unannounced must've been when she'd gotten the code.

How, I wasn't sure. Though, it was safe to say that would be changing the second they were off my property.

"Okay." Reeling in my anger was difficult, especially when all I wanted to do was get them the fuck out of my house as quickly as possible. The problem was the cops were more likely to throw me in handcuffs if I started threatening anyone, no matter how justified and deserved it was. "I'm going to be straight with you, I know exactly what you're doing."

Steele let out a short laugh. "I'm sorry?"

"It's not his. And you know that."

To his credit, the expression that crossed his face looked like genuine confusion. To the point where if I didn't know any better, I would've fallen for it instantly and backtracked my accusations.

Being from the corporate world, or rather the upper echelon of it, I was accustomed to people trying to pull a fast one on me. Either to get a better deal, screw me and my company over, or simply cause chaos in order to confuse my shareholders into backing out and finding somewhere else to burn their wealth.

My specialty in smelling out bullshit had felt like a curse growing up, one that ostracized me from a lot of my peers because I demanded authenticity over popularity. Now, though, it was my super power. One I used to protect myself along with my assets.

"I'm... not sure I follow, Mr. McAllister," he said.

Stepping forward, I watched the moment of hesitation in Steele's eyes as he contemplated giving in to his baser instincts to step back and give me more space. Whatever he was reading on my face, I hoped it was making his heart pound.

"The baby, Steele. It's not his. It's *yours*."

His lips parted in surprise.

Heels clacking over marbled floors dragged my attention away from him briefly in order to focus it on the Russian model storming over to me.

"You lie," she spat out.

"If that's the case, you wouldn't mind doing a DNA test right now." I jerked my head back toward the front doors. "Come with me and we'll settle this once and for all."

Steele moved to put his body in between Ana and I. "Mr. McAllister, the DNA test was already done. The results were sent to your lawyer to give to you."

"You know what's funny about going to any medical center?" My gaze flitted between them both. "They have cameras set up everywhere. Even in the parking lot."

Both of them remained quiet, even as I shoved my hand into my pocket and pulled out my phone, bringing up the picture stills Ted had sent over to me after we'd gotten off the phone.

Zooming in on one of the clearer shots, I flipped it around to show them both.

"Given the timeline of your relationship, and the fact that my dad was snipped long before you met him, I'm pretty confident that I'm right."

"This is *his* baby!" Ana shouted. Her hand darted out to snatch my phone, nearly touching it right as I stepped back to avoid her. "His baby. Your brother."

"Ana," Steele grabbed her arm in a gentle hold.

She ripped out of his grasp with a ferocity I hadn't been expecting. "No! No more. This is his baby. We did test to prove it. End of story—"

A radio crackling from behind us cut Ana off. "What's going on in here?"

Turning to greet both officers, I spotted Brandon bringing up the rear. His eyes were filled with worry, the obvious want to clear the distance between us and glue himself to my side was palpable, so much so that I nearly reached out my hand to beckon him over.

Before I could, one of the officers—Sergeant Boise—held up his hand. "Mr. McAllister, a word?"

"Actually, officer..." Steele moved around me,

ripping the notice out of my hand. "We have a court order stating we have the right to be here."

"That was gained under false pretenses," I argued.

"Regardless, if it's signed by a judge, there's not much we can do," Boise countered with.

Such bullshit.

Why was the legal system always so vulnerable to corruption? One measly piece of paper that falsely stated Ana's baby was my relative was all it took to be able to grant her access to my home, my property and the right to trespass for as long as she damn well pleased.

And there was nothing any of us could do about it.

Anger surged in me. Burning so bright and brilliant that I was surprised I didn't have smoke blowing out of my ears. As I turned to Ana again, both of my hands fisted at my sides. Her satisfied smirk, coupled with her hand circling over her belly in an almost mocking attempt to garner sympathy was more than I could take.

"You're a fucking snake," I hissed at her, keeping my tone low.

Her eyes shot to me. "Hold your tone."

"Why? Pretending like you belong here will

be the worst mistake you'll ever make. I can promise you that."

"We will see when I leave you out on the streets. You are spoiled, rotten boy."

Now that I thought about it, her and my father were a match made in heaven.

I turned my body to fully face her, the seething anger slowly morphing into glee. Going toe-to-toe with this woman wasn't something I ever wanted to cross off on my bucket list, but if she wanted a fight, she was going to get it. I'd make her regret ever choosing to mistake messing with my family's legacy as a smart move—one that would be worth her while as long as she played her cards right.

If I was going to be forced to live with this woman and her bastard child for the rest of my life, I was going to make it hell for her. After all, wasn't that the McAllister way? I was simply passing down my father's wonderful legacy to her, making her a part of the family she'd soon regret wanting to join.

"I'm glad my father picked you up off the streets." Her eyes widened at my words. "I doubt your career would've lasted much longer anyway. I'm going to enjoy every goddamn minute of making sure you regret ever saying yes to that rock on our finger and not sticking to selling magazine covers. You think being a McAllister is all about blowing money on expensive cars and getting your hair and nails done every week? You've got another thing coming. And I'll be *happy* to help you earn your stripes. Whatever back alley that modeling agency scooped you out of is what you're going to wish you could return to once I'm done with you."

I heard the slap before I felt it crack across my face. Belatedly, it occurred to me that threatening a pregnant woman as unhinged as Ana seemed to be was probably not one of my finer moves. However, I wasn't about to take back any of those words. Not when she, out of anyone, needed to realize what the fuck she was getting into.

I wasn't letting her off that easily with her inflated ego and the false belief that as long as she had a lawyer willing to draft up any motion she desired and warm her bed at night was going to get her whatever she wanted in life, it was my job to show her otherwise.

My cheek burned from where her hand had caught me, small pin prickles that radiated pain from what I could only assume were her long nails having dragged across my poor skin.

As I lifted my hand to touch the side of my face, she swiped at me again with the other hand.

"You are nothing!" she screamed. "He said so. He told me all about you. How disappointed you made him. How you and your mother wasted his best years!"

I caught her wrist and held it in a tight grip, nearly missing the other one that came swinging at me as she pivoted her weight to the other side. She screamed again when I grabbed onto the other one, too, holding both of her arms firmly no matter how hard she yanked to be let free.

There was no doubt in my mind that my father had told her any of those things. In fact, it sounded just like him, right down to their callous delivery. The only problem was Ana was five years too late for me to care. I'd heard those same tired words my entire life and had vowed on my wedding day to never let them affect me again.

She could hurl whatever insult she wanted, none of it was going to matter.

"Hey! Let go of her!" Steele shouted.

Before I could even turn around to tell him to back off, he had two fists full of my shirt and was yanking me away from Ana. Out of instinct, I let go of her, stumbling back from the force of another grown man propelling me backward.

There was barely any time to react as a fist came swinging at me, nearly catching me right in the jaw. I jerked my head back out of instinct, giving me enough of a torque on my body to slip free from his hold on me.

"Knock it off!" Sergeant Boise's voice boomed.

Unfortunately, it seemed Steele was too enraged at seeing me put hands on his mistress, despite it being self-defense in the first place. He reared back once more, clocking me on the shoulder on his way up from swinging and missing my face yet again.

There was a brief moment where I spotted Brandon darting away from the two officers and coming at Steele and I full force. In that instant, my heart clenched with worry. As noble as it was of him to come over here and help defend me, I in no way wanted him hurt in the process.

Thankfully, both officers suddenly seemed to decide that springing into action was a far better choice than waiting for Steele to actually land some kind of hit that would result in me having an open and shut lawsuit against the Palmerston police department for negligence.

The second I stepped to the side, the other office tackled Steele to the ground, flattening him on his stomach. The man let out a shrill howl the moment his arms were yanked behind his back and a pair of cuffs was slapped on his wrists.

My cheek burned, the skin tender when I tapped at it gently.

Bitch...

"No!" Ana screeched, jabbing a manicured finger at me. "Arrest *him!*"

"Slaps count as assault, ma'am," Boise stated, motioning for her to turn around. "We can do this the easy way or the hard way."

I wasn't afraid to admit how satisfying it was to watch Ana fight with the officer before she, too, was forced into cuffs. Her shouts for them to arrest and charge me with assault rang on deaf ears, even as she was forcefully dragged out of my foyer literally kicking and screaming.

"Jesus..." Brandon mumbled, his arm looping under mine. He tucked his body against me, allowing me to lean my weight into him while we stood by and waited for Steele to be peeled off the floor and taken out to the police cars parked in the driveway.

As soon as the foyer grew quiet, a long sigh of relief left me.

"Let me see." Brandon maneuvered my face around, his touch gentle. "Oh…"

"How bad?" Judging by his reaction, I had a feeling it was already bruising. For someone so small, Ana sure had a killer wind-up.

"It's… well, you can definitely see the impression of her fingers. And her manicure."

I rolled my eyes. "Mind taking a picture? I want to send it over to Ted for evidence. Maybe charging her will keep her off my property."

After Brandon snapped a few photos and sent them over to me, he slipped his phone back into his pocket in order to cup my jaw again. "We should get you some ice."

"We should follow up with the cops first. They'll probably want us to fill out a report first before they leave."

"Good point. Hopefully, they'll stay in jail over the weekend. It's the least they deserve."

I slipped an arm around his waist, pulling him to my side again.

His warm body was comforting, a solid

weight against me that instantly soothed whatever lingering anger I had surging through me. He was my own personal white noise machine, cutting through the chaos in my mind with that unshakable steadiness he wore so well.

My cheek pinched when I leaned down to kiss him, a hiss escaping me.

"Careful," he murmured.

It was those damn nails. Like fucking razor blades.

The moment I reached down to grab his hand, he laced our fingers together. A warmth spread through my body, starting from my chest where it rapidly trickled down to my toes. The feeling beat in time with my heart, cocooning me in these tender emotions I had for my best friend.

What would I ever do with him?

"Come on," he said, nodding for the doors. "Let's get this over with. Then I can get back to babying you."

With a firm nod and a hand squeeze, he tugged us forward.

I absolutely loved the sound of that.

CHAPTER 30

BRANDON

"MOMENT OF TRUTH." The words were soft as I said them to myself, my hand slightly jerky while lining up the key to the ignition.

It slid in like butter, the grooves of the key clicking pleasantly when it pressed flush to the lock cylinder.

I wasn't sure why I was nervous to be doing this. It wasn't like I was some wannabe mechanic and this was my first fixer upper. I had plenty of cars under my belt at this point, from beaters to the occasional luxury model that rolled through town with an out-of-state license plate.

What made Avery's classic so damn nerve wracking?

Maybe because you don't want to disappoint him.

The thought had me rolling my eyes. Even if there was a sliver of truth to it. If it turned out his cars were better off laying in a scrap yard, I doubted he'd care. It would be one less thing on his plate he'd need to juggle in terms of finding and selling the vehicle off to a collector. Not to mention the pain it was to get all of the stickers and paperwork up to date.

Though at the same time, failing would guilt me immensely. Especially, when he'd spent the last four months paying my damn shop's bills.

I had to remind myself over and over again that to a billionaire, a couple of thousand dollars worth of expenses a month was a drop in the bucket. If that. Actually, it was probably a misting.

Getting used to being spoiled by Avery was kind of a funny thing. Back when we were kids, I was adamant about not taking a dime from him, regardless of how many times he begged me to let him.

As clever as he was, after a while he'd come to

figure out other ways to spoil me that I wasn't so easily able to refuse. Bus fare to our favorite hangout spots, bringing me lunch every day at school, being the sole filler of gas for his car that we *both* drove.

Added up, they were all a culmination of Avery's care for me. Shown through his generous heart and desire to make me happy.

Now that we were older and I had my own income, I'd made it harder for him to revert back to those old ways. Yet even still, his cleverness never ceased to amaze me.

Case in point, my shop's bills. So far he'd behaved himself and wasn't going too overboard with taking me out after work. Though, I had a feeling if left to his own devices, I'd soon be eating those words.

It felt strange to be taking advantage of him like that, even if I wasn't *really* doing so. Seeing as he was my—

My... boyfriend?

Leaning back from the steering wheel while letting the key go, I sunk back into the seat to cover my rapidly heating face with my hands.

Boyfriend.

That word had been echoing in my head for

the past few weeks. Since we'd slept together the first time, actually.

With the fiasco involving Ana and her lawyer-turned-baby-daddy still ongoing, Avery had enough on his plate to deal with without me adding to the mix with a 'what are we?' conversation.

I'd reveled in the peace we'd had since they were thrown into the back of two police cars and booked for jail, regardless of their stay only lasting two days before they were both bailed out. Since then, no one had come around to try and slap another bogus subpoena on the McAllister's front door, demanding some kind of fucked up version of eminent domain.

I hoped this reprieve lasted. At least for a little while. Avery deserved some fucking time to himself where he wasn't dealing with crisis after crisis. How he still had a head of thick blond hair with no grays intermingled throughout the strands, I'd never know.

But it was rather impressive.

"Taking a break?"

I jumped, slamming my knees against the steering wheel hard enough to pull a pained grunt from my throat.

Goddamn it. Of all times to sneak up on me…

Avery let out a sympathetic hum before ducking and reaching through the window to settle his hand over my knee. He worked his thumb along the bone, helping to rub out the pain.

"You come for a test drive?" I joked.

His smile had my heart skipping a beat. "Is it road ready?"

"I was in the middle of testing to see if it started first."

He chuckled. "Kind of looked like you were taking a nap."

"On the job? I'd never."

"You're right." There was a subtle twinkle in his eyes when he turned them to me, his hand sneaking up from my knee to between my thighs. "You'd be doing something else to help you relax."

Well, that was one way to put it.

I'd been wanting to have a sit down serious conversation with Avery for a few days now, however, each time I worked up the nerve to pull the trigger and spill my guts as to how I'd been feeling, something always seemed to crop up at the last second.

Whether that was some divine sign or my own avoidance rearing its ugly head, I had a hard time getting myself to go through with it, regardless of Avery's poking and prodding at me.

It was at least obvious to him that I'd had something on my mind and while he wasn't privy to the subject of it, he was courteous to know not to push me on it. Figuring that I'd tell him eventually.

I wanted to.

I *needed* to.

The problem was the fear of rejection. Of him telling me—or rather reminding me—that his stay here in Ellington Heights was coming to an end. Soon, he'd be on his way back to the city where we would no doubt have yet another falling out. Gradual, of course, as we'd always done so.

At least this one wouldn't leave me wondering if he was dead or not. That was at least a *little* comforting, though tragic all the same.

"Hey..." He cupped my face, pulling me out

of my daze. "I was only kidding. You can tell me I'm being an ass, Bran."

Oh, how I loved this lovably oblivious man.

Reaching up, I wrapped my hand around his wrist in order to keep his hand pressed to my face while I leaned forward to grab the key still hanging in the ignition. Torquing it forward, the car's engine stuttered twice before finally roaring to life with a healthy rumble.

The seat under me vibrated from the horsepower, getting me a little horny in the process.

I loved the power of a good and well taken care of engine. It spoke to the humanistic genius that was machinery.

Avery's laugh cut through the sound of the motor. "Oh, that's a nice sound."

He leaned his upper body against the frame of the door, keeping his other hand in place on my knee. If I wanted to, I had the ability to pull him down into a kiss—and he'd let me do it. In the middle of my damn shop where just anyone could walk in. He wouldn't care in the slightest if we were caught.

Didn't that mean something? Wasn't that a prime example that I was getting too much in my own head about his feelings for me? He told me he liked me, spoke those words that I'd been longing to hear since I was sixteen.

Yet, I was still convinced that he could easily walk away from me at any time. We had no label. There was nothing keeping him here other than an old friendship. I wanted more so badly but didn't know how to ask for it.

How could I when it would mean asking him to give up his life in the city?

"We taking it for a joyride?" he suggested.

I killed the ignition instead, letting go of his wrist. "Needs new tires first. I only wanted to make sure I wasn't working on a dead machine."

"Makes sense." He stood back in order to pop my door open for me. "You hungry?"

The butterflies in my stomach kicked up at the sight of the plastic bag that had been set down by his feet. Always bringing me food. Always making sure I was taken care of.

Ugh, my poor heart couldn't take it.

"Av..."

He trapped me against the side of the car the second I climbed out of it, cradling my face in a tender hold. I was kind of thankful the shop had cleared out for lunch. I wasn't at all ashamed or embarrassed about Avery being here or getting caught with him—quite the opposite, in fact.

The thing was, I wanted to keep these moments private and between us without the annoyance of other parties poking fun at us. Commandeering Avery's attention and time was a precious thing at this point, and wasn't something I was going to be apologizing over, either.

"I missed you." He whispered the words against my skin, sending a shiver racing up my spine.

I fisted my hands around the fabric of his shirt, pulling him closer to me until we were practically molded together. *This* was perfect.

"I'm surprised you're out and about." A smile teased at my lips. "Thought I wore you out too much last night."

He breathed out a laugh. "What, are you calling me old?"

"Never."

He nipped at my ear lobe. "Liar."

I slapped his back in response. "You didn't need to come all the way out here just to bring me lunch. Though, I do appreciate it."

"I wanted to." He leaned back to look at me. "Plus, I had a meeting earlier."

"Don't tell me there's another lawsuit coming your way."

I wouldn't put it past Steele to drag this on for the next few years with lawsuit after lawsuit, no matter how many of them got thrown out. If there was a way to waste Avery's time and money, that was the golden ticket.

"Actually…" He nuzzled his nose against mine. "It was over me quitting my job."

That had me jerking my head back instantly. "*What?*"

He frowned slightly. "My VP swung down from the city. I handed over all of my passcodes and admin privileges to him over breakfast."

"That—for…" I could barely get the words out. "*Why?*"

His mouth opened and shut a few times, clearly at a loss as to how to answer my question.

Why the hell would he throw away a career like that just because he was going to be faced with some hiccups regarding Ana and Alexander Steele?

That was letting them win. That was letting them get in his head while convincing him there was no way to fight them unless he was stuck here in Ellington Heights.

The worst part was that stupidly selfish greed to be happy over his decision. I couldn't let him do that to himself, or his career. What kind of... whatever-I-was would I be?

"Avery, you can't stay here."

His eyes widened. His Adam's apple bobbed with a hard swallow. "Why? You don't want me to?"

Yes, of course I do. "That's not the point."

He seemed hurt by my words for some reason, attention flickering away. "All right."

I tightened my hand around his shirt, not letting him move when he began to pull away. This was a serious conversation. I was going to drill it into his head not to let someone like *Ana Liapovich* convince him he needed to be trapped here on the front line in order to protect his family's assets.

"Avery, listen to me. You don't need to stay here. That's letting them win. You're so much stronger than that."

His brows pulled together. "What the hell are you talking about?"

"The court case? Or whatever's going on with Ana and Alexander Steele. Don't let them get into your head about having to stay here. If anything, I can stop by the estate and check on it every day before and after work to make sure no moving trucks have somehow snuck in."

For some reason, he stared at me for an unforgivably long pause. The weird tension was causing my stomach to clench hard enough that I was beginning to feel nauseous. I hoped he wasn't taking this as me pushing him away.

Hell, I *wanted* him to stay and would give anything to keep him here. But unfortunately that wasn't the reality of this situation. Unfortunately, I was going to have to be a damn grown up and get over myself.

Could we do long distance?

Suddenly, he burst out laughing. "Brandon, sometimes I wonder about you."

Before I could retort, he sealed my mouth into a kiss. I curled my toes when his tongue rolled along the seam of my lips, egging me on into parting them for him. He tasted like his favorite coffee—a dark roast with a little bit of cream and sugar to offset the rich flavor. It was my favorite thing to wake up to every morning, aside from being wrapped up in his arms.

He ground his hips into mine, drawing a soft moan out of me.

We probably had time for a quickie before the guys got back. Unless we were able to sneak off to my office before we got too far into it. There, I could give Avery's cock the proper attention it deserved. Namely in the form of me dropping to my knees for him.

To my dismay, he soon parted from me. "I didn't quit because of the court case."

My lashes fluttered open. "So, why..."

Avery shook his head at me. "I quit because of *you*."

"What?" I mumbled.

"Brandon. I quit because I wanted to stay here. With *you*."

I could only stare in response.

My brain was short-circuiting with the newfound information. All cylinders were rapid firing with no information crossing the threshold of my brain to properly help me formulate a sentence. There was no way he was serious about that. Quitting his seven figure job just to play house with me.

He couldn't.

He wouldn't?

But he did.

"Are you upset?" he asked.

Belatedly, I realized my eyes were beginning to water. "No."

"Bran..."

It hurt to swallow, mainly from how choked up I was getting. "Are you serious? You want to stay here with me?"

His expression softened. "Of course I am. I can't leave you again."

Oh, fuck.

Now my eyes were really beginning to sting.

"You don't have to. Stay, I mean. I'll be okay." Even to my own ears, I knew how lousy that sounded. How barely put together I was.

Of course Avery could see right through me. Just like he always had. "I *want* to. Every time I thought about going to the city, I dreaded it. The thought of having to be away from you again was killing me. So, I quit my job. What was holding me there, anyway?"

"Your friends?"

"They'll move here."

I swallowed back more tears. "Carrie?"

"I called her earlier. She said she was really happy for me and wished us well."

A single tear slipped past my waterline.

"Weren't you living in a really nice penthouse or something?"

"My mansion's way nicer." He glided his thumb under my eye, collecting the drop there. "Speaking of which, you should move in."

My knees nearly buckled. This conversation felt like a fever dream.

Was I even alive?

Maybe I died in my sleep last night and this was my little slice of heaven—getting Avery to stay and for us to live out our happy, merry lives together.

It certainly sounded like something I'd manifest in the afterlife.

"What are we?" I croaked.

"Whatever you want us to be," came his soft reply.

"I..." I wanted everything. I wanted more than he could probably ever possibly give me. I wanted it all. I wanted... "I want you."

He smiled. "Then you shall have me. Forever. Or until you get sick of me."

Yeah, that was so not happening. Not in this lifetime, at least.

There wasn't a day in my life that ever went by

where I thought to myself how ecstatic I'd felt with Avery out of my life. Quite the opposite, in fact. So, it was safe to say that he'd never be leaving.

My stomach tightened at the thought, a pleasant warmth sinking deep down into my bones.

"Come to my sister's wedding with me?" I pressed the question to his lips, reveling in the smile that upticked against mine.

"I'd be honored."

EPILOGUE

AVERY

WEDDINGS WERE NEVER REALLY my thing,
least of all for people I hardly knew.

However, seeing Brandon dressed up in a
suit?

Wow.

I'd been sporting a half hard on since leaving
Ellington Heights with him earlier this evening.
The sight of him wrapped in a fitted black tux
that hugged every part of his solid frame was
downright punishing for my poor libido.

With this being his sister's wedding and with

plenty of kids around, I was forced to keep my hands to myself and behave.

For now, at least.

The ceremony had been beautifully done with barely a dry eye in the church. Seeing Brandon's new family for the first time had been a little jarring, especially after having not been a part of the Anders (now Carmichael) family for so long.

I'd been welcomed by his sister, though, when she'd come over after the ceremony to do her rounds with her new husband. Witnessing her and Brandon go toe-to-toe was a sight to behold and one I readily looked forward to come holiday season.

"Avery!" A glass of champagne was set down in front of me, sloshing dangerously inside of the drinkware. "Long time no see! When Brandon told me he was bringing you, I thought he was pulling my leg."

The man who settled into the chair next to me had a familiar head of curly red hair, styled off to the side in an artistic way that framed his handsome face well.

Jonah.

"Look who the cat dragged in. How've you been?"

He grinned at my words. As soon as he thrust his hand out to shake mine, I took it.

He threw back half of his glass of champagne. "Could ask you the same damn thing," he bellowed, his voice drowning out the music playing from the dance floor. "Bran told us he was bringing someone special but he was tight-lipped about who. If I knew you were coming, I would've brought my hacky-sack."

Wow, that certainly brought back some memories. Out of all of Brandon's brothers, Jonah had always been my favorite. His laidback and happy-go-lucky attitude melded perfectly with everyone around him, no matter the circumstances.

"He told me you were some bigwig in the city now," Jonah went on.

"Not anymore. Recently divorced from the city life, actually."

"No shit?" He shook his head at me, downing the rest of his glass. "Can't imagine why you'd do something like that. Oh, wait..."

The smug narrowing of his eyes had me nearly bridging the distance between us to give his shin a swift kick. Lovingly, of course. No matter how much time passed, Jonah still knew how to push my buttons at an expert level and apparently still loved doing so.

I liked to imagine he was giving me the older brother treatment I never received as a kid—a rite of passage, as it were. However, now that we were adults, I was allowed to give it right back to him and feel fine doing so.

"Speak of the devil." He grinned, his eyes shifting to something over my shoulder.

Craning my neck around, I spotted Brandon laughing as he headed our way, another one of his brothers, Reece, in tow. The two of them were peas in a pod—similar builds, the same wavy, dark hair, and twin smiles that could melt even the coldest of hearts.

Together, they were a deadly combo save for one simple fact: their complete opposite personalities.

As soon as they were within shouting distance, Reece broke away from his brother's side in order to beeline straight toward me. I only had around three and a half seconds to try and brace myself before a pair of beefy arms were being wrangled around my neck and a set of knuckles were thrust down against the top of my skull in a rather haphazard noogie.

"Avery McAllister!" I could *hear* the devious grin in his voice. Bastard. "As I live and breathe!"

"Reece!" Brandon scolded.

Flashbacks of being fourteen again and Reece wrestling me to the ground to pin me like we were in some official WWE match while Jonah and Jace egged him on in the background were suddenly thrust into the forefront of my mind.

A charming time back then but not at all one I wanted a repeat of two decades later.

Twisting my arm around, I jabbed my fingers up into Reece's armpit and dug them in deep, hard enough to be felt through the thick fabric of his suit jacket. He yelped, quickly disentangling himself from me while cupping his hands under his armpits.

"Low blow, McAllister," he chided.

Jonah barked out a laugh. "You left yourself wide open, man. What did you expect?"

"You both are ridiculous." Brandon stuck his hand out toward me, wiggling his fingers until I took it. He hauled me up from my seat, still shaking his head. "I'd blame it on the drinks but I know for a fact you two have already blown through your free tickets."

Reece moved past me to steal my seat. "Yeah. Now we're onto stealing all of the auntie's tickets when they're not looking."

I had to hand it to him, I could appreciate the mischievousness. At least Brandon's brothers were making their own kind of fun and keeping out of their sister's hair while she was celebrated for the rest of the evening.

"The least you two could do is be nice to Avery. Remember how we were all *begging* for him to come home? Don't make him regret his life choices."

I held in a laugh and threw my arm around his shoulders. No amount of hazing from the Carmichael brothers could ever get me to reconsider staying in Ellington Heights. That decision had been single handedly the easiest one I'd ever had to make. Choosing Brandon, and choosing my life with him, was always a no-brainer.

Anyone who thought otherwise was playing ignorant.

"Oh, come on, Bran. You know how it goes. You bring a boyfriend around, we get to pick on him. It's all a part of the ritual." Jonah nudged me with his foot, shooting me a wink at that last part.

Funny, considering I'd already been through this process long before Brandon and I were even past puberty, let alone at the point where we were dating officially. Though, I supposed with my absence, I had a bit of catching up to do.

"Animals," Brandon muttered, gripping my hand tight in his while he turned and tugged me away from their table.

He weaved us through the crowd expertly, the music from the party soon growing soft while we wandered away from it.

The venue was on a beautiful property up in the sticks. With little to no light pollution and the sun having set hours ago, the stars were out in full force, shimmering like diamonds against the dark night sky.

I watched them while I let Brandon guide me, trusting him to not let me fall as he navigated down to a small, private dock that overlooked the lake. The air was peaceful and quiet, a stark change from the energetic celebration raging on a few hundred yards away.

Brandon breathed out a sigh, his body finally

relaxing once we were alone. "I'm sorry about them. They're—"

I wrapped him up into a hug, squeezing him. "Just being annoying older brothers," I said, finishing for him.

He sagged into me, nodding with his chest pressed to my chest. "They'll calm down. Eventually."

I doubted that, but I'd keep that opinion to myself. With Brandon and I out and actually dating, I had a feeling it'd be a while until the dust settled over the newness of our relationship.

Coming from our background and now ending up where we did, it was a wonder we weren't getting pulled away by Brandon's mother while she tearfully lamented about how she always knew we were meant to be together.

Though, maybe that would be in due time. After all, tonight wasn't about us.

"You okay?" I asked, smoothing a hand along the back of his head.

"Now I am."

My chest ached with fondness for him.

A few weeks had passed since we'd made it official and since then, we'd been practically inseparable. I didn't want to jinx anything by predicting too early on where this was headed, however, deep down in my heart, I knew that come next spring, the wedding bells would be tolling once more.

That was something to look forward to. A future I never knew would've been possible six months ago, but now was clear as day as the only path I ever wanted to travel. Letting him go had been the biggest mistake of my life. I had the rest of forever to make it up to him, and I one hundred and ten percent planned on doing so.

Leaning back slightly, I cupped a hand around his jaw, moving his face away from my chest so I could trail a line of kisses from his forehead, down to his mouth. Treating him tenderly, loving him in the way that he deserved to be, was all I needed.

This right here was what true and divine happiness really felt like.

"I love you, Brandon Carmichael."

His eyes fluttered open, blinking a few times as tears formed at the corners of his lashes. "I do, too. I love you, Avery. I have for so long. I... I never thought..."

"Me too. I think I've loved you forever."

My heart was his.

My soul was his.

His breath mingled with mine, a soft trailing of his finger working its way across my cheek to circle around my lips and trace the outer edges of them. His dark eyes were glossy from his unshed tears, casting a slight sparkle to them that drew me in. "Thank you for staying, Avery."

I kissed him once more. "I'll never leave you again."

***

MARLOW

"You're actually going through with it?" My best friend's straightforward tone, while normally charming to a fault, was beginning to grate on my ears.

Save for the fact of this being the third time he was bringing up the same subject, I was beginning to wonder how many times it would take for me to repeat myself before Silas finally gave up and accepted the fact that I was doing this.

Coming from his perspective, I supposed I could understand the bewilderment to a certain extent. After all, sitting behind a desk while staring at numbers on a screen all day, every day, wasn't exactly screaming extreme sports enthusiast.

I was a fit man and took care of my health as much as I could given my work schedule, but even that had its drawbacks. There were only so many trails in Ellington Heights I could run before I began to go stir crazy.

Hence the need for a change.

"For the millionth time, *yes*. Can you get off my dick about it?"

On the other end of the phone, Silas scoffed. "You can't expect me not to worry about you. You're going to a fucking wilderness camp where there's mountain lions and bears around. It would be shitty of me *not* to worry about you."

While he had a point, his loud opinion about it certainly wasn't what I wanted to hear. This year, I was on a mission to better my health—to get myself into the best shape of my life and have fun doing it. As wild of a concept as it was to do just that at a wilderness camp, I didn't care.

Not if it kept me from keeling over like my late pops.

"Thank you for caring about me," I said.

The zipper to my bag only barely stayed together, the opposite side of it bulging with how much stuff I'd managed to cram into the small carry-on sized case. In the welcome packet that had been sent to me a week prior, there were hardly any specifics on what I was supposed to be bringing along with me, outside of the basic toiletries.

Which left liberty for creative freedom.

"Wow, try not to sound like you're being held at gunpoint next time."

"Don't you have lives to save? An organ to stitch back together perhaps?"

"Nope." He let out a grunt that slowly morphed into a deep sigh. "Got the next forty-eight hours off. Lucky me."

Was it really luck if he'd been on a nine-day rotation before this?

While I admired Silas's work and his chosen career path, the life of a surgeon typically sounded like torture to me. Even on the good days where he got to brag about attaching some kid's limb back onto their body.

"Though, I'm sure you'll be calling me your first night there," he said, his tone slipping from that usual nonchalant tone to one that never failed to instigate me. "You'll see one bug bite on your skin and end up losing your mind because you'll convince yourself it was a snake bite instead."

What the hell was with the stray balls?

I got that he was pissy I was leaving him for six weeks, but damn, he didn't have to go for my jugular like that. At least Avery had the decency to sound happy for me, even if he, too, didn't get my decision to go.

I wasn't looking for understanding, I was looking for support. Simple as that.

"How much?" I said.

"What?"

"How much are we betting? Seeing as you're *so* confident I'm going to come crying to you on day one."

"Night one," he corrected. "And you definitely will. Or at least, in the first week."

"How. Much," I gritted through my teeth.

The other end of the phone was silent for a moment, allowing me to finish the rest of my packing while he continued to devise what was probably a very diabolical punishment for me if I was to actually lose this.

Ironic, seeing as how my toxic trait was being

competitive as fuck. Turning it into a super-power for my job was the ultimate fuck you to the universe and subsequently everyone else who dared to think they'd be good enough to win against me.

Finances were a game played on a massive scale where the stakes were the difference between buying a second vacation home or getting evicted and kicked out onto the streets. The potential to ruin someone else's life simply by making one wrong move was thrilling if not downright boner inducing.

But I digress.

"It's an IOU," he finally said.

Raising my brow, I repeated. "IOU?"

"You remember what it stands for?"

If only I could reach through the phone and strangle him. The worst part is that he'd probably like it.

"What are the parameters of this IOU?"

"The usual. One favor at any time, any place, anywhere. Winner gets to choose the timeline on when the favor needs to be redeemed by."

"Fine," I said, hauling my bag off of my bed in order to swing it around and dump it next to my door. "You've got yourself a deal. I look forward to proving you wrong."

"Me too. Though, I doubt you will."

Oh, he was so lucky he wasn't standing right next to me. "Goodbye, Silas."

"Call me before you lose service. So I know where to send the forest rangers when they have to come rescue you."

Rolling my eyes, I slammed my thumb down on the 'end' icon and tossed my phone onto my bed.

What was it with surgeons and being giant asswipes?

It had to have been taught somewhere in medical school: 'how to be a douche 101'.

Or maybe it was an upper level class. A real 304.

Whatever. I wasn't about to let him get in my head about this. I'd made my decision weeks ago when I'd signed up and sent in my yearly physical for medical approval. Surviving a wilderness camp for the next six weeks was going to be fine.

I was going to be fine.

All that I'd walk out of there with was probably a mild case of poison ivy and a whole favor richer.

Ah, I could taste the sweet victory lap I'd be doing now while Silas got to eat his words—both metaphorically and physically, because the second I got back from this trip, I was going to make him write down his doubts and then force feed it to him.

A real, put your money where your mouth is type scenario.

Cruel?

Maybe, but he started it.

Good thing I was happy to end it.

My phone chimed with my alarm, reminding me that I needed to get in my car and head over to the pickup site, pronto.

Grabbing my phone and my bag up off the floor, I slung it over my shoulder and gave my bedroom one last cursory glance before shutting off the light and leaving it, and the rest of my problems, behind for the next six weeks.

Click now to read *Marlow*, the next book in the Billionaire Bad Boys & Blue Collar Men series.

DEAR READER

Dear Reader,

Thank you for reading Avery, book one in the Billionaire Bad Boys & Blue Collar Men series.

If you enjoyed this taste of my new small town billionaire boys series, then please let me know.

You can simply return to the online retailer where you made your purchase and leave me a short review.

Your thoughts may just encourage other readers to try my books, and help me continue writing the characters we all adore and root for.

Even a few words would mean the world to me.

~Love, Evie Riley

Other Books By Evie

My action-filled, romantic suspense, and darker-themed books:

Rock Hard Mountain Men

Magnus

Brody

Creed

Federal Protection Agency

Mason

Rafe

Ryzen

Cooper

Noah

Damien

Sebastian

Gabe

Logan

Ruthless Empire

Courting Danger

Chasing Danger

Kissing Danger

Smokejumpers

Hawke

Cyrus

Jase

Gage

Jackson

Xavier

From The Edge

Shattered

Runaway

Jaded

Rescue

Hidden

Tormented

Gray Vale Pack

His Fated Mate

His Wounded Warrior

His Healing Heart

My more romance-themed books:

Billionaire Bad Boys

& Blue Collar Men

Avery

Marlow

Silas

Rock His World

Hollow Heart

Wild Stars

Grave Misgivings

Jasper Springs

Cade

Dawson

Drew

Grayson

Riley

Mitch

ABOUT THE AUTHOR

Evie Riley believes too much time spent at the beach is barely enough. She enjoys spending time puttering in the garden, cooking yummy things for her family, and has a quirky personality, described by her partner as ranging from cute to deadly, depending on her blood-chocolate levels.

Evie crafts steamy gay male romance filled with all the edgy angst, or dark and gritty romantic suspense where her men must overcome difficult obstacles and may find love along the way while dishing out their own brand of justice.

Evie spends her nights writing bad boys in love, and her days wrangling the sweet boys she loves.

www.ingramcontent.com/pod-product-compliance
Lightning Source LLC
Chambersburg PA
CBHW070338170726
48291CB00001B/90